GAIL ANTHEA BROWN

# CASTLES OF STEEL AND THUNDER

FUZZY
FLAMINGO

First published in 2020 by Fuzzy Flamingo
Copyright © Gail Anthea Brown 2020

Gail Anthea Brown has asserted her right to be identified as the author
of this Work in accordance with the Copyright, Designs and Patents
Act 1988.

ISBN: 978-1-8380944-3-0

Editing and design by Fuzzy Flamingo
www.fuzzyflamingo.co.uk

A catalogue for this book is available from the British Library.

# ACKNOWLEDGMENTS

When I was in High School, I was offered the chance to illustrate a book by a local author, the late Donald Omand – the book was called *Caithness: Lore and Legend*. Whilst I still believe Mr Omand was rather generous in allowing my amateur drawings in his publication, the stories he recounted ignited a spark of interest in me that never went away.

Years later, I came across a copy of the book in our attic, and found myself as fascinated as ever by the tales of Fae folk, mermaids and other-worldly beings. I decided to use some of the stories as a jumping-off point for the book you see before you now.

In writing this book, I am therefore indebted to Donald Omand and his wife, my High School English teacher, who made the introductions between us. I also owe thanks to my family, especially my husband, children and parents, who have offered a huge amount of support and encouragement along the way. I am grateful to my friends, to June, my first reader, and to all the people who have read and commented on my blog over the years, encouraging me to believe that I might just be a writer. I also owe thanks to George Gunn and all at the Ravenskald writing group, for their constructive feedback.

And to Nana and Iain – who probably didn't believe in faeries, but always believed in me.

Gail Brown, 2020

*On the day it ended, blood fell from the sky like raindrops. It trickled down the cliff and into every crevice, scarring the obstinate stone with a streak of restless, seeking red. I heard her cry out, a sound both young and ancient in the darkness. And then silence, piercing the air like a steel blade cutting through the sky. They thought it ended then, as the sky seer flew and the mountain turned over into slumber. In truth, it had only just started.*

*Like the buds pricking open on the hillside, I had only just begun.*

# PART ONE

# NEVER NIGHT

# CHAPTER ONE

Even on something as innocuous as market day, Sysa felt the fear of the *sheean* around her, hanging in the air like putrid laundry. As she followed Grey through the street that wound down to the market, she saw the necklaces threaded with small pendants of iron, the horseshoes overhanging doors and the arrowheads gathered from supposed faerie darts.

'My father collects them,' Hugh, a scruffy-looking boy from the next croft said, appearing at her shoulder and jerking his head towards an arrow tethered with a piece of twine to a doorknob.

'They fire them at you when you least expect it. Like this,' he continued, drawing back his arm and flicking his thumb against his forefinger in display, a hissing sound escaping from his mouth as he mimicked the action of the Fae.

'They don't even need a bow, Sysa,' he said, continuing with his story as Sysa stared at him blankly. 'They just flick the arrow with their fingers, and it goes right into your body, without even piercing the skin.' Hugh paused for a moment, his grubby face searching Sysa's for some reaction to this revelation.

'Is that so?' she said, turning her head towards her Grandfather, who was now engaged in conversation with a nearby vendor, but caught her eye over Hugh's shoulder, shooting her a quick, apologetic smile.

'Yes, it is Sysa.' Hugh continued with his tale, apparently unworried by Sysa's lack of interest.

'It goes right into your body, wounding all your vital parts. Just imagine, your heart, your lungs, all your insides struck with a blow like thunder that doesn't even make you bleed!' He looked at her expectantly.

'Terrible,' Sysa replied, nodding gravely back into Hugh's wide-eyed, searching expression.

'But don't worry, Sysa,' Hugh continued, 'like I said, my Father collects the arrowheads, you know, to use against them. They can protect you against the faerie magic. The crops and animals too. I can get you some if you want them.' Hugh raised his chin and looked at her, crossed arms containing the small swell of pride across his chest that made him look to Sysa like a puffed-up, scruffy chicken.

'Oh well, that's very kind of you Hugh but…' Sysa's voice trailed off as she saw her Grandfather approaching. She moved towards him as Grey Steel greeted the pair with his usual easy smile.

Grey's eyes glistened as he threw a wink in Sysa's direction.

'What's this about arrowheads then Hugh?'

The young boy dropped his arms to his sides, his shoulders slumping as he lowered his head and hissed to Sysa under his breath.

'Why does your Grandfather have to hear everything? Isn't he meant to be a deaf old man by now?'

'I like to keep my ears clean, Hugh,' Grey answered as Hugh jolted upright.

'I didn't mean…' the boy stammered, flushing and fidgeting, looking around for any glimpse of his Mother among the throng of market goers, suddenly eager to be gone.

'By the looks of you, you could do with a wash behind the ears yourself, Hugh lad,' Grey laughed. 'Be off with you. And less of that nonsense about faerie darts. If a faerie wishes to harm you, Hugh, those darts will be of little use to you.' With a gesture of his arm he waved the boy away.

Sysa watched as Hugh scuttled off through the market towards his Mother. He was quickly lost amongst the cobbles, stalls and swishing folds of skirts. Sysa looked at Grey and burst out laughing. Grey shook his head in the direction of Hugh's retreating figure.

'Deaf indeed,' he said, a twinkle of amusement in his eyes.

'Why does everyone think the faeries are so terrible?' Sysa asked Grey as they meandered along the track on the way back to the cottage.

Grey turned, little clouds of dust rising from beneath his feet as he swivelled to look into her face. Sysa saw the fields spread out behind him, rolling over and down as they approached the river bank. In the distance, she could see a slice of blue sea and the cliffs of the headland beyond. Grey stood against the picture, the edges of his tall, angular frame softened by the bursts of colour. Sysa blinked, wishing for a second that she could capture him there, like a painting, with her eyes.

'Have I ever told you of the difference between Seelie

and Unseelie Fae Courts, Sysa?' Grey said, interrupting Sysa's dream-like wonderings.

'No, I don't think so, Grandfather,' Sysa replied, grateful for Grey's willingness to impart information that ordinarily seemed the domain of only adult exchange. Since she had been a tiny child, Grey had overlooked the fact that she was smaller, and supposedly less knowledgeable than her grown-up counterparts. He spoke to her as he would any other adult, and Sysa had responded with a maturity far beyond her years.

'Children know all the secrets of the world,' he had said to her one day. 'But as adults they forget them.'

Grey, it seemed to Sysa, had that unusual ability to be grown up whilst not forgetting the things that made him young.

'Well, the Seelie are mostly made up of what we would call good Fae folk, the type who use light magic and don't like to cause any trouble in the human world,' Grey said, as Sysa nodded along beside him, desperate not to miss a single sentence.

'The Unseelie use dark magic,' he continued, 'and they've been known to cause a bit of mischief. The Unseelie are the ones the humans are frightened of, but because they don't always understand what goes on in the faerie world, people often assume the whole lot of them are bad.'

'Things never seem to change in that respect,' Grey sighed, looking down the track towards their cottage, and the Hawthorn that stood aside it.

He picked Sysa up and twirled her round, the rush of air against her body dispelling her concentration. She laughed, unsteady, as he lowered her down on the long grass that hedged the path towards the glen. 'I love you Grandad,' she said, running off ahead and into the cottage, her dark hair lit with sunlight.

'I love you too,' Grey called out behind her.

As if in answer, the leaves of the Hawthorn tree rustled, whispering to unseen blossoms as his words drifted on the wind.

# CHAPTER TWO

Sysa watched as the fire flickered and danced in the distance. Shuddering against the chill morning air, she pulled at the collar of her jacket, enjoying the sudden rush of warmth against her skin.

'Cold?' asked Grey, pulling off his coat and wrapping it around her shoulders. It hung loosely around her frame and dragged along the track as they walked towards the flames.

Sysa rubbed at her eyes with one hand while the other clasped the edges of Grey's coat, holding it tight around her neckline. Grey followed her with his eyes, noting the small curves of her knuckles as they pressed against her face. He had woken her early, at her own request, standing beside her bed as she stretched and grumbled sleepily. A few moments later she had emerged for the breakfast he was making, the scent of warmed porridge overlaid by the smell of hair, warm blankets, child and sleep.

Their annual pilgrimage to the village festival for Beltane was a short one. Each year, Sysa would persuade Grey to make the walk along the track to join the townsfolk in the kindling of the dawn fire. As the empty fields narrowed, Sysa would feel her excitement building, although Grey's mood never seemed to match her enthusiasm. Considering his love for magical stories, Sysa couldn't understand why the prospect of the fire festival didn't fill him with the same sense of anticipation that she felt. Hadn't he told her himself that Beltane was one of only a few times when the veil between the human world and the otherworld could be lifted? As the fire welcomed the return of the sun after winter, the natural way of the world, for a while at least, could be dimmed. Indeed, it was not unusual to hear of Fae sightings amongst the firelight. Once, someone had said they saw a troop of Fae on horseback surround the fire. But when Sysa had rushed, breathless, towards the throng of onlookers, there had been nothing but the flash and curl of flames, moving ever upward. Sysa had returned to where Grey stood, under the curving branch of a tree, a faraway look in his eyes. Sysa had halted for a moment, following his gaze until his face loosened, snapped back into the moment as he caught sight of her. He threw her a grin and Sysa thought she saw a flash of relief wash over him, the same expression he wore when she emerged unscathed from a fall or tumbled without injury from the branch of a tree.

'Nothing to see then Sysa?' he had asked, and she had shaken her head glumly.

'No Grandfather,' she'd answered as he took her hand and led her away from the flames.

'Let's go home then,' he'd said, as she'd looked over her shoulder and watched the fire recede to a dim glow behind them.

'All right,' she conceded, glancing back up at her Grandfather, still looking for all the world as if he belonged entirely somewhere else.

★

This morning, there had been no Fae sightings either, and the two of them walked back to the cottage, leaving the cacophony of chatter and fire crackle behind them.

'Can we walk along the riverside to home?' Sysa asked, brightening after the disappointment of another Beltane without a faerie sighting. Perhaps Samhain, she thought hopefully, rallying at the prospect of the winter festival, and the fires that would be lit then to seek a hasty return to sunlight.

'Yes, of course, if you'd like to,' Grey replied, returning Sysa from her thoughts. The walk would be a little longer, with a final uphill through the glen to reach the cottage, but the air was clean and crisp now and felt light, as it often did in the hours close behind the dawn. Sysa was in no rush to get home to chores and the feeding of the animals. She relished the chance to spend more time out in the glen with Grey, and it appeared he also felt the same.

Sysa swung at her Grandfather's arm as they walked through the longer grass, lush and damp beneath them. The air felt sharp somehow, the early hour heightening the scent of grass, gorse and the carpet of tiny pebbles nestling in the bank. Soon the days would stretch out, until night and day would merge almost into one, the barrier between light and dark virtually imperceptible.

'Never Night, that's what the Fae folk call it, this place of ours,' Grey had told her once as they'd looked out over the glen one summer's evening, the sky bright and clear despite the waning day. Sysa had breathed in the evening air, its chilly bite the only indication of her approaching bedtime.

'Never Night,' she'd repeated, enjoying the thrill of the

words dripping from her mouth like velvet. She'd followed Grey's eyes off into the distance, imagining a world where a lack of darkness also meant a corresponding lack of sleep.

'Will you tell me a story while we walk, Grandfather?' Sysa asked, her thoughts returning to Beltane's most recent disappointment.

'I will,' Grey answered, apparently happy to seek out a diversion to Sysa's quiet mood. 'Just let me think of one.' Grey paused for a moment, his back to the edge of the river, the rising sun trickling gold across the water. As he searched out the entry point to his story, Sysa noticed something, a shadow splitting the rays that now suddenly faltered at his rear.

There was something moving towards them under the water, something that even in the most simple of movements, manifested a sort of darkness. And not just darkness – cold, too, Sysa registered, as a trickle of ice made its way along her spine. Something shifted uneasily in her stomach, some sort of awful recognition. She had a sudden sense of understanding, altering quickly to a sense of not understanding anything at all. Before she could cry out, the shaggy form of the thing was creeping out of the water, nudging closer to Grey's legs, all the while staring at her through bright blue eyes that seemed to bore under her flesh to the very depths of her. It was a rodent-like creature, much like a shrew, but many times larger, she observed, as she began to regain control of her senses and her strangled, stolen voice. The thing crept closer to Grey, long pointed nose and large ears twitching as it moved towards him.

'Grandfather!' Sysa finally shrieked, as the creature came level with his foot. In an instant, Grey whirled round, seizing the creature by its long tail, as it displayed a set of large fangs and let out a hissing sound that bounced and echoed off the water.

'Sysa, run!' Grey commanded, grappling with the creature which railed and jarred against him. 'Run!' Grey shouted once more, with a quick glance at Sysa, who realised with a jolt she had been standing rooted to the spot.

Sysa ran, onwards and upwards, coming level with the cottage. Satisfied she had gone far enough, she turned, breathlessly searching across the hill for some sign that Grey was following behind. She stepped up on tiptoe, unable to see over the curve of the hill that led down to the river.

Panicked, she called out – 'Grandfather, Grandfather!' – but the only response was a flash of bright light somewhere in the distance, that rose up and over the hill for a moment, before retreating as quickly as it came. Sysa jumped back, holding her hand to her forehead, shielding herself from the onslaught. She heard a splash, and then everything went completely still, as if the birds and insects had quickly scurried off somewhere; the sky and the land no longer theirs to fly and hum in, the world momentarily belonging somewhere else.

Sysa jolted herself out of the soundless air that suddenly seemed to press in on her, and stepped slowly towards the grassy mound where the land curved over to the bank. Reaching it, she peered over the arc, the voice that escaped her nothing but a whispered croak.

'Grandfather?' she pleaded, realising that for the first time in her life she was completely alone amongst the grass and the gorse bushes. Seeing only the empty expanse of green laid out before her, Sysa looked back towards the cottage, as if some shelter from the fear and loneliness might be found within its walls.

'Sysa!' a voice called out behind her. Turning back towards the river, Sysa saw Grey fill the empty space she had looked into just a few seconds before.

'But Grandad? How?' she called back to him, wiping one arm over her eyes and the tears that had been falling down her cheeks in panic.

'It's all right,' Grey said as he moved up the hill towards her. 'It's all right,' he repeated as she threw herself down the hill to meet him and he swept her up in his arms, kissing her forehead, his mouth against her hair. Sysa squeezed him tightly, satisfying herself of his weight, his presence.

'I thought you were gone,' she whispered into the fabric of his tunic. 'Grandad, are you all right?'

'I'm fine, Sysa, see?' he said brightly, pushing her to arm's length so she could make her own appraisal. Sysa looked at him closely. To her surprise, her Grandfather did seem to be completely unharmed.

'And I wasn't gone, I was just over there, seeing to that creature,' Grey continued, a flick of his head indicating the direction of the incident.

'Everything is fine now Sysa, please don't worry. Everything is all right. Now, let's get you home and warm.'

'But what *was* that Grandfather?' Sysa continued, taking Grey's hand as he led her back towards the cottage.

'That was the Lavellan,' Grey answered, his face tight as he strode towards their home.

'What's the Lavellan?' Sysa asked, 'I've never heard of

that before. It had horrible fangs, Grandad, and I think it planned to bite you. Did it bite you? I was so worried Grandad, I'm so glad that you're okay.'

'It didn't bite me, Sysa, although it does have a nasty bite, if you're so unfortunate. The Lavellan is a creature that lives, some of the time at least, in the deep pools and rivers of Caithness. It can kill a person or an animal with that bite, and its fangs are venomous.' Sysa gasped, looking up wide-eyed at her Grandfather. 'But I don't mean to scare you, Sysa,' he said, patting her hand, his face softening. 'You have nothing to fear from the Lavellan so long as I am here.'

'But why would it come here, and why would it try to attack us Grandfather?' Sysa continued, her words coming quick and breathless as they continued up the riverbank. 'We've never seen it here before, why did it come here now?'

'That's just what I'm wondering,' said Grey, pausing a moment to cast a sideways look at her. 'But it's gone now,' he continued, offering a smile that didn't quite reach the green pools of his eyes.

'Did you kill it?' Sysa said, turning to face him, eyes round and bright as she stared at him.

'No, I didn't kill it Sysa,' Grey answered, shaking his head as he looked off towards the pebbled water's edge. 'I just sent it on its way, that's all – it shouldn't be bothering us again.'

'Oh,' Sysa said, following his gaze now. 'Was that the splashing sound I heard?'

'And did you see the flash of light, Grandad?' she continued, when Grey didn't answer her question. 'Where did that come from? Did the Lavellan do that, Grandad?' she continued, tugging at his sleeve.

'Perhaps,' he said, that same faraway look in his eyes Sysa had seen before by the tree on that other Beltane. 'Do you know, Sysa, I didn't actually notice that.'

'Hmm,' Sysa said, squeezing her eyelids together before shaking off the shiver that rose quickly up her arms and then down again. 'Well, I'm happy the Lavellan didn't manage to harm you, Grandfather,' she said, quickening her pace before running off ahead.

'It wasn't myself I was worried about, Sysa,' Grey said into the air as his words disappeared on the breeze behind them.

As he looked back towards the river, he considered the lie he had told his Granddaughter. He shook his head, dismissing the thought, and strode onwards, leaving his thoughts on the tracks behind his feet.

On the Hawthorn tree, the new blossoms whispered into the morning.

*What does one more lie matter?* they seemed to say to one another.

Grey had been lying to Sysa her whole life.

★

In the weeks that followed, Sysa noticed small changes in her Grandfather. He was quieter, somehow, as if his thoughts were often far away. Sysa would come upon him at the table by the window, looking out over the glen, his eyes fixed on a point in the distance. It wasn't the same look she saw when he sought out the start of his stories. There was no flicker of revelation in his eyes as he found the answer he'd been looking for, nothing but a weary smile

15

and a look of resignation as she startled him back into the world.

'Sysa,' he'd say, as he pulled her onto his lap and cradled her against the window. Sysa would look out to the sloping glen, framed by stone, breeze flowing through the gap.

'Will you tell me a story?' she'd ask, and as always, he'd oblige her. But the stories were different somehow, as if he told them with someone else sitting with them in the room.

As time passed, they ventured less and less to the village and the market. Visits to the fires of Beltane and Samhain became less frequent as the seasons passed in their never-ending exchange of light and dark. Sysa accepted it all without disagreement. She had seen the change in her Grandfather's face when they ventured from the cottage; etched with worry, and suddenly older than he seemed. She had no desire to bolster the darkness that seemed to accompany them every time they chanced away from the cottage, and so she never complained, never argued. Instead, she withdrew with Grey to the world of their own making.

All the while, Grey's light seemed to diminish before her eyes.

Eventually, Grey asked her to stay away from the faerie brochs and hillocks that dotted the Caithness landscape. The mounds through which unfortunate townsfolk disappeared to Fae lands were places he suddenly begged her to avoid. Grey never forbade her anything, but Sysa saw his weary face and knew, pressing her hand to his and nodding her promise. Yet his stories continued – tales of selkies, mermaids and giants, and the Fae folk, resplendent in their velvets and their silken mantles of green and gold.

Sometimes, lying in bed at night, Sysa would watch Grey, standing at the entrance to the cottage and staring out across the glen before him. At sunset, she'd see him silhouetted against the evening, the sky blazing back at him like a dragon had opened its mouth and roared. Grey would just stand there, waiting and watching in the half-light until Sysa's eyelids fluttered in time with the drapes that curled around her window. She'd drift off into sleep, dreaming of his stories.

When she opened her eyes there he'd be, staring out into the world, as if seeking an answer in the sky.

# CHAPTER THREE

## NINE YEARS LATER

Sysa awoke to the sound of birds singing as they dipped and fluttered around the glen outside her window. The half-light of the early hours cast a dim glow across the cottage as Sysa propped herself up on her elbows and squinted into the grey. As she yawned and stretched, she saw that her Grandfather was already awake and fully dressed, busying himself outside the open cottage door and wrapping up his knapsack.

'Ah, Sysa, good morning!' he called as he looked up and saw his Granddaughter watching him. 'I'm glad that you're awake. I have a surprise for you. We're going somewhere special. Up you get and dress now, Sysa, I have your porridge ready for you. Once you've had your breakfast we must set off.' He looked around, as if he were convincing himself of something, and then muttered, 'yes, we must go while the day is new.'

Sysa wasn't sure if Grey was talking to her, or to himself.

Still heavy with sleep, Sysa blinked, taking in the sight of Grey rushing around the cottage. She watched as he hurriedly spooned her porridge into the bowl on the table, beige globs of oatmeal attaching themselves to its sides and dripping onto the wooden top beneath. Grey was rarely in a hurry to go anywhere, normally carrying himself with a peaceful, easy demeanour that Sysa had always found comforting. Today he seemed unsettled; a look of worry etched on his face as he went about his chores.

'Where are we going Grandfather?' Sysa asked him as Grey looked up suddenly from the table and paused, the porridge pot still in his hand, his mouth still open from his murmurings. His eyes met hers for a moment and Sysa saw something flash across them. Was it sadness? Sysa couldn't tell. She rose from her bed, padding across the floor towards him, face tilted in query.

'We're going to a faerie hill, Sysa,' Grey replied quietly, lowering the pot to the table. He stared down at it for a moment before speaking again. 'I thought it was time you saw one for yourself.'

Sysa felt something quicken in her chest, like a little bird escaping from her ribcage.

'Oh thank you Grandfather,' she squealed, rushing closer to grab his cheeks in her hands and place a kiss on his face, surprised by the prickly stab that met her lips. Grey shook his head and carried on with serving Sysa's breakfast.

'But I thought you didn't want me to go near a faerie hill, Grandad?' she called, as she quickly retreated to dress behind the screen at the far end of the cottage. Flinging her bedclothes over the edge of the wooden screen, she chastised herself for the question, frowning into the blouse that fell over her head and skimmed the pale skin of her shoulders. Grey was finally allowing her to visit a faerie broch, the last thing she wanted to do was provide any opportunity for doubts to surface in his mind.

'You're almost eighteen now, Sysa,' Grey answered,

casting a glance over his shoulder as he began scrubbing the empty porridge pot. 'Virtually a grown woman. It's time I let you do the things you need to do.' He sighed, pausing for a moment from his activity. 'I know your life has been limited, living here in this cottage with me. I hope it's been enough for you Sysa.' He spoke into the blank face of the stone wall in front of him. 'You and me here together, I mean, I hope it's been enough.'

'What? Of course it's been enough, Grandad, why are you saying these things?' Sysa, now fully dressed and all remnants of sleep discarded, made her way across the room and curved towards Grey, fixing him with a raised eyebrow as she spoke.

'I just mean that you've been everything to me in life Sysa, I hope you know that,' Grey answered, as Sysa took a step back, a questioning line etching her forehead.

'Of course I know that, Grandad. We've been everything to *each other*. You're worrying me with this sort of talk Grandad. What on earth is wrong?'

'Nothing's wrong, child,' Grey said, his expression softening. And the last thing I mean to do is worry you.' Grey sighed, his shoulders rising and falling like a wave. 'I just hope you know how much I love you, and hope someday you'll understand me limiting you the way I have these past years. I know there are lots of things you've wanted to do that you've been unable to. When…' Grey paused for a moment, looking up at the wooden beams of the ceiling. 'When you're a bit older I hope you'll understand, and maybe forgive me a little bit.'

Sysa stood with her hands on her hips, incredulous. 'Grandad, there's nothing to forgive, don't be so silly!

You call this life here with you limited?' She waved her arm around. 'Limited? It's been the greatest adventure I could have ever had. And today, we're going on another adventure together, aren't we?' She pulled at his sleeve, tilting her face into his elbow. 'Come on Grandad, let's get ready.' She flung her arms around his shoulders, Grey's arms gathering loosely about her waist, the pot he had been scrubbing still jutting from one hand.

Sysa gulped down her breakfast, keen to depart for the long walk ahead of them. As they left the cottage, she looked around the glen and felt something strange come over her, almost as if she was seeing her home, the river and the sky from a viewpoint far away. She shuddered; Grey's odd mood was making her nervous. Grey smiled and patted her hand lightly, his eyes following hers across the scene behind them.

'Come now, Sysa,' he said after a moment. 'We better start walking.' He looked up, taking the measure of the early morning sky.

As the pair made their way along the track, Sysa saw an orange light in the distance. She squinted her eyes, blinking towards the watery glow that smeared the sky. Fire. *Of course, Beltane,* she thought, looking towards Grey, whose eyes remained steadfast on the route ahead of them.

'Look, the fire festival,' Sysa said, gesturing towards the fire that burned and flickered to the east. Grey paused, glancing over towards the flames, a rim of orange edging the sharp planes of his profile.

'Yes, it's been a while since we've seen that.' Grey stopped for a moment, his face expressionless despite the leaping flames reflected in his eyes.

21

As they walked on, Grey told Sysa that he was taking her towards the west, where she'd be able to see out to the water, to Orkney, and to the horizon. Sysa, who was used to the imposing landscape of the glen, watched as the world opened up across endless moors in rhythm with her steps. Grey, though, seemed sombre, his usually smooth face etched with worry. His green eyes, strangely flat and lifeless, betrayed the weak smile he cast at her as he made vague attempts at idle chat. Sysa grimaced, knowing Grey had never been one for small talk. The excitement building in her was tempered with a growing sense of dread. She flicked glances at her Grandfather, seeing a strange shadow across his features. Without warning, the darkness that had hovered around their lives these past few years was back.

The pair carried on, stopping now and again for water or something to eat from Grey's sack, or just to look out over the barren, bleak landscape that surrounded them in the half-light. Eventually, as Sysa saw the faint glow of sunrise peering out at them, they reached a grassy field which rose steeply to the right.

'Here we are,' said Grey as they turned in towards it. 'Not much further now.'

Sysa breathed in the smell of wildflowers and dew, suddenly feeling alive and alert again. The air held the remnants of rain, wafting around her like a sharp, beautiful assault against her nose.

They started to climb, making their way up the hill as the sunrise poured red and gold over the landscape. They rose steadily, clamouring over land stained green and brown and peppered with buttercups and cotton that sprang back against their feet. Sysa strode ahead, calling every so often to her Grandfather who tailed slightly behind, catching his breath now and then as the hill rose sharply above them. Sysa looked up at the peak, feeling for a moment as if an invisible line tugged at her, pulling at somewhere deep inside her ribcage, in that same place she'd felt that sense of lifting when Grey had told her of his plans.

Scrambling to the top, Sysa looked round to see what seemed like the whole world laid out before her, the sky so endless, and the land so big, letting her see all the way to Orkney. Taking a deep breath, she tried to breathe the landscape in, fresh air filling her lungs, euphoric with nature and the joy of simple things.

'Oh Grandfather, isn't it beautiful?' She turned to Grey, who was still making the final few steps towards her. She twirled around, her arms spread like out wings against the sunrise, all earlier worries forgotten. She stopped, giddy with life, fresh air and wonder.

'Isn't it just the most beautiful place you've ever seen?'

'Yes Sysa, it's lovely,' Grey said quietly, pausing for a moment to regulate his breathing. Sysa's thoughts were interrupted by the growing realisation that she had never seen Grey struggle after any kind of exertion in her life. 'And here is the place I wanted to show you,' Grey continued, the object of his gesture quickly diverting Sysa's anxiety. A little to their right, he motioned to a large hillock rising from the ground, a hill upon a hill, with a long chamber-shaped vessel protruding from the land beside it. 'Na Tri Shean,' he said, 'the three faerie mounds. Sysa, let's rest a little here.'

Grey moved towards the grassy hillock and on reaching it, sat down, resting himself against the moss, heavy and solid with the weight of stone behind it. Sysa followed, sitting down beside him, arching her back against the mass. She stretched her legs, looking out over the scene below them and the sunrise now reaching its final climax. As the last embers of gold and red lingered in the sky she looked towards Grey who took her hand and held it between his palms. His eyes were bright as he looked out over the vista. But as Sysa followed his gaze she felt a faint burr, the heat of a tremble beneath her skin. A screeching noise, at first distant, and then growing, began to ring in her ears and all around her. She smelled something like burning, but not like the flames from the peat fire, this was the burning of air and water and stone. She turned to look at her Grandfather, her mouth open.

'What's happening, Grandad?' she yelled as the noise and trembling whirled around her head, until she covered her ears against the scratching, desperate magnitude of the whirring. She was faintly aware of Grey looking at her, his lips forming words that seemed to say 'it's going to be all right.'

'You'll understand soon,' he called, the moisture in his eyes brighter now, as he stood above her. Sysa found herself standing too, the noise deafening, the whirring pulling irresistibly against her limbs. It took every ounce of her strength to extend her arm towards him.

'Grandad, help me, please don't leave me,' she called, her face contorting against the angry whirring that now swirled like waves and wind around her.

'I'll never leave you,' Grey said, grabbing onto her fingers and clutching them. 'But this is a journey I can't make with you,' he shouted, his fingers slowly loosing their grip as he backed away.

Sysa looked at him, into those bright green eyes she had seen so many times before. She had never seen them like this, so bright, yet so completely empty. As Grey backed away, Sysa lost sight of him amidst the chaos. His tall angular frame had simply disappeared behind a wall of air and noise and fear.

The din continued, the sound of a thousand fingernails on a blackboard. The whir rose higher, piercing the air in a cacophony of shrieks. Sysa felt the tang of the burning smell, saw a flash like lightning, heard a crash as though the sky had fallen in, and for a moment thought the world was going to burst before her. Then she saw the faces of a brown-haired man, a woman, a fair-haired girl, a Giant and a boy. Before she could see any more the world behind her eyes seemed to crack and shatter into tiny pieces.

Then darkness.

The world she knew was gone.

PART TWO

# CASTLES OF STEEL AND THUNDER

# CHAPTER FOUR

Aware of the light behind her eyes returning, Sysa forced her eyelids open. Groggy with the residue of sleep, she propped herself up onto her arms and squinted against the bright sun poking at her face. Raising a hand to her forehead, she looked around and wondered vaguely if she was dreaming.

'Grandad?' she managed, her weak voice disappearing into air.

The only reply was the sound of birds chirping and insects rustling underneath her. Sysa listened closely, tilting her head towards the ground. She could hear the soft sway of every grass blade, the breath of every wildflower. She inhaled, picking up the fresh, sweet scent of buttercups, and something else too – the tracks of an animal perhaps? Everything was sharper, clearer somehow, as if a misted window had been wiped without any prior knowledge that it needed cleaning. Sysa shuddered, shaking herself, feeling every whisper of the meadow that made contact with her skin. She bolted upright, looking around at the unfamiliar landscape. She was awake, of that she was certain. So where was her Grandfather and what on earth was going on?

She looked around, confirming without surprise that she was no longer in Caithness. This place was nothing like her home, with its vast and open fields. Brown and oatmeal coloured tundra had been replaced by a lush, green landscape flecked with wildflowers that smelled like sugar. Sysa marvelled for a moment at the hues of pink, purple and yellow laid out like a carpet across the scene. The wide open skies of her childhood were now divided by tall trees reaching up towards a ceiling of bright blue, sharp like crystal. Not far from the clearing in which she sat, a stream meandered slowly, glistening and sparkling in the light. Between the flowers, butterflies and birds in every colour of the rainbow dipped around the landscape. They hovered amongst the grass, spinning and twirling in the sun.

Sysa shook her head, closed her eyes, and opened them again, only to remain confronted with the unfamiliar scenery. She felt a sort of panic rise within her; a bubble floating from her stomach to her throat, where it lodged itself, so that she didn't think she could scream, or even speak, in a bid to call out to anyone for help. Where was her Grandfather, and what was she doing here? And what was it he had been saying to her before she fell asleep?

As she looked around wildly, Sysa heard the rustle of footsteps in the distance. Her heart pounded as she turned to see their owners emerging from the trees. Three figures appeared from the darkness, apparently their own light source. Sysa watched, frozen, as they moved towards her, faintly glowing from inside.

She registered two fair-haired women and, alongside them, a dark-haired man, his jaw cloaked in a beard that did not hide the marble-like beauty of his features. The trio strode purposely, almost gliding, and as the distance between them narrowed, Sysa regained control of her senses and scrambled to her feet. Oddly, she didn't feel frightened now, on the contrary, she felt a growing sense of calm as they moved closer towards her. It was as if she knew these people, these three strangers who approached her, and as the man drew closer, she recognised a familiar softness in his eyes.

He edged slowly towards her, arms outstretched, palms outwards, as if placating something that might attack him.

'Sysa, is that you?' he half-whispered, his voice straining, his face etched with an emotion Sysa couldn't place.

'I am Sysa,' she replied, standing aloft now, chin forward, her chest thrust out slightly.

'Who are you, and where am I?' she asked the tall man, as the two fair-haired women suddenly appeared behind him.

With their long flowing robes and golden hair they made Sysa think of angels, of sunlight, and of Kings and Queens atop impossibly shiny, gilded thrones. She couldn't help but be momentarily distracted by that faint glow which accompanied their presence, before returning her attention to the man before her, his green eyes imploring, his right palm pressed to his large chest as he spoke.

'Sysa, this is going to be hard for you to take in. You are in Fyrish, our homeland. I am Bruan, and this is my wife Elise,' he said, gesturing to the older of the two females behind him.

'And this is my daughter Elva,' he said, pointing to the other. 'This won't make much sense right now, so I'm just going to say it quickly,' he continued, everything about him looking awkward.

'Elise and I are your parents, Sysa, and Elva is your younger sister. We are so very glad to see you. We've waited a very, very long time for you to come back home.'

Sysa stared at the three people before her, the man searching her face, the two women smiling, the older one – her Mother he had said? – lifting a hand towards her lips, tears running down the planes of her cheekbones. Sysa felt a rush of shock sear through her. Her parents were dead, Grey had told her as much. *Hadn't he?* The man made a move towards her and Sysa jolted backwards, looking around, half expecting Grey to suddenly appear.

'But I don't understand. How can you be my parents? I don't have any parents – it's just my Grandfather and me. He took me to a faerie knoll and I fell asleep and woke up here. Where is my Grandad? Where's Grey? I don't understand!'

'Of course you don't,' said Bruan, backing away again.

'This is all too much for you to take in.' He sighed, looking around himself for an answer that did not appear to be forthcoming in the trees. Sysa recognised the gesture and felt the tightness across her chest release. She had seen that look many times before, back in Caithness.

'Come with us, back to our home here.' Bruan waved towards the trees he and the two women had emerged from. We'll explain everything once we get you home.'

He gestured again in a way that indicated Sysa should follow him, and despite herself, she did exactly as he asked. The presence of the three pulled at her, without them even touching her. She fell in behind them, the one the man had called Elva sneaking backwards glances, a shy smile playing across her face.

Sysa followed the three of them into the trees, her

mind swimming in a waterfall of confusion. Her silence harboured the racing of a million thoughts which arrived and retreated behind her eyes. How could these people be her parents? Yet were they? She rubbed at her temples, feeling the start of a dull ache growing. As they made their way through the woodland every crunch of fallen leaves pierced a sting against her brow.

Eventually, she saw a tall tower protruding from between trees in the distance, its roof arrow-like, staring at the sun which beamed back at it. As they grew closer a track emerged, and as the view opened, Sysa saw a white castle, and next to it a winding path, a forest, and in the distance the sea and a stony, shingled shore. Sysa paused for a moment, feeling the faint breath of salty air and the sound of rasping waves curl against her senses. Closer, from the track ahead, she heard the chirruping of birds, and listened to the faint murmur of a butterfly flap its wings.

They arrived at the castle doors, already swung open in readiness of their coming. Several figures stood waiting, lining the arched entrance which was tiled in gleaming black and white. An aproned woman held her hand to her chest and Sysa heard the sharp intake of a muffled breath as she pressed her fist against her mouth, crying out softly.

'Sysa, welcome to the Castle of Steel,' Bruan said, turning quickly enough to catch the flicker in Sysa's eyes at the mention of her name.

He paused for a moment, as if he planned to say something else on the matter but then thought better of it. He turned back towards the woman, who was still quivering with excitement, her apron now bunched in the fist she was dabbing across her cheeks.

'This is our housekeeper Ida,' Bruan said as he waved an arm between the pair in introduction. Sysa aimed a weak smile at the woman, getting the sense that her small, stout body was almost ready to explode.

'Oh my dear, you've come back!' the housekeeper half-shouted, unable to contain herself any longer as she advanced, pulling Sysa close to her rounded figure. Sysa stood, limp-armed and squashed against Ida's ample bosom as the woman held her with a ferocity that suggested unusual strength for a lady of her size.

'Come now, Ida, she's tired. This has all been a bit of a shock for her,' Bruan offered politely, venturing his outstretched arm towards Sysa as an exit. Sysa ducked under it as the woman pressed her lips together and prodded at her eyes with a large handkerchief she had produced from somewhere in her dress.

Sysa peered out from under Bruan's arm as they passed the other men and women lining the entranceway. Servants, she thought, by the looks of them, smiling tightly at the faces of several youngish-looking men and women, all in the process of either curtseying or dipping their heads low as she passed. Through tufts of hair, she noticed ears peak-tipped, like tiny mountain summits. A large dog, flecked with grey and white scuttled and barked around the women's skirts, nails clipping on the marble.

'Telon, come!' Bruan commanded over his shoulder, and the dog scrambled over obediently to his heel.

As they were about to round towards the inner entrance to the castle, Sysa heard a beating sound behind her, slow and steady in the distance. Eventually, the sound ceased, leaving Sysa with the odd impression that something had planted itself behind her and was waiting expectantly at her rear. She turned to see a golden eagle perched on the branch of a tree overhanging the path which was leading to the left of them. Sysa looked around quickly, but found no sign of any surprise in her family's – was that what they were now? – returning stares. Instead, Bruan turned to look at the huge eagle, a slow smile curving on his lips. Sysa looked again at the bird and back towards the man who called himself her Father, and gasped involuntarily. They appeared to be communicating.

'Is that... are you?...' she asked, her words trailing off into the air.

'Yes,' Bruan answered, looking back at her.

'That's Arno, he's what we call a sky seer, and we can talk to him. Come, we'll tell you everything inside,' he continued, moving her gently along towards the inner door.

Sysa glanced back towards the huge bird who sat statue-like on his perch behind them. She wondered at the strength of the tree able to hold him, yet the slim branch showed no sign of straining with his weight.

'Things are made stronger here,' the woman called Ida whispered towards Sysa, winking.

The bird looked at Sysa for a moment, cocked his large head and then appeared to nod. Transfixed, Sysa stared at him, his beady amber eyes holding hers, unblinking. Finally, she was released from his stare by the light pressure of Bruan's fingers guiding her inside. Sysa watched as Bruan nodded back to the bird, held his eyes for a moment, and then whispered something. At his request the bird opened his large wings and flew away, his drumming wing beats echoing around the hall.

Sysa followed the others through a hallway, up a curving staircase, and through another doorway. They finally arrived in a large room laid with dark and heavy slabs. To one side, an orange fire glowed in a hearth, its warmth beckoning the dog, Telon, who ventured over and plopped himself, limbs sprawling, on a rug in front of the fireplace. He emitted a loud sigh before falling asleep in front of the crackle of the flames.

To the other side of the room was a huge wooden table, lit by a hanging candelabra that ignited with a flick of Bruan's wrist as he entered. The table was adorned with several bowls of fruit, which reminded Sysa that she hadn't eaten for some time. The fruit shone under the light of the candelabra in golden arcs of ripe sweetness – a prospect which invited a growl from Sysa's stomach in response.

'Are you hungry?' the woman, Elise, ventured quietly, noticing Sysa's gaze on the table and gesturing towards the colourful platter.

'No, no thankyou,' Sysa said, the stories of not eating or drinking in the Fae lands echoing through her. *Not yet*, she thought, *not until I know more about them*. Her mouth watered involuntarily. She pursed her lips together, swallowing the saliva that rushed up inside her throat.

Bruan had seated himself at the table and now beckoned Sysa to sit at one of the chairs opposite him. He gestured for the two women to sit on either side of him.

'Please,' he said, watching Sysa's fingers linger on the chair. 'We'd never hurt you Sysa.'

He smiled again, that faraway look in his eyes reminding her of Grey. Something about the set of his mouth, the way his lips curled – she'd seen it all before. Sysa waited

36

for the two women to sit down, hearing the sliver of silk as they smoothed their robes beneath them and looked at her expectantly. Sighing, Sysa sat too, her chair scratching against the grey slabs underneath her feet. Bruan looked back at her and nodded, his hands clasped against the table.

'Thankyou Sysa,' he whispered, meeting her eyes again, the sound of his exhale fluttering around her ears. He bowed his head low and opened his mouth before closing it again.

*He's nervous*, Sysa thought, feeling her own hands tremble as she pressed them to her lap.

'Go on,' she said, her face softening under the candlelight. She leaned in across the table. Something about this man made her want to listen to him speak.

'I'm going to tell you the story of how you came to be in Fyrish, Sysa,' he said as he lifted his face towards her. 'It's a long and difficult story, and I'm sure in many ways it will leave you feeling full of questions and confused. But I'll tell it the best I can and hope you'll understand it. It's the story of our family and this land of ours. And it's the story of you, and Grey, and why he sent you back here. And why you had to leave in the first place.' His voice cracked a little. Sysa watched as Elise gripped his hand, her knuckles white against the skin.

'Many years ago, this land of ours was ruled by both a Faerie King and Queen, and a King and Queen of Giants,' Bruan continued, clearing his throat quickly. 'If you didn't realise it by now, Sysa, the faeries and giants your Grandfather told you about were real. They lived in harmony and ruled separate areas of the kingdom. Your Grandfather was in fact my Father, and he was once our Faerie King.'

Sysa gasped. Grey? A Fae King? Why had he never told her?

'But he can't have been!' Sysa blurted, thoughts looping around her head, twisting and threading through her mind. *But could he?* she thought again, remembering the flash on the hill that day of the Lavellan. Then she thought of Grey making her breakfast, tucking her into her bed, doing things that could be described as little more than ordinary. Was what this man was telling her even possible? Could Grey have really been a King?

'I know it makes very little sense just now,' Bruan said, raising a palm up as if halting the stream of thoughts within her.

'It's the truth,' Elise offered from beside him, her face tilted towards Sysa, eyes moist under the glow from the candelabra hanging above.

'It is, isn't it?' Sysa answered, looking between them, understanding flooding through her. She felt it trickle down her throat and spread to her stomach, across her limbs and right down to her feet. They were telling the truth and she knew it, perhaps she had always known it. An image of Grey staring out at the sunset on the glen flashed across her mind. She sighed, wanting to reach out to him, to run to him and tell him she understood now. Before she could speak, he turned and smiled that faraway smile. Then the image cracked, splintering and shaking across her consciousness, retreating as quickly as it had come to her.

'Tell me the rest,' she said, arching her spine before sinking again into the wooden back of the chair.

'As a boy, I played with the Giant Prince, Rogart, and

we spent many years enjoying our childhood together as the sons of royalty,' Bruan continued.

'But things changed when we grew into young men and fell in love with the same woman, the woman that now sits beside me as my wife,' Bruan said, placing a hand on Elise's arm. Sysa saw the look that passed between them, the shared history as their eyes met. She winced inwardly at some internal hurt, a small ache that pulsed steadily, growing and gripping against her bones.

'Rogart was filled with jealousy when he discovered that Elise and I were sweethearts, but we would not betray the love we felt for one another,' Bruan said, looking back at his wife again. 'Jealousy darkened inside Rogart, and after his Father's death, he took his darkness to the throne. When he found out that Elise was pregnant – with you Sysa' – Bruan looked across at her, eyes gleaming – 'he cursed the fruit of her belly to be banished from Fyrish forever. The fruit of her belly was you, Sysa. You were our beloved unborn child.'

Sysa tried to imagine herself growing inside this woman's rounded belly. She tried to imagine the hurt and confusion the two young lovers must have felt in the knowledge that their unborn child was cursed. She squeezed her eyes together, pressing against the misery and chaos. When she opened them again, something between a cough and a snort escaped from her throat and rose up in her mouth.

'Your Mother, who was skilled in magic,' Bruan continued, his face etched and painful, 'managed to reduce the curse so that although you might be banished, you could return to Fyrish before your eighteenth birthday.'

Bruan tiptoed over the words, placing them slowly in front of Sysa as she absorbed each tiny revelation with a nod.

'She also managed to enact a glamour which meant that Rogart would never again be able to curse a child within her.' *A glamour*, Sysa thought, looking towards Elise, whose head was bent slightly towards the table. *She made her womb invisible to him.*

'I so wish I'd done that before, Sysa,' Elise said, stretching a hand across the table towards her. Sysa stared at it blankly.

'We didn't know then what Rogart was capable of. We never thought…' Elise's words trailed off as the proffered hand slipped back across the wood.

'It was too late by the time we realised the lengths he was willing to go to Sysa,' she said, her eyes moist pools of guilt and pleading.

'You have to understand, Sysa, he had been our *friend*.'

'And so as soon as you were born my Father took you away to the human world, so he could assist in your return when you were older,' Bruan interjected, his words piercing the cloud of pain that lingered between Sysa and her Mother.

'The stories he told you were imbued with a magic, which meant that the powers he possessed were passed directly on to you. Every night, when he was telling you those stories, he gave you a little more of those powers, so that by the time you were ready to return here you'd have the power of a King within you. Well, more accurately, the power of a Queen, Sysa.

Because that's what you are here Sysa. You are the Faerie Queen.'

# CHAPTER FIVE

'Can we just go back for a moment?' Sysa said, rubbing at her temples. The throbbing was back now, pulsing and squeezing beneath her brow. 'If I was your child, why didn't you come with me?' She watched as another flicker of pain spread its way across Elise's face.

'We wanted to, Sysa, believe me, we wanted that more than anything.' Tears were running down Elise's cheeks but her voice didn't falter.

'It was impossible, though, your Grandfather convinced us of that. As the King, he held within him all the magic he was due to pass down to your Father. He'd passed on some of it of course, but by that stage, it just wasn't going to be enough. If we had gone to the human world with you, we'd all have died within a few years. There's no way Grey would have stayed here and allowed that. It would have been a death sentence. For all of us. I'd have given up my life a hundred times over for you Sysa. But we couldn't take you to Never Night just to let you die.'

Sysa searched her memory for some of Grey's stories. His *teachings*. She remembered his words, about Never Night, the place she knew as home. She thought back to those nights on the rocking chair, her feet dangling over Grey's solid, long limbs as he spoke to her. Could there really have been a weakness under that exterior? She remembered what he'd told her: Fae folk could not survive in the human world for long.

'The only one who was powerful enough to go with you was Grey, Sysa. The strength of his power meant that he'd be able to survive in the human world – and keep you alive – for many years longer than we could. In that time, he'd be able to pass on all the powers you needed, and once he'd done that, return you here before your eighteenth birthday. It was the only way Sysa. I promise you. Sending you away without us was the hardest thing we've ever had to do.'

'The powers I needed?' Sysa asked, her thoughts swimming in dark pools of confusion. 'I don't have any powers!' She jolted back against her chair, the screech of wood on stone singing across the room.

'Let me explain a bit more, Sysa,' Bruan said, pressing his palms to the table. He looked weary, Sysa thought, years of worry and remorse drawn in fine lines across his forehead. He rubbed his beard, soft and dark, not the prickly kind Sysa was accustomed to seeing in the menfolk of Caithness. She exhaled, unwinding in response to his open face.

'And what about your Mother? Grey's wife, my Grand-mother. Where's she?' Sysa looked around the room as if she expected the woman to somehow materialise.

'My Mother died when I was very young. I don't remember her.' Something painful in the set of Bruan's jaw diverted Sysa from her line of questioning.

'All right, tell me the rest, then please,' she managed finally. 'It's just a lot to take in, that's all.'

Bruan nodded. 'I know it is. This is strange for us too, Sysa. I'll do my best.'

'Your Mother and I have waited here for many years for Grey to return you, as we always knew he would when the time was right for it.' Bruan's voice was steady now. 'We have carried on here in Fyrish as the Faerie King and Queen and in the meantime you have a sister, Elva,' Bruan said, reaching a hand towards the young woman who squeezed it, an easy display of affection that made something flutter inside Sysa's chest.

'As you know, Rogart was unable to curse Elva in the same way he did you thanks to your Mother's glamour. From a young age, Elva has known all about you.' The girl beside him nodded. 'We have lived here together all these years waiting for you, Sysa. We have thought about you every single day.'

'But whilst you have been gone I'm afraid Fyrish has fallen into disarray, with Rogart persecuting faeries and many other Fyrish people,' Bruan continued, his voice smooth and deep across the table.

'Rogart has only grown in power, while our own powers have become less and less. You see, without the presence of Grey, our magic has diminished. You are much more powerful than any of us Sysa. And so, Fyrish is now relying on you to help us defeat Rogart. You're the only one who can do it Sysa. We've always believed that your return would save our way of life.'

Sysa looked into Bruan's eyes, which flashed with shame and guilt and sorrow. *For what he's telling me?* she wondered. *Or for what they had to do when they let me go away?* She also saw the light of something else there, a flicker echoed in the glances her Mother stole towards her. That same look she had seen in Grey's eyes when he kissed her goodnight or told her that he loved her. It was there in their eyes too, waiting for the tiniest morsel of hope.

Sysa's thoughts were interrupted by a loud snore from the fireplace. She glanced over at Telon, who was evidently in a state of blissful dreaming, completely unperturbed by the events unfolding as he slept.

'So you're telling me... that I'm more powerful than you? Fae people?' Sysa finally croaked out, her throat dry and tingling from the breath she had kept sucked in through Bruan's revelations. 'And that Grey, he passed these powers on through, what, talking, or the air? Through the stories he told me? The powers skipped a generation and came to me instead of you?'

'In a manner of speaking, yes that's what happened,' Elise said, nodding at her daughter. 'We do have some powers, but they're a shadow of what they were.'

'Can I give them back to you?' Sysa said, feeling faintly ridiculous at the question. She was bargaining over powers she didn't even recognise as being hers.

'I'm afraid not, they belong to you now,' Bruan said, a small smile slipping across his face, transforming his features. 'Now that you're back, it may be that your presence returns some powers to us, we'll have to see about that as time goes on. But what matters now is you being here with us again Sysa. I know this is hard for you, but you don't know how long we've all dreamt about this day.'

Bruan paused and looked over at his newly returned daughter, willing her to understand his story. Sysa let his kind eyes wash over her, and despite questions raising up from every corner of her being, knew somehow that he was telling her the truth. But still the questions raced through her mind until they settled on the one that had been creeping and retreating. *Faeries cannot survive in the human world for long.*

'But what about Grey?' she croaked, her voice escaping in a way she didn't recognise. 'What about my Grandfather? What will happen to him now?'

Bruan's head dipped, heavy with the weight of sorrow. When he lifted it again, the look across his features left Sysa with a dull ache that slowly stabbed across her heart.

'You'll know from the stories Grey told you,' he began, 'that when faeries leave our world for the human world they can normally only survive for a year or less. Things were different for Grey, as they are for High Fae possessing of such power. His abilities meant he could survive for many more years than that – that was the reason he went with you. Grey used those years to pass all his powers on to you, so that you could one day return to Fyrish with all the powers of a Fae Queen.'

Sysa listened as Bruan reiterated his earlier story. Grey had given his powers to her so she could live. The knowledge pricked at Sysa's throat as she imagined his gift, pressing through the air between them. He had given her his powers, and the strength to survive within the glen. The realisation that the place where she had lived so easily could have slowly killed her was unthinkable. And there was another thought, pressing down on her chest as her heart thudded to meet it. *No, she would not think of that just yet.*

'That's why Grey forbade you from visiting a faerie

hillock – for fear that you might return too early,' Bruan continued, piercing her thoughts as she avoided the inevitable.

'Grey had to make sure he had time to pass on all his powers to you before your eighteenth birthday, so that he could return you to us with all the powers you need. He couldn't risk sending you back early, before you were ready.'

*Ready*, thought Sysa. *I have never felt less ready.*

'He knows about me, doesn't he? Rogart I mean,' Sysa said, throwing her words across the table. 'Things happened, before Grey asked me to stop going far from the cottage.'

Bruan looked at her, his mouth forming a silent 'o'.

'There was a creature, a *thing* one day' – Sysa spat the word out with disgust – 'that tried to attack Grandfather at Beltane. After that he changed, he seemed to worry about me more.' *Beltane*, she thought, that look in Grey's eyes when he thought she might see the trooping faeries. 'He was worried I was going to leave early – or that someone was coming to take me away.'

Bruan exhaled, and looked down towards his fingers. 'Yes, it's likely that Rogart knows about you by now, Sysa, and that he sent some of his followers to track you. He has Fae folk within his ranks, some shape shifters, some of our own Seelie folk he's managed to twist into the dark. I admit that even we ourselves couldn't always resist the temptation to see you now and again.' Sysa thought of the townsfolk and their whispers of sightings of the Fae Queen, the trooping faeries at Beltane.

'You watched me?' she said in a whisper.

'Yes, sometimes,' Elise answered, her eyes glistening in reply. 'But it was too risky. Mostly we sent Arno to watch over you. He would come back with visions for me. How I loved it when I could watch you sleep.'

Sysa shivered, imagining her Mother watching her through the amber eyes of the eagle. 'Arno? The eagle we saw back there at the door?'

'Yes, Arno – his kind are our friends and messengers,' Elise said, her green eyes warm across the table.

'They are able to move between the Fae and human worlds easily. He often watched you, and carried messages from Grey. That's how we knew you were coming home today, of course.' Elise spoke as if Sysa had popped out on an errand.

Sysa traced the corners of her mind for a memory that suddenly came loose behind her eyes. A small girl looking up at a huge-winged bird in the sky and squinting at the sunshine. Grey, looking out into the sky for answers at the dawn. And the bird, back at the entrance to the castle, peering at her through eyes that could see right through to her soul, to the bones within her. Of course they could, she thought – he had always known her. And then the question came back, pressing and crushing against her, taking her breath away.

'And Grey – what will happen to him now that I am gone?'

# CHAPTER SIX

'Please tell me,' she asked again, more gently this time. 'What happens to Grandfather now that I am here? Will he continue to live in the glen alone? Who will keep him company now that I'm no longer with him?' The lightness in Sysa's voice scratched at a wound that had already opened somewhere in her chest.

Bruan's eyes dropped to the table, and he spoke more quietly than he had done previously. 'I'm so sorry Sysa, but now that Grey has passed all of his powers to you his strength has weakened. He will no longer be able to use those powers to keep him alive in the human world. You deserve to know the truth my darling.' He said the word with such tenderness that Sysa thought her heart was going to break, just spill out over the table and fall into the deep ridges of the wood. She sat upright, though, eyes stinging and burning. She knew this, somewhere in herself she'd known this – somehow Grey had already made her understand.

'So he just dies?' she said bluntly, her eyes brimming, full of regret for the life she'd taken from him. For the life he'd given to her so easily. Bruan nodded. She felt something fall inside her, lurching to the floor of her stomach with a thump.

A sound escaped from her, something like the wail of an animal, a noise she hadn't known existed. Bruan and Elise rushed towards her as she slumped suddenly to the floor. She felt arms under her shoulders as the world disappeared into a muffled, dizzy haze around her. Then they picked her up, the room spinning. Across the table she saw Elva chewing on her lip, her face a blur behind the tears.

Bruan held Sysa away from him, his hands on her shoulders, eyes pleading. Finally she sunk into the arms that wrapped around her, the touch of Elise's hands warm against her back. Elva hovered at the edges, hesitating as she placed long fingers on Sysa's shoulders. They stood together like that for a while, sobbing through ragged, punctured breaths. Sysa felt the warmth of them around her, standing enclosed completely between her Father and her Mother. They were the only things in the world keeping her from falling. From now on, she realised, they were everything she had.

But still she couldn't accept Grey's fate as settled, she had to ask, she had to rail against it.

'But can't we bring him back to the faerie world?' she said, pushing herself with a gasp out of the embrace. 'We can't just leave him there to die can we? I can't bear the thought of it!' She squeezed at her eyes, wiping the tears away, pacing back and forth across the floor.

When she turned, Bruan's face was dark, shadows crossing his features. In the dim of the room, she saw the light of the fire reflected in his eyes.

'I understand your feelings Sysa, believe me,' he said, stepping towards her. 'Grey is my Father, I want nothing more than to live with him here again. If there were any way he could rejoin us I would make it happen, I would Sysa. But there is just no way that we can do it. He knew that, when he sent you back here. He wanted nothing more than for you to get back safe.'

Sysa made a strangled noise as Bruan continued.

'When Grey passed all his powers to you he became weakened, his heart less of a faerie, and more like a mortal man. He was happy to bequeath that power to you. He made those sacrifices gladly, knowing that one day he could return you here to claim your throne with us. Grey believed more than any of us that you would be Fyrish's saviour. From the moment you were born he felt the strength of your love inside you. He knew that love would one day be strong enough to save us all.'

Sysa sat down again at the table, defeated. A single hot tear rolled down her cheek as thoughts of Grey rolled over in her head. Grey, who had sacrificed everything because of how much he loved her. Who had spent so many years preparing her for this day. Who had given her all the power and magic he possessed in life. As her family's arms encircled her, Sysa swore to herself that she would not let him down.

*

The hours that followed were spent weaving through the memories lost in years of separation. In a game of back and forth, Sysa took her family through the corridors and passages of her life. She listened as they did likewise, veering between regret for what was gone, and curiosity. And something else that had lain dormant in her chest somewhere – the simple sense of who she was. Sysa found herself amazed at how quickly she slotted back into her family, how keenly she allowed her Father's arms to wrap around her, how much she enjoyed the touch of her Mother's hands as she held her face, declaring how much they'd missed her. She found the quiet joy of a new-found sister, as she and Elva got to know each other, at first nervously and then in fits of giggles as Sysa regaled her with stories of her many happy years with Grey. Somewhere, amongst the loss and the sorrow and the misery, there was still that, the memories beating steady like a drum inside her. The pain that had cracked open within her over Grey had left a hole, an entranceway her family could use. They were there with her now, she wholly given up to them, and they likewise. Amongst it all, she felt something like happiness lurk within her chest. There was only one thing missing – Grey himself, her beloved Grandad, the man who had raised her, the Fae King who bequeathed her with powers she still could not believe in. The loss of Grey was devastating, shattering somehow, and Sysa felt that dull stab of sadness pierce the bubble that had been created around the room. It felt right to be here with her family, but so wrong that it had been at the cost of the life spent with her Grandfather. How was it possible, she thought, to feel wonder and joy and grief all at the same time? How was it possible to love someone so much and to wake up and find them completely absent from your life?

★

Some time later, Sysa looked up from the table to see a dark-haired boy peering around the large oak door of the dining room. Half-in, half-out of the room, he hesitated, a smile spreading across his face as he wrapped one arm around the frame.

'Brodie, come in, come in boy!' Bruan boomed across the table, gesturing to the boy in welcome. The boy was more of a young man, Sysa noted, as he moved with long strides across the room. The air in the room pricked with energy as Brodie swept towards the table, Telon barking and flitting in the background. Sysa watched as Elise and Elva jumped up to meet him, reaching out to him in a manner that indicated he was familiar with the intimacies of such scenes.

'Brodie, this is Sysa, our daughter,' said Bruan, eyes glistening with pride under the candelabra. He slapped Brodie on the back in greeting and the boy lurched forward slightly in reaction to the force.

'Sysa is here Brodie, she's come back to us. Come and meet her Brodie, our daughter has returned!'

'Oh I know, Bruan, Arno came to find me, and to tell me, and I rushed straight back from the forest,' Brodie said breathlessly, his eyes darting around the table.

'I'm so happy to meet you Sysa,' he said, turning from Sysa's Father to face her, grasping her hand and shaking it until everyone ended up laughing because he had been shaking it for so long.

'I'm sorry,' Brodie laughed, revealing a set of white teeth and a smile that reached up to meet the corners of his eyes. For a moment Sysa found herself blushing, overwhelmed by her sudden status as centrepiece. Then, annoyed at herself, she lifted her chin, meeting the bright blue eyes that swivelled towards her face. She thought she saw Brodie's expression flicker, but just as quickly his features rearranged themselves; the upturned corners of his mouth suggesting something like amusement. Irritated, Sysa sniffed at the air, feeling a wet nose thrust itself into her fingers. She looked down to see Telon in the space between them, nudging at her palm with his muzzle and rubbing his head against her legs.

'So how do you all know each other?' Sysa asked, shooing the dog away and gesturing in a way that encompassed Brodie, her parents and Elva. Behind her, Telon, evidently now bored with the proceedings, turned several half-circles on the rug, before flopping down again to resume his interrupted rest.

'Oh, we've known Brodie forever. He's one of the family really,' Elva said, moving to Brodie's side and putting an arm around him. Sysa couldn't help but notice the way Elva's fingertips gripped his hand, holding it for a moment longer than was really necessary, Sysa thought – albeit with her very limited experience of boys. Brodie smiled back, taking a small step away to the right – which placed him right in the path of Elise, who had, in the interim, curved into the space beside them. Brodie looked between the pair and gave the tiniest of shrugs, obviously resigned to the petting and prodding of the two females who now flanked his either side.

'I found him, on the shore out there, when he was just a baby,' Elise said, stroking at Brodie's arm and squeezing his cheek lightly. Brodie half-shrugged, half-nodded as he looked at Sysa. He glanced back at Elise, awaiting the start of an obviously familiar tale. Sysa flinched a little, feeling a sense of being on the outside of a well-trodden path, the route unknown to her. She thought of the cottage, the track, and the glen rushing down to the river in Caithness. All as known to her as her own reflection in a looking glass. All part of a story which had only ever belonged to her and Grey.

'I was out walking, not long after we lost you Sysa,' Elise continued, apparently oblivious to Sysa's thoughts as she started in to her story. Sysa nodded in encouragement, grateful that her Mother's powers didn't appear to extend to observing the inner workings of her mind.

'At that time, I often strolled along the beach in the morning. I found a lot of comfort in the waves,' Elise said, her gaze drifting to the window that framed a perfect rectangle of hazy, azure sky. One morning, I found him out there, wrapped up in a sealskin, just a little baby, and right then I vowed that we would watch over and protect him. And from that day on, he lived with us here. Well most of the time anyway.' She nodded towards Brodie, fussing over his collar.

'He's a bit of a free spirit, our Brodie. He comes and goes as he pleases. It's always been that way.' She pecked him on the cheek and sat down again, leaving Elva to linger at his side.

'So where did you come from? Are you a selkie?' Sysa asked, swivelling to look at Brodie. She thought back to Grey's old stories of the seal folk who shed their skins to take human form around the earth. The females, so beautiful that mortal men would steal their skins so that they could possess them, take them as wives and keep them from the sea. The males, devastatingly handsome and possessing of a sort of magnetism that mortal women found impossible to resist. Sysa felt heat rush towards her face as she looked at the tall, angular boy across the table. A muscle in his cheek twitched as he fixed her with an unusually piercing blue stare.

*I'm not a mortal woman*, Sysa thought, shivering slightly.

'No, I'm not a selkie, Sysa,' Brodie said, holding her gaze in answer. Despite wondering what that actually made him, Sysa did not ask him any more.

'No, Brodie isn't a selkie,' Elise said, looking between the pair, jolting them back into the present. 'We kept the seal skin we found him in, but it held no power to transform him to a seal. Brodie is just Brodie, aren't you, my dear?' Elise said, placing a hand on his shoulder as he took a seat, his chair scratching on the floor.

'We think of him as a gift from the universe, sent to help our hearts after we lost you, Sysa. He and your sister,' she said, gesturing towards Elva who had sat down next to Brodie.

'I see,' said Sysa, looking between the pair, who could, she thought briefly, almost pass for siblings, despite the marked difference in hair and eye colour. Brodie drummed his fingers lightly on the table, absently enough, Sysa thought, to indicate nothing of his thoughts. She opened her mouth to ask another question, and then closed it again abruptly. Something in the way he looked at her told Sysa not to pursue this conversation any further than she had.

Although his affection for the family was apparent, Brodie did not, Sysa noticed over the coming hours, assume the familiarity of an immediate family member. He called her parents by their first names and poked fun gently at Elva as they talked. Sysa learned that over the years he had spent much of his time away from the family, living a sort of solitary existence and returning as and when he wished to. No one seemed to mind this, and Brodie was treated with all the affection and cordiality afforded to a friend. Her parents laughed as they told stories of Elva and Brodie learning to fly the young eagle Arno as toddlers. Sysa watched her sister's eyes rest on Brodie as he mimicked a tiny Elva clinging onto Arno and sliding across his wings. That Sysa wasn't stunned by stories of children riding golden eagles made her laugh suddenly.

*Grandfather,* she thought to herself, *you certainly prepared me well.*

Pausing, the group looked round to her, and rising to his feet Bruan lifted his glass in address to the watching room.

'To Sysa, my dear daughter who on this happiest of days is returned to us. And to Grey, my dear Father. I'm so sorry we couldn't say goodbye.'

# CHAPTER SEVEN

'We need to let her see what Fyrish has become, Bruan,' Sysa overheard her Mother whisper as she made her way along the long hallway leading from her new bedroom. Sunlight poured in through a large window at the end of the hall, which faced out onto the walled garden and the sea and sky beyond. Sysa watched every dust mote curl and dance around the hallway as she made her path along the carpeted passage. Peering around the edge of the door from which the whispers originated she saw her Mother standing over Bruan, who was rubbing rhythmically at his brow. Elise's hands rested on his shoulders, which were hunched over his knees, coiled and weary.

'It's too soon, darling,' said Bruan, 'it's too much for her. We're expecting such a lot of her, and we've only just got her back.'

Sysa indicated her arrival with a cough which jolted Bruan immediately upright. His eyes brightened when he saw her, and he made his way over to his daughter and wrapped his arms around her tight.

'Good morning. I didn't see you there,' he said, holding her away from his body, looking over her as if for the first time.

'How did you sleep darling; how do you feel today?' Elise interjected, hugging her shoulders and kissing her with lips that felt like velvet. Sysa sighed. In truth she hadn't slept terribly well in her new surroundings, having been led to a huge high-ceilinged room that was nothing like the tiny cottage she was used to sleeping in with Grey. Tossing and turning for most of the night she had spent hours grappling with the enormity of everything she had discovered, before eventually falling into a half-sleep that left her neither rested nor refreshed when she awoke from it. But seeing the concern on her parents' faces she had no desire to distress them any further. 'I slept very well, thankyou,' she lied, gripping her Mother's hands and holding them in the space between their chests.

'Father, I heard you talking,' Sysa said as she drew away slowly, tiptoeing into the subject. 'And you don't need to worry, because I'm ready to see whatever it is I need to see. I want to help you and the sooner we get on with it the better. I'm not the baby who left here Father. I'm strong, and I want to see my home.'

Bruan looked at her, his eyes twinkling, a small smile sending fine lines dancing around his face.

'Indeed you are strong,' he said, shaking his head and laughing despite himself, the skin around his eyes crinkling. 'You're as strong as can be, and just as stubborn. Soon, we will take you to see what's become of the place. But first, we want to welcome you home properly. After that, we take you to see your land.'

*

Sysa bristled as the silk of her dress rustled underneath her. She pulled at a piece of material at her shoulder and grimaced as it slipped back down her skin. Ida, with her fussing and fawning in the bedroom, had cajoled Sysa into a sparkling, swaying creation of green silk and chiffon.

'You're a vision!' the servant had declared triumphantly when her preening was complete and Sysa was permitted to look in the oval standing mirror.

*A vision of what*, Sysa wondered as she looked over the ringed curls and folded pleats staring back.

She turned in small half-circles, barely recognising the girl in front of her, so different from the one who'd left the glen with Grey so recently. She had to concede, though, that the dress brought out the bright green of her eyes.

'So beautiful!' Ida said, her head appearing in the mirror in the space above Sysa's shoulder.

'Thankyou, Ida,' Sysa answered, smoothing down a strand of hair that had come loose from its containment. The woman squeezed her shoulder and hurried off, making small squealing sounds on her way out of the room and onwards down the hall.

'Beautiful indeed,' Bruan said, his head appearing around the doorway. 'May I come in?' he ventured.

'Of course,' said Sysa, scratching at her neck and looking squarely at her feet.

'I feel ridiculous,' she announced, shrugging off any pretence of comfort in her restrictive outfit.

'Well, you look wonderful,' Bruan offered, his eyes bright against the glare of Sysa's dress.

'Oh, let me look at you!' Elise, who had appeared in the room in a blur of silken elegance, cried out, clasping her hands to her chest and virtually floating across the floor.

'Let me see my beautiful daughter,' she implored,

grabbing Sysa's hands and raising them, turning her this way and that to get a better view. Sysa dipped her chin, looking out from under dark lashes and raising an eyebrow.

'Will I do?' she asked. Her Mother pulled her to her chest in answer.

'No, I'm going to crease your dress,' she sniffed, pulling away and wiping her eyes quickly. 'Come, let's go now, the guests are arriving. Everyone is so excited to see you.' With a pull on Sysa's hand, Elise dragged her gently from the room.

Elva was waiting in the hallway, resplendent in a long ivory satin gown, flecked with swirls of lace which traced an arc across her body. Her face brightened as her sister and parents emerged from Sysa's bedroom.

'You look wonderful!' she cried out, rushing up to Sysa and clutching at her hand. 'Come on, everyone's waiting,' she instructed, already pulling Sysa towards the staircase. As they reached the top of the curving stairs, Sysa looked down at the throng of people gathered in the entrance hall, the hum of their conversation sweeping up to meet them.

'I can't do this,' she gulped, swivelling on her heel and attempting to push her way back to the bedroom via the space between her parents' chests.

'Oh no you don't,' smiled Bruan, pressing his fingers lightly on her shoulder and steering her back towards the stairs.

'It'll be fine,' said Elva, briefly scanning the crowd before announcing, 'Oh look, there's Brodie!' and pointing towards the marbled floor beneath them.

Sysa peered over the banister and saw him looking up at her, his bright blue eyes twinkling as Elva waved, her cheeks flushing as she tried to get his attention. Still

Brodie held Sysa's eyes, a small smile tugging at his lips. He gestured in the tiniest of bows before turning his attention towards Elva and their parents. Sysa inhaled, an unfamiliar warmth rising up to meet her features. All of a sudden, she felt ready to descend.

'I present to you, Sysa, daughter of Bruan and Elise and sister of Elva. Returned to us from the land of the Never Night!' a voice boomed out from the entrance hall below.

Sysa looked over to see one of the servants who had greeted her the day previously, now dressed in formal attire, a band of ruffles at each wrist and just below his knees.

'It's going to be fine,' she whispered to herself in refrain as they descended, a hush falling across the hall as a sea of soundless faces peered up at her. Elise glanced at her with a smile obviously well versed in the formality of such scenes.

'I'm all right,' Sysa assured her, something squeezing at the space inside her throat for a moment as she carefully picked her way down the steps beneath her, pinched fingers lifting the material of her ballgown.

Suddenly, the sound of applause, at first a slow clap and then a thundering drum of hands and feet drew in like a wave across the hall. She looked over at her parents, their eyes glistening as they stood on either side of her, Elva slipping into the space at Bruan's shoulder. Sysa felt her hands lifted as the family stood in unison, facing out towards their people.

'Our daughter has returned and tonight we celebrate,' Bruan said, his deep voice cutting through the noise. 'Tomorrow we start our fight, tomorrow we start our challenge,' he boomed, nodding to a few hurrahs around the hallway.

'But tonight is for dancing, giving thanks and being with family.' Sysa felt his hand press round hers tighter. 'So come, raise your glasses and let us enjoy an evening of good cheer.'

The crowd dispersed, parting to form a corridor as Bruan and Elise led Sysa towards the Great Hall, which sat through an alcove down the hallway. Over the sea of heads, which bobbed and dropped as she passed them, Sysa could see groups of dancers, twirling in large circles across the floor. She heard the sound of pipes and fiddles, their melodies lilting and echoing across the marble and up towards the vaulted ceiling. As they rounded the alcove, Brodie appeared again, perched against the pillar of a stone archway.

'M'lady?' he enquired, raising an eyebrow and offering an outstretched arm to Sysa. She took it, while Elva scuttled in to Brodie's other side, flanking him as they followed Bruan and Elise down a carpeted passage towards a stage at the far end of the Hall. Sysa looked around at the blur of faces, paused in their motions to stoop, bow and curtsey at the passing family. She smiled at them, her hand quivering slightly as she surveyed tables laden with fruits, meat and foliage, which cascaded down heavy wooden legs. She peered up at the ceiling, heavy with candelabras which flooded a golden warmth across the room. She felt Brodie squeeze her fingers, lightly enough to make her wonder if she'd imagined it. When she turned her head towards him his eyes faced forward, only the tiniest shadow of a smile visible on his face.

Finally they reached the steps to the stage and the four sumptuous velvet thrones which awaited them. Brodie bowed towards Sysa, swivelling in a half-circle to face Elva and stooping low as she appeared to stifle a laugh, her eyes twinkling in his wake. He walked to the edge of the stage, looking out towards the throng of party goers, his eyes scanning the warm mass of smiling bodies. They all looked relatively normal, Sysa thought, save for the slight pointed tips to their ears, that feature Sysa had already registered in her own family, and with some surprise since her arrival, in herself. All but Brodie and a few others appeared, in terms of their physical features at least, human-looking – albeit with the brightness turned up. They were all more beautiful, more colourful, their features more defined and sharper somehow than the faces she had been used to back in Caithness. As she looked around the Hall, she noted that the characteristic didn't just apply to Fyrish's people – the whole place was brighter and more vibrant than anything she had ever seen before. As she pondered that thought, her Father's voice rang out in a toast towards the revellers.

'To family!' A huge cheer rose up among the dancers in collective celebration.

'To family!' they responded in unison, goblets held aloft above their shoulders, splatters of liquid dropping like raindrops to the floor.

Sysa smiled and seated herself, glad at least that the first formalities of the evening were now behind her. She arched her back, enjoying the feel of smooth velvet as she settled into her throne and watched the dance resume below. The servant who had announced her arrival stepped forward, offering a platter filled with grapes, meat, cheese and other delicacies from the feast. Sysa accepted the proffered food, all thoughts of not eating long since banished by her rapidly returning appetite, which sent waves of liquid to her mouth. As she bit into a grape she made a small sound of pleasure.

'Good?' Elva asked, indicating Sysa's plate.

'Very good,' Sysa replied, delving hungrily into the pile of food in front of her – somehow sweeter and sharper than the food she had been used to, as if the sea had sprinkled salt on it, and the sun had warmed it in response.

'Dancing later!' Elva squealed, oblivious to Sysa's rapture as she squeezed her sister's hand and then dropped it.

'Perhaps,' Sysa replied, emitting a different kind of groan, before licking her lips and quickly smoothing out the creases in her dress.

The next hours passed in a haze of spectating and introductions. It seemed that everyone wanted to meet Sysa, ascending the steps in eager columns to kiss her hand, or just tell her how glad they were that she was home. As the final group of well-wishers resumed their dancing, she pressed at her jaw, now aching from a prolonged period of smiling. She pressed back into her seat, scanning her eyes around the room. From her vantage point she saw Brodie, at the farthest edge of the Hall, talking to a dark-haired man amongst a group that numbered five or six. Sysa pulled herself upwards, craning to get a better view, finding as she did so that Brodie had turned around, and was looking directly at her, smiling broadly. She shrank back into her seat, shielding her face, which was beginning to burn pink beneath her fingers.

'Oh look, Brodie's coming over!' Elva said from beside her, brightening – Sysa had the impression Elva had found the evening so far tedious at best.

Sysa felt the flush of air that seemed to move across the room as Brodie weaved his way through the twirling dancers.

'Permission to ascend?' he asked at the foot of the steps, his eyes twinkling in the light.

'Oh don't be silly, come up here,' Elise laughed as he took the steps in two long strides, and appeared in front of the party.

'Would you like this dance?' Brodie motioned towards Sysa in a flourish. From beside her, Sysa felt her sister stiffen in her throne.

'Oh, I'm not much of a dancer,' Sysa laughed, brushing off the invitation and turning towards Elva. 'Perhaps you and Elva should dance together.' She gestured between the pair vaguely. 'You know, the two of you can show me how it's done.'

'Nonsense!' Bruan interrupted, smiling towards Brodie and Sysa.

'You're of Fae blood Sysa, and dancing is one thing you'll be able to do without anyone teaching you anything at all. Get up and dance with him!' he bellowed, chuckling to himself as he leaned back into his seat again.

'Go on,' Elva said tightly, gulping down a drink from her goblet. Brodie looked back at Sysa, eyebrows arched in anticipation. She took the outstretched hand he offered and followed him down the steps.

The crowd parted to allow the pair to enter, dancers twirling away from them as they rounded across the room. Brodie held his hands up in a manner indicating she should take them.

'Shall we?' he said as she stepped into the space between his arms.

'Who were you talking to back there?' Sysa spoke into his shoulder, her mouth lightly brushing the fabric of his jacket.

'Oh them,' Brodie swivelled his head around, seeking out his former companions.

'That was Frode, and some of the other selkie folk I know.'

'They're friends of yours?' Sysa asked, looking up at his face as he craned his neck around the room above her.

'Yes, they are,' he said, his eyes back on hers, his mouth twitching slightly. 'Old friends. I would introduce you but I don't know where they've gone.'

'Mmm,' Sysa said, stepping from side to side awkwardly as Brodie led her around the dancefloor. She could feel the pressure of his arm as it rested on her waist. His body moved beside hers, pushing her lightly this way and that way.

*How can I be a faerie*, she thought to herself blankly as she tried to keep up with his footsteps. *Look at me. I can barely even dance.*

'How are you settling into your new home then? Does castle life suit you?' Brodie enquired politely.

'What?' Sysa mumbled, trying to keep up with the rhythm of his steps.

'Do you like it here?' he repeated, looking down at her, his movement slowing momentarily.

'Oh yes, it's very nice.' Sysa went back to following her feet in the space between their chests.

'You're shaking,' Brodie said after a moment, as he lifted up her hand to demonstrate.

'Am I?' Sysa muttered, embarrassed. This night was getting worse and worse.

'I'm just a little nervous, this is all new to me, and it's cold in here.' There was an edge to her voice she hadn't intended.

'Oh,' Brodie said, glancing towards the fire roaring deeply at the other side of the Hall.

'I'm fine. Let's just dance,' she snapped again, putting her hand back into his palm and resuming her sideways shuffle.

'As you wish,' he said, bowing his head and smiling that half-smile of his again. Was he mocking her? Sysa wondered, irritated. She sighed loudly as he began to spin her slowly around the room.

The other dancers smiled as they glided past them, moustached men bowing their heads slightly, women tilting their faces as they rounded the room in elegant, sweeping arcs.

*Why am I so clumsy?* Sysa thought, her face burning next to Brodie's lapel. She couldn't shift the feeling that he was laughing at her. The nearest she had ever come to dancing with a boy was a few sidesteps years ago at a ceilidh with Hugh, who hadn't really counted as a boy in her mind at seven in any case.

She was so busy in her humiliation that at first she didn't notice the hush that fell on the dancefloor. Or the thud that signalled the throwing open of the doors. The way the music petered out abruptly, and left the dancers clinging to each other without movement. But she felt the chill, she felt that all right. If she hadn't been cold before, she certainly was now.

'Ah, a ceilidh!' a voice boomed out from behind them. Sysa turned, seeing the dancers part like curtains, moving

67

out of the way of the voice that seemed to enter the Hall before the body it inhabited. A man; young, tall, with shoulder-length white hair and skin the colour of snow swaggered through the doors.

'A party, and you didn't think to invite me Bruan? Tut, tut.' He twirled his long index fingers around in some imaginary loop.

'No, I didn't invite you, and you shouldn't be here,' Bruan said, risen from his chair and making his way across the floor now. He rounded past Sysa and Brodie, sweeping an arm behind him, shielding them from whatever threat this man presented.

'What are you doing here?' Her Father's voice was cold. 'You know you shouldn't be on our side of the forest. You should leave.'

'Oh, the rules! How awful of me!' the young man said, clutching one hand to his chest and tilting his head towards Bruan.

'I'm so bad, aren't I, King Bruan?' He lifted his eyes towards the ceiling and shrugged.

Sysa saw her Father's fingers twitch beside his thigh. This man was mocking him. She felt a surge of anger rise up within her. These people seemed to be stunned into silence through the mere presence of this man. Were they afraid of him? She looked at him, his bright blue eyes flashing around the Hall – he was enjoying himself. She bristled as a wave of recognition hit her. There was something familiar in his eyes.

Behind them, Elise and Elva stood huddled amongst the dancers.

'Who is that?' Sysa hissed to Brodie under her breath,

who was shaking his head and looking surprisingly complacent amidst the scene.

'Just Lavellan. One of Rogart's lackeys. Shape shifter. Likes to make an entrance.'

'Lavellan?' Sysa answered, a little louder than she expected.

The room suddenly seemed to freeze over, throwing the question out of her mouth like an icicle, arcing towards the man and hanging suspended in the air.

# CHAPTER EIGHT

'Ah, now here she is!' Lavellan trilled, clapping his hands together and tilting his head to one side as he looked past Bruan towards Sysa. 'Oh, we've been hearing so much about you! My master is so pleased to hear about you returning. It's all been getting a bit boring around here, if you know what I mean,' he said, with a sideways glance at Bruan as he passed.

He fixed Sysa with a blue stare, his eyes seeming to peel away at the layers of silk and chiffon. Sysa felt a prickle of humiliation light up her body.

'Pretty, too,' Lavellan drawled, looking her up and down.

'Get away from her!' Brodie darted out from behind Sysa and stood between them, all traces of nonchalance wiped from his features. Sysa saw his back uncurl perceptibly before her. From her vantage point, she could see his fists tighten and a muscle twitching at his jaw.

She sighed, shoving Brodie out of the way and shaking her head towards her Father.

'I can deal with this, thank you.' She placed herself back in front of Lavellan and fixed him with a green stare of her own.

'I know you,' she said, looking squarely into his face, daring him to reveal himself.

'Oh you do?' Lavellan replied brightly. 'How wonderful, because I think we're going to be firm friends.'

'Somehow I doubt it,' Sysa replied, as Lavellan watched her through arched eyebrows. 'You're that – that *rat* thing, that tried to attack me and my Grandfather by the riverside that day.'

'Me?' Lavellan pointed at himself, pushing his bottom lip out and widening his blue eyes in a display of childlike innocence. 'I'm burned! As if I would do such a thing, and especially to a Princess like yourself. And by the way, I'll have you know that was NOT a rat. The Lavellan is a species misunderstood amongst our human counterparts.' Lavellan turned, waving a handkerchief he had produced from a pocket somewhere.

'You've hurt my feelings now. It's time for me to leave.'

'Good riddance.' Sysa heard a voice from behind her. She turned to see Brodie, arms crossed, watching as Lavellan swaggered down the Hall. As he reached the doors he turned, holding his handkerchief aloft in one hand, the other resting on his hip, as if signalling the start of a dance – or a duel perhaps, Sysa thought.

'I bid you good evening Seelie folk. My master would wish me home to tell him *all* about your charming party. And you, Princess, I hope to see you again very soon.' He flashed a smile towards Sysa, showing white teeth that glared against the candlelight. And then in a flurry of colour and cold and movement, he disappeared behind the doors and off into the night.

'What was that all about?' Sysa said, turning to the others as Bruan clapped towards the musicians.

'Music please!' he boomed out across the Hall as the sounds of fiddles awkwardly resumed.

Sysa prised her way through the dancers, most of whom

71

were gathering up their belongings and making apologetic exits. The fire, which had gone out when Lavellan had entered, defiantly burst back into life as Bruan threw an arm towards it. Its flames did little to stoke the spirits of the Fae folk, though, who were now retreating as quickly as possible towards their homes.

'That was Lavellan making sure we understand that Rogart knows you're here, Sysa,' Bruan answered when she caught up with him. She could tell he was angry.

'It was a display, that's all,' he said, his eyes softening as his fingers touched her arm. 'He's a shape shifter, so used to being someone else that he has no idea who he even is any more. He's an actor, pure and simple,' Bruan said, making his way towards Elise and Elva who were standing together at the edge of the dancefloor.

'And a fool.' Brodie said, from behind them. 'Just another one of Rogart's fools.'

'What was all that about rules?' Sysa asked, looking around the group for answers.

'Just one rule really,' Elise replied, stepping forward. 'Dark hearts cannot enter our side of the forest, since you left it's always been the way. Before he took you away, Grey glamoured our side of the forest with a magic that meant they were just not able to pass over. Unfortunately, he had to do it in a hurry, and it doesn't seem to apply to Fae folk who can change their form. That's why Rogart sends Lavellan, a shape shifter, to do his bidding for him.' Elise looked towards Bruan, biting at her lip.

'Unfortunately, Grey's glamour also couldn't extend to keeping the creeping darkness out of the light forest,' Bruan continued.

'As Rogart's power increases, it edges into our side of the forest a little more every day. One day, it could overtake us altogether – that's why we need you to help us stop him. There's nothing we can do against this darkness that exists without a heart.'

'Well then. Tomorrow we leave, and you show me,' Sysa said simply. 'For now, I think we should all go and get some rest.'

Bruan's eyes flickered with pride as he nodded. Sysa linked arms with her Mother and Elva and walked towards the heavy doors.

As she made her way over the threshold, she slipped back and turned to Brodie, who was hovering behind them, his feet clipping at her heels.

'Thank you for trying to help me back there but I don't need rescuing. This isn't a fairytale.'

She turned and made her way up the stairs as Brodie stood watching from the hallway, smiling at her retreating figure as she shifted out of the light and into the dark corridor that lay beyond.

★

'Ready?' Sysa asked, looking towards the group as they reached her at the large oak tree outside the castle entrance. She looked up at the branch that had supported Arno just a few days earlier, when she had entered the castle, bewildered and confused.

'Ready,' her Father nodded, his eyes at first on hers, and then drifting above her shoulder. As if on cue, the eagle was swooping down towards them, his wings drumming a heavy beat.

'You're coming?' Sysa said as he perched beside her, his amber eyes flicking around the party. 'Very well,' she directed her answer at his eyes, before settling back towards her parents, Elva and Brodie at her other side.

'Let's go then,' she said, swivelling on her heel and heading out through the forest, the sun glinting between arced branches and dancing on the knotted floor below.

Sysa lifted her hand to adjust the floral crown Elva had presented her with before they left, that now sat awkwardly over her forehead.

'For my sister!' Elva had cried, arms extended towards her as she bestowed the crown matching those she and Elise already wore.

They had laughed as Sysa curtseyed when Elva placed the ringed display upon her. Sysa now felt ridiculous wearing it, its perky bravado completely at odds with the seriousness of their plight. Nearby, Elva was humming to herself and picking wildflowers as she wandered along behind them, the picture of youth and foolishness. Sysa frowned, feeling a pang of jealousy stab at her for a moment before she batted it away, ashamed. It wasn't Elva's fault that she was the one fated to determine the forest's future. Still, it would help if her sister at least *attempted* to take things a little more seriously than she did. As Sysa pondered this thought, Elva caught up, smiling in a way that made Sysa feel terrible. She offered her brightest smile in answer, pulling her sister along to join Bruan and Elise who were leading the way ahead.

They continued on until they approached the edge of the forest. Sysa glanced over her shoulder at Brodie, who appeared to be deep in conversation with Arno, the huge bird hovering silently at his side.

'Nearly there,' called Elise, gesturing back towards them. Sysa looked around, registering with a faint sense of surprise that their journey had taken them hardly any time whatsoever. She thought back to something Grey had once told her – that anyone watching a faerie make a journey would see them move as fast as an arrow, fleeing from a bow.

*Super-strength hearing, eyesight and speed,* she thought to herself. She possessed them all now, yet felt them within her as natural as the air.

Where the forest ended, the group paused, and looked towards the space in front of them. Where the trees met the rest of Fyrish the light abruptly ended and ahead was a vast expanse of grey. It was as if two worlds existed, like falling off a cliff edge into darkness. The ground was barren save a few withered remnants and the sky was bruised with black. In the distance, Sysa saw a castle, not beautiful like her parents' one, but dark and vengeful-looking, its towers poking up like arrows waiting to be released into the murk. As she made to step into the space in front of her, rain fell like daggers, battering at her skin and blinding her with wet shears that stung against her eyes. As she forced her eyelids open, lightning cracked in angry welts over the looming castle, scarring the grimy sky and everything it touched with white-hot fingers. Sysa felt the thunder rumble, felt it vibrate, felt the earth trembling beneath her. The wind howled, whipping wet strands of hair over her face, lashing at her cheeks until she tasted it, salty and damp against the corners of her mouth.

'That,' Bruan called out, his voice straining over the racket, 'is the Castle of Thunder. And this is what Rogart has done to Fyrish, Sysa,' he shouted, the arm that had been lifted to shield his face now gesturing to encompass the scarred land that lay beyond.

'He has sent the place to ruin, and persecuted so many that once lived here. This – darkness –' Bruan paused, as if he were seeking another word, but could find no better alternative – 'this darkness has been creeping over Fyrish since Rogart started his campaign. So far we have managed to keep this evil from our forest, but every day the darkness seeps in a little closer to us. His power only grows with it, the only fuel he needs is the air you see, and this air' – Bruan jerked his head towards the castle – 'it's a kind filled with a darkness that only encourages the evil in him to grow.'

Sysa nodded, thinking of Grey and one of his stories. *A giant who could live on fresh air alone.* She exhaled, her breath slipping slowly through the gaps between her teeth. *What part of my breath might reach him?* she wondered vaguely, before the thought lost momentum as more imminent concerns pushed their way into her consciousness. She looked around at the darkness, a ripple of gooseflesh that had nothing to do with the cold singing its way along the skin beneath her cloak.

'But what of all the people who lived here? What has become of them?' Sysa shouted, straining against the onslaught of the wind and rain that battered them.

'Many were killed,' Bruan answered simply, as he looked out on the vastness, his eyes fixed on a space beyond the castle towers.

'Others managed to escape into the forest lands, under our protection. Those remaining succumbed to darkness, became Rogart's.' He sighed, his eyes gleaming with the sheen of memory. 'It is those who carry out his wishes to cause mischief in the human world.'

Sysa's thoughts flashed for a moment to the stories human people told about the Fae folk and other magical beings. Of how they abducted humans, caused injury, and did harm to crofters' crops. Grey had told her of these stories but also warned she guard against them. Had this been what he'd meant all those nights she'd sat upon his knee?

'Most faeries and other Fyrish people are good, Sysa,' said Bruan, returning her to the present. 'Rogart was once a good man too,' he added, 'although, granted, you might find that hard now to believe. Fae folk have no quarrel with humans and the mischief they've been doing is because they've lost all hope in life. Rogart promised to hunt them down no longer if they succumbed to him, and somewhere along the way his attentions turned not only to Fyrish but to disrupting the human world. I promise you we did everything we could to try to stop him. The truth is, without you here, our powers alone were not enough.'

'What about Lavellan?' Sysa asked, her thoughts turning unbidden to last night's gatecrasher. 'Was he turned by Rogart? Was he once one of your people too?'

'Not exactly,' her Mother sighed, joining the conversation as she looked out into the bleakness. 'We think Lavellan was turned by Rogart when he was nothing but a child. There are those we can turn back to us, but it's harder with hearts who have no light left inside them.' She glanced at Sysa, her eyes deep pools of regret that glistened in the dark.

'But with your help,' Elise continued, brightening a little, 'we may be able to bring back some of those we lost, and stop Rogart and his creeping darkness. Grey believed your love would save Fyrish and we too believe it. We need you to do this for us – I'm so sorry to ask it of you, but you're the only one who can.'

'If I'm the only one who can do it then I'll do it gladly,' Sysa replied, thinking of Grey, his twinkling eyes, his smile, his stories. As she opened her mouth to continue, she heard it; a distant, beating sound moving towards them across the gloom.

Turning around, she saw three enormous bat-like creatures swooping towards them, flying through the murky air, huge black wings cutting through the darkness.

'It's Rogart's spotters!' Brodie called out to Sysa. 'Everyone, get back into the forest. We need to go.' He pulled at Sysa, who was staring at the approaching creatures, while Arno flapped towards them, rearing up as he dared them to proceed.

'Sysa, come on, we need to go RIGHT NOW!' Brodie called out again. He pulled at her arm, as Bruan and the others hesitated beside them.

'Come now, please, Sysa,' Bruan shouted over the cacophony. 'Brodie's right, we have to leave.'

Sysa turned, grabbing Brodie's hand and following the others who were moving at lightning speed back through the forest. Looking over her shoulder, she saw the spotters rear up and circle as they met with Arno, cawing and howling as they turned and flew back in the direction from which they'd came.

'They can't stand the light,' said Brodie, by way of

explanation. 'Dark hearts and all that.' He slowed off slightly, looking down at the hand he was holding.

'Come on, let's get you back to the castle and dry again.' Sysa nodded, marching ahead to the others who were panting under the shelter of a tree, its branches cradling them as they dripped beads of wet darkness onto the forest floor.

★

'So what do the spotters do?' Sysa asked later, over dinner. They had walked back in silence, each apparently understanding Sysa's need to turn things over in her head.

'Eyes and ears, that sort of thing,' Brodie said, chewing at a chicken leg as they sat at the large dining table. 'A bit like Arno does for us I suppose,' he continued, a slick of grease dripping from his lower lip.

'You have something just here,' Elva said, motioning a finger towards her own bottom lip and patting it. 'Let me get it for you,' she continued, drawing out a tissue and dabbing Brodie on the mouth.

Sysa frowned, pushing the bowl that sat in front of her aside, its contents suddenly becoming less and less appealing. *How can they eat, with all this going on around them?* she wondered, a sting of resentment adding to the knot that already churned at the centre of her core. She looked towards her parents, their returning stares tinged with a sort of hesitant expectation. *Of course, none of this is new to them,* she thought bleakly, inwardly chastising herself for the second time since morning. *This is their reality. It's only new to me.*

'Rogart will be angry, of course, Sysa,' said Bruan, interrupting her thoughts and flashing a quick, bemused glance at Elva and Brodie before resuming the conversation. He licked his lips and leant forward on his elbows, long fingers steepled against the peaked bows of his mouth.

'He will be looking to seek revenge.' Bruan spoke as if he were still processing his own thoughts on the matter, and finding them uncomfortable viewing.

'When the spotters saw you they would also have been able to see glimpses of your time with your Grandfather, and Rogart will know that you're here now to challenge him. He'll be keen to move the darkness into the forest as quickly as possible.' Bruan sat back on his chair, long arms hanging loosely aside him, and exhaled loudly through his nose.

'This means we don't have much time to waste,' continued Elise, patting Bruan's arm and picking up the baton of explanation.

'We need to retrieve those lost beyond the edge of the forest before it's all too late. Only by unifying our people again can we stand a chance against Rogart, Sysa. For each one we turn we can push back the darkness a little more.'

'You know I want to help Mother,' said Sysa, pushing her hand across the table to her Mother's and encircling it. 'But I have no knowledge of my powers, or how to use them, so how do I go about bringing back those who are lost? I'm not frightened or unwilling, I just don't understand what it is I have to do here. Whatever it is you wish me to do I'll do it. But first, I need to understand what I'm capable of.'

Her voice rose with a hint of desperation. 'Can you tell me what it is I need to do?'

'Oh Sysa,' her Mother said, her face streaked with a line of sorrow. 'I know you're frustrated. We ask so much of you, and you ask nothing in return. All the powers you need are inside you already. Grey put them there with the words he spoke.'

'They're right here,' she said, walking around the table and placing her fingertips just above Sysa's chest, holding them there.

'All you have to do is be exactly who you already are.'

'Let her try something,' Elva's voice broke in from the corner of the table. Sysa looked over at her sister, who was smiling widely, clearly intent on lightening up the mood.

Elva stood, pushing her chair back with a loud scrape against the stone as she pointed to an empty chair beside the fireplace. Sysa watched as she moved her arm in a swooping motion which had the effect of lifting the chair several inches from the floor.

'Try it Sysa,' Elva smiled, bobbing her head towards her sister as the chair hung, effortlessly suspended, while Telon looked on from the rug and yawned with the appearance of one not easily impressed by such demonstrations.

'I don't know,' Sysa said, her wide eyes brimming with frustration. 'I can't do it, Elva. I don't know what to do.'

'Just do what I did,' said Elva, dropping her arm, and the chair, down abruptly. 'Just see the thing in your head, then do it – it's easy, go on, try.' Elva nodded as she spoke.

Sysa sighed, jerking her head as she pointed her arm towards the table. She squeezed her eyes shut, willing the table to move with every fibre she possessed. She felt a prickle along her skin and then a dull sort of weight along her forearm. As if a reflection of her movement, the whole table, every chair and all the occupants rose up towards the roof. Sysa blinked, looking up at the group who were laughing down at her with a hint of trepidation.

'Just don't be too hasty on the down,' Bruan smiled, raising an eyebrow towards her.

'I won't,' Sysa replied, lowering her arm carefully as the table met the cold stone floor with a gentle scuff.

'See, you're more powerful than me already,' laughed Elva, nudging her sister with a playful flick of her hips and pinching the skin lightly on her forearm. Sysa noticed a flicker behind Elva's eyes as she looked back towards the table, her bright smile just a fraction too sparkling as she beamed with perfect teeth towards the group.

'I am?' Sysa said, looking at her arm, turning it this way and that as if trying to decipher its secrets.

'Of course. You're meant to be.' Elva spoke slowly, her smile wavering for a second before it suddenly reappeared.

'Come on, let's go and tease Brodie for a while.' Elva pulled on Sysa's sleeve and scuttled away towards the others.

'Do you see now?' Elise said, as Sysa scraped the chair next to her across the floor and sat down, still looking with some alarm at this wonderous new limb she suddenly possessed.

'I do,' Sysa said. 'At least I think so.' She looked at her Father, who was sitting back in his chair with his arms crossed, pride beaming across his features.

Sysa waggled her fingers, feeling the last flecks of whatever had been in there fall away from her hand like stardust. She watched as the steel coloured motes twirled like dancers in the air.

She nodded across the table, lifting her chin to the waiting faces.

'I'm ready,' she said, her voice steady.

The room carried her words like the tiny shards of steel that flitted up towards the roof.

PART THREE

# THE PIPER

# CHAPTER NINE

With the light of the peat fire crackling and murmuring in the background, Sysa adjusted herself on Grey's knee and listened.

'Tonight I'm going to tell you the story of the Piper of Windy Ha',' Grey said, his eyes lighting up in resolution. Rubbing his chin with his knuckle, he looked into the fire, which rasped back at him, as if an aide to his intentions.

'Yes, that's the one I'll tell tonight,' he repeated, a little more firmly this time. Sysa couldn't tell if he was speaking to the fire or to himself.

Sysa looked up at her Grandfather as he began to tell her the story of a man named Peter Waters. A man who stopped for a drink at a well in a place called Olrig after a day of driving cattle, and fell asleep on a faerie hill under the glare of the balmy summer sun.

'Peter woke several hours later to feel someone shaking his shoulder,' Grey said, as Sysa nuzzled into the space under his armpit.

'And from above him he heard a voice like velvet telling him to wake up. When he opened his eyes, Peter saw the prettiest face he had ever looked upon staring down at him. As he squinted into the sunlight, he saw that the face belonged to a beautiful young woman with golden hair, and a green silken gown.

Peter scrambled to his feet, wondering whether he should make a run for it, but something about the beautiful lady's smile fixed him to the spot,' Grey continued, the look in his eyes making Sysa wonder if Grey himself had ever been rooted to the spot by a female.

'The young lady assured him he shouldn't be afraid of her, though, and told him she had come to make a man of him,' Grey continued, his eyes clearing as he adjusted on his seat.

'Silly Peter though, mistook her statement for an offer of marriage.' Grey raised an eyebrow and winked at Sysa conspiratorially. 'Peter mumbled something about needing to get to know the lady better before deciding to be wed to her.'

'Silly Peter!' Sysa repeated, covering her squeal of amusement with a small bunched fist raised up towards her mouth.

'The beautiful young woman just laughed at Peter and shook her head,' Grey continued, looking down at Sysa, who shook her head back, as if in answer. 'She told Peter that what she intended was to make a man of him, not through marriage, but out in the wider world.

She told him she was able to offer him the chance of fame and fortune, a chance to rise up above his current station.' Grey swept his arm around, mimicking the golden-haired lady.

Sysa nodded up at Grey in rapture as he continued with the story, her long hair bobbing as it fell over the light fabric of her gown.

'Peter thought of his Mother and Father, who were simple crofters,' Grey said, glancing at the fire again. 'Unfortunately, the thought of making a fortune made his ears prick up with greed.

The lady told him she had one of two things to offer him,' Grey continued, sighing, as if in disappointment at Peter's grasping nature.

'And upon each of her hands, apparently out of nowhere, suddenly appeared at first a book and then a pipe. The woman raised up her left hand, which held the book, and told Peter that if he chose it as his prize, he would become the best-known preacher in the Highlands. And then she held up her right hand, which had the pipe in it, and told him that if he chose that, he would become the best piper in the land. She then removed a small golden timepiece from a front opening of her dress, and told Peter she would give him five minutes to come to his decision. Then, she sat down on a tree stump, laid the pipe and the book down beside her, and waited for Peter to declare his choice of prize. In her hand, she held the ticking timepiece level with her eyeline. As it swayed in front of her, Peter was left alone to decide which of the two options he would choose.

Looking at the objects which sat perched up against the tree stump, Peter thought what fine examples they were,' Grey continued, raising his clasped hands and then lowering them onto Sysa's lap again.

'The book was, he saw, a beautifully bound copy of the Bible in gold and silver, and the pipe was attached to a silken bag of green tissue contrasting against a line of gold and silver keys. How wonderful it would be, Peter thought to himself, to be a fine preacher living in a manse and to enjoy the company of lairds and ladies, yet how marvellous to become the most famous piper in the land. The second thought attached itself to him and he thought of all the riches such a talent might bring him.

He told the woman he planned to take up her offer of the pipe, and thanked her for her generosity. He did, however, also tell her it might be some time before he could play it, given that he had never so much as held a chanter in his life. The lady smiled back at him; a dazzling sort of smile that made Peter's cheeks flush like someone had spilled red ink all over them. She thrust the pipe into Peter's hands and told him to blow into it, and listen to the beautiful music he could play.'

Grey paused for a moment, tilting his head towards the window.

The movement made Sysa follow with her own gaze; half expecting to hear a melody lilting across the river and up into the glen.

'While Peter coughed and scuffed around in embarrassment, the lady shook the pipe at him, and repeated her instruction to blow it,' Grey continued, whatever trance they had both been party to dissolving.

'She tilted her head towards him, her dark eyelashes fluttering in persuasion, until Peter reached his arm over to grasp the instrument and tentatively placed the pipe between his lips. Upon blowing into it he was surprised to hear the tune of "Maggie Lauder" played without any effort whatsoever. The music was so good that even the best piper in Scotland could not have distinguished himself from the man who played. From the corner of his eye Peter watched, amazed, as the cattle he had been driving lifted their heads to the music and began to fidget and flail about in the field beside them. Ready to begin his new life of advantage, Peter removed the pipe from his lips and, feeling a surge of confidence returning, began to thank the young woman so that he could away and take his leave.

Before he left though,' Grey said, his voice adopting the solemn tone that often accompanied the conclusion to his stories, 'the woman told him of a condition attached to their arrangement. That on the same night, seven years forwards, Peter was to come back to the same spot to meet with her once again. She looked to the well he had been drinking from and asked him to swear by it, her index finger curving towards the dark water.

Keen to get away, Peter swore to keep the future arrangement, and bidding the woman goodbye, rushed his way along the steep farm track towards his home, a place called Windy Ha'.

On reaching the croft, he burst in and proudly showed off his prize to his assembled kin, who were gathered around the hearth fire. Hearing how he obtained it, the elders of the family did not share Peter's enthusiasm for his pipe.

His Mother cried out that her son had been lost to the faeries, while his Father, a mean and bitter man, asked what use a pipe was to a man who could not play the instrument.

Peter embraced his Mother and assured her that the woman who had given him the pipe was not a faerie.' Grey shook his head in a way that made Sysa wonder whether Peter was really a very silly man indeed.

'Peter became angry with his Father, and suggested that before speaking again, the older man should listen to him play,' Grey said. 'And with that Peter blew into his pipe and played the most alluring music, which immediately set his whole family off to jigging and dancing around the room despite themselves. Even Peter's ninety-year-old Granny frolicked about, breathlessly sending stools flying and scattering the remnants of the peat fire as she whirled around the room.

Peter's Father roared at him to stop, crying out that he'd be the death of all of them if he continued with this nonsense. Indeed, the old Granny, who was by now bent over, spluttering and coughing with the exertion, looked as though she might be the first to go.

In answer, Peter removed the pipe from his mouth and stared long and hard at his Father.' Grey's tone grew ever more serious.

'He was struck with a sudden sense of power over him, a new confidence that seemed to emanate from the reed that hung beneath his lips.

Peter told his Father that from now on, he had no right to tell him what to do, his voice a deep echo of the drone he'd just been playing.

And as his Father looked on in astonishment, Peter turned and walked out of the home he once belonged to, planting a kiss upon the *heads of his breathless Mother and his Granny as he left.*

*In the years that followed,' Grey continued, his voice lilting in recollection, 'Peter found all the fame and fortune that he had been promised, and was asked to play at every celebration in the Highlands. He had his choice of the lassies, and as his vanity and pride grew the goodness of his heart shrank with every passing day. He stopped visiting his Mother in the old croft house and spent his money on drink and parties. But in time he reached the seven-year anniversary of his meeting with the young woman at Olrig and as the sun set, he slowly made his way up the hill towards the well beside which he had fallen asleep all those years ago. As to what happened at the meeting, no one has ever been any the wiser. But it is said that the larks stopped singing that night and the wail of a single plover was all that could be heard across the moor. As for Peter Waters, he never returned from his visit to meet the mysterious woman. And as for the pipes of Windy Ha', they have never again been heard to play.'*

*Grey, whose eyes had been near to closing at the end of the story, raised his head to Sysa and smiled his familiar faraway smile, the fire hissing like an epilogue behind him. Sysa, who was now far too awake for sleeping, began to besiege him with questions about what the story meant.*

*'Did the lady take Peter off to the Fae lands, did she Grandfather, did she?' The words tumbled out of Sysa like a waterfall. 'Is he still there, do you think, Grandfather, and why has he never come back home?'*

*'If the lady took Peter off to the Fae lands then she had her reasons,' Grey said softly, lifting Sysa from his lap and planting her small bare feet onto the floor beneath them.*

*'And if she ever lets him come home to Caithness, then she'll have her reasons for that aswell. Peter let his vanity get in front of*

him Sysa. One day he might discover that it's love and kindness, not fame and fortune that make a person grand you know.' Grey rose from his seat, signalling the end of the evening's entertainment. Sysa's brows furrowed with a hundred questions, the cold bite of the stone floor snapping and singing at her toes.

Grey gestured towards Sysa's sleeping area, dropping a kiss on her forehead as she passed, sighing and frowning her way across the cottage.

'I'm not tired at all!' she wailed, eager to avoid the inconvenience of sleep. 'Can we have another story?' Sysa offered Grey her widest smile, with pleading eyes to match.

'I'm afraid the stories will have to wait for another day,' Grey answered, lifting her bedcovers and sweeping her into the cavity between the blankets. Sysa turned to look at him, her face lighting up again as she tucked her chin above the sheet.

'When I get big we could show Peter, Grandfather, all about kindness and love and being good you know. I'd bet together we could bring him back to Caithness,' she yawned, heavy eyes drooping.

'We'll see,' Grey smiled as he ruffled her hair and pressed his lips to the cool skin of her forehead.

He blew out the candle as her eyes closed, a quiver of smoke clinging gently to the dark.

# CHAPTER TEN

Sysa opened her eyes, sat upright and looked around the room, searching out her Grandfather. With a sense of realisation, she arrived back from that small hollow that separates the sleeping from the awake. She had been there a lot lately, grasping on to those moments when she opened her eyes and thought for a second that Grey was still with her. She flopped back onto the pillow, feeling the dull ache that slowly spread through her stomach and seeped out towards her limbs. How she missed him, the sight and the smell and the warmth of him. She rubbed at her eyes and thought about her dream. It had been a long time since she'd heard that story – and she couldn't help the feeling that she had been meant to hear it again, right now in her bedroom. Sitting upright, and swinging her legs out of the bedcovers, she padded across the tiles towards the window, where the light fell in, dropping golden shafts across the floor.

As she peered out, she saw Brodie and Elva talking in the castle gardens. Brodie appeared to be telling one of his funny stories and Elva was smiling up into his face. At the end of the story Elva nudged him, almost pushing him into the flowered display that sat inside the walled border of the gardens. Brodie ran off towards the fountain, Elva chasing behind him, shrieking and giggling in his wake. She held up her skirt, laughing as she tried to pull him into the water. Sysa pulled the netted curtain a little higher, registering with an odd feeling how much Elva laughed when Brodie was around.

Opening the window further, she leant out and coughed in interruption.

'Good morning you two.' Brodie swung around, panting, his arms still entwined in Elva's, trying to extricate himself from her strong but playful grip. He smiled up towards the window, his face so open that Sysa had to look away to still the uncomfortable sensation that was rising up within her. Annoyed, she looked back, setting her features in what she thought was a haughty manner.

'Brodie, Elva, I'm coming downstairs to meet you. I need to talk to you. I know who we're going to bring back first.'

★

'So it's agreed, then, myself, Brodie and Elva will go out into the forest,' Sysa said, looking around the room for confirmation.

Bruan inhaled deeply, looked down at his hands, and shook his head. His face furrowed and the white line of his jaw sat tight against his skin. When he looked up again, a sort of helpless expression cloaked his features. For a second, Sysa could see how he must have looked in his younger days, and a small prick of regret poked its way inside her chest.

'Bruan, we've been through this,' Elise murmured, the hum of her voice a salve to Sysa's sadness.

'Between Sysa and Elva, they have more power than both of us, and Brodie knows his way around the forest.' She pushed her hand across the table and squeezed Bruan's arm gently as she spoke.

'Besides, we must stay here and watch over our people – you know that, my love.'

Bruan rubbed the skin on his forehead between his fingers, making little effort to conceal the sigh that escaped loudly from his mouth.

'You're right of course, Elise, but it doesn't mean I have to like it. For the love of Fae, Elva has never crossed over to the dark side of the forest in her life! No, you'll stay here with us Elva, and Brodie will go with Sysa,' he said, reneging for the umpteenth time that morning.

'Sysa has more powers than you, it makes more sense this way. The dark side of the forest is dangerous Elva – it's no place for you. It's no place for any of you,' he muttered, looking at Brodie and Sysa. 'I'm so sorry that any of you have to do this.' Sysa avoided his gaze, not wanting to see the hurt and shame that lingered behind his eyes.

'Father, that's not fair, we've discussed this,' Elva interrupted, her pale skin colouring. 'I've told you already, I want to go – I *will* go – I want to do my bit to help. It may be Sysa's *destiny*' – she rolled her eyes and waved her hand around in a grand gesture – 'to save Fyrish but I want to help my sister, and Brodie, and the rest of us. I'm going Father. I won't forgive you if you don't allow me to play a part.'

Elva looked quickly around the room, daring anyone to refuse her. For a moment, Sysa thought, she looked like an animal, eyes darting soundlessly around a pack. In the high-pitched quiet, she stood there, tight and curled, awaiting her Father's answer.

Finally, Bruan looked between them and rose to his feet, the corners of his lips twitching in an uneasy line.

'It looks like I have two headstrong daughters,' he said, moving towards them and placing his hands on Elva's shoulders. As he dropped down to meet her eyes something in Elva softened.

'You can go, Elva. I'm not sure I could stop you even if I tried.'

★

'So this woman is called Krystan?' Sysa asked as they made their way back along the forest path.

'Yes, it certainly sounds like it could be her, from the story you told us, and what I've heard of her,' Brodie answered as he nodded by her side.

'She hasn't been seen in this side of the forest since she was a child,' he continued, as they crunched along, dry leaves rustling on the path before them. 'Your parents lost track of those Rogart turned in the end,' he said, glancing back at Elva, who was admiring something sprouting from the bottom of a nearby tree trunk.

'Eventually, they only had enough power to focus on protecting the ones Rogart left behind.'

'But how on earth will we know how to find this Krystan?' said Elva, catching up with them. 'She could be anywhere in there.' Elva pointed to encapsulate the expanse of the dark land that lay beyond.

'I'll think of something,' Sysa said, turning towards

her sister, who was framed in a shaft of golden light that filtered down through the tree tops. *She's so beautiful*, Sysa thought, with an uncomfortable pang that might have been envy. She shrugged the feeling off, grabbing Elva by the hand and pulling her along between herself and Brodie.

'Don't take too long about it, then.' Elva giggled, humming and skipping as they made their way together along the path.

As they approached the dark edge of the forest, they passed the homes of several Fae folk, who peered out from wooden doorways. Smiling and curtseying, they waved at the passing party, one young faerie running towards them and thrusting a bunch of fragrant blue flowers into Sysa's hands. Sysa smiled at the young faerie and crouched down to look at her.

'So kind, thankyou,' she said, touching the girl's cheek with her fingers. The young faerie looked up at her brightly, her freckled face dimpling as she smiled.

'My Mother says you're going to save the forest,' she said, white teeth and green eyes glistening. 'Are you?' she ventured bluntly, her chin jutting out in question. This girl reminded Sysa of herself.

'Well – I very much hope your Mother's faith in me is rewarded,' Sysa said, hoping her smile didn't betray her own uncertainty.

As she turned to walk away, she heard the young faerie call out, 'When I grow up, I want to be just like you.'

'I have no doubt you will be,' Brodie called over, flashing a smile towards the growing group of onlookers.

'We have to go now, I'm afraid.' He gestured to Sysa, as he made off with Elva to resume their journey through the trees.

'Thankyou for the good wishes.' Sysa nodded around the group and followed the others, clutching the blue flowers tightly to her body. As she walked, the petals fluttered against her ribcage, like fragrant silk kisses answering the beating of her heart.

★

As they carried on towards the dark edge of the forest, Brodie regaled the girls with light-hearted stories. He laughed as he told Sysa about the tricks he would play on Elva when she was young.

'I once told her there was a baby giant outside her window,' he said, eyeing Elva with that crooked half-smile of his. 'Naturally, she believed me. She wouldn't go back out on her balcony for weeks.'

Elva responded by nudging him in the stomach, mock insult playing across her features. Brodie pretended to be injured, clasping at his ribcage and falling to the ground.

'Get up, you silly fool,' Elva said, laughing and reaching out a hand to him. Brodie took the proffered hand, prompting Sysa to look away, strangely unsettled by the display of leisurely intimacy between the two.

'Oh, look, it's Arno,' she said, relieved of the diversion as she watched the eagle beat a path slowly towards them. As he perched on a nearby tree stump, he looked at her quizzically and cocked his large head to one side.

'Ah, you're spying on us are you Arno?' Brodie jumped up, smiling towards the huge creature. 'It seems Bruan and Elise have found a way to keep tabs on us after all.'

Brodie went to the bird, stroking and cooing at him

in murmured whispers. Brodie seemed to have an easy intimacy with everyone, Sysa observed, watching him converse with his avian friend. She felt a sudden emotion flash over her, rippling across her insides like gooseflesh. *Am I jealous of all of them?* she wondered, annoyed at herself, and at all these new feelings somehow finding their way inside her head. She shuddered, batting the thoughts away from her. She had to concentrate. She squeezed her eyes shut, wishing her eyelids could form some sort of barrier to stop unbidden thoughts from getting in.

'Nearly there,' Brodie said eventually as they got closer to the dark side of the forest. They had walked in silence since Arno's arrival, Brodie's stories tailing off without warning and Elva's face growing serious as the light before them fell. Sysa looked out into the space between the trees where the land became unrecognisable, scissored away like a bleak, blank canvas.

'Ready?' Brodie asked as they prepared to step into the murky depths of the other side.

The wind began to howl and the rain fell like pellets, lashing against their skin and their clothing. Sysa nodded, inwardly noting that she felt anything but.

She dropped her head against the wind, which answered with a distant thudding. Sysa wondered if it was the sound of her own heart beating, raising her hand to her chest instinctively as the drum beat echoed its thunder around the sky.

Sysa looked in the direction of the noise, which was suddenly coming closer. It echoed around them, circling their bodies like a bird. Sysa looked to her sister and heard a small voice:

'Rogart.'

Before Sysa could say anything in reply the ground around them vibrated and shook as if thunder and lightning were shaking hands. She looked up to see a face she had seen before, and wondered for a moment if she was dreaming. Then she remembered. Not a dream, a memory.

It was the last face she had seen in Caithness.

Before the world she knew had died.

# CHAPTER ELEVEN

Rogart's face seemed to block out the sky for a moment. He was huge, about twice the size of a normal man, but as Sysa stared up at him, she realised he bore very little resemblance to a human man at all. He was half-beast, with large curling horns that protruded over smaller, horse-like ears covered in brown fur that reminded Sysa of soft velvet. The rest of his face and body were covered in a similarly textured mane, kept short over his limbs and torso and flowing longer around his head where it fell over his face and horns. The fur – which, Sysa thought with surprise, reminded her of the soft coat of a baby chick – grew into his face and arced around his features, leaving only the profile of a long snubbed nose, a straight mouth and amber-coloured eyes that arced ever so slightly up. Beneath his huge chest, his lower half was adorned in some sort of armoured gear ending just above his feet – which were not feet at all but hooves, Sysa saw. She gasped in spite of herself. He was beautiful. For a moment it occurred to her that he could just squash the three of them, right there were they stood.

For now, though, they were still on the light side of the forest, which meant that, according to everything she had been told so far, Rogart would not be able to come any closer.

*Unless I'm ready to go in there, testing out my powers against Rogart might have to wait for a while*, Sysa thought as she looked up at his face.

Drawing away from his eyes she saw Lavellan, who was not far behind his master, standing with his arms folded, white hair sleek and dripping as he smiled at her.

*He followed us along the coast*, Sysa thought. *He told Rogart we were coming.* She glared at him, but he just continued smiling back at her, blue eyes wide in an innocent *who me?* facade. Above his head, Rogart's spotters circled idly. Brodie and Elva looked on wordlessly, apparently dumbfounded at the sight of Rogart and his entourage. For a second Brodie looked like he was ready to step forward, but then thought better of it – perhaps, Sysa thought, bearing in mind her reproach at the ceildh the other night.

'You're back.'

Sysa's eyes returned to the owner of the voice who spoke quietly above her. Behind Rogart, the sky circled in whorls of purple and yellow, like the lingering remnants of a bruise.

'I'll give you this, you and your family have some nerve.'

'We're not the only ones,' Sysa replied evenly, surveying the devastation Rogart had wreaked around the other side of the Fae lands.

'And you.' He spoke again, turning his attention towards Elva. 'You're lucky you didn't receive the same fate as your sister.' Sysa felt Elva tremble at her side.

'And your parents, how the mighty have fallen, sending a group of children to fight their battles for them. They think the three of you are going to steal away my faeries, my land, everything I've worked for? I should kill the three of you now. Luckily for you I like to play.'

As Sysa opened her mouth to speak, Rogart turned his attentions towards Brodie. His eyes narrowed for a moment and one of his large hands curled itself into a fist. He looked over the three of them briefly, his amber eyes flickering and burning. Then something flashed across his face. He suddenly turned, his hooves thudding against the ground, taking him and his spotters away as quickly as they had come. Only Lavellan waited in the darkness, looking over his shoulder towards his master. He turned to look back at Sysa and the others with a wide, white grin on his face.

'Game on,' he said, and swivelled towards the dark castle, kicking up the gravel beneath him as he turned and walked away.

Sysa looked around in disbelief and turned to see Arno, who had appeared behind them during the commotion, wings outstretched, staring into the empty space that Rogart and the others had left behind them.

'What was that?' she asked the group in general.

'That was your introduction to Rogart,' said Elva, shivering, and pulling the collar of her cloak a little tighter to her chin.

'For a minute there I actually thought he might just finish the three of us off for good.'

Sysa put an arm around her sister and held her close, looking over her shoulder towards Brodie.

'I'd like to see him try,' she said, sounding a little braver than she felt.

'Okay, we need to gather our thoughts and decide how

we go forward,' Sysa continued, trying to portray an air of self-confidence.

'If we want to achieve anything, sooner or later someone is going to have break this stalemate and cross over to the other side.'

'You're right, Sysa,' said Brodie. 'But now that Rogart knows we're here, once we cross over to the other side he can hurt and attack us if he wants to. Until we know how powerful you are against him we have no idea what we can withstand.'

'Well, hanging around here waiting isn't going to change that Brodie,' Sysa said, exasperated. 'What did we come here for if it wasn't to go over to the other side? Getting hurt or attacked is just a risk we have to take – and if you don't want that risk, neither of you need to come with me.' Sysa avoided their eyes and looked out into the dark.

'Of course we're coming with you,' Brodie rounded in front of her, something between anger and hurt flashing across his features.

'Me too,' Elva said quietly from behind him. In the distance, Sysa heard the dull beat of a spotter's thrumming wings.

'Okay, that's settled then,' she said, feeling guilty again – an experience she was now becoming accustomed to.

She surveyed the expanse of light forest that lay behind them.

'Let's set up camp here and sleep a while. At sunrise tomorrow, we go in.'

★

Sysa woke to find the sun rising where she lay on the light side of the forest. As she turned her head, she saw that the darkness of the other side remained just as it had before. She had slept restlessly, visions of the Giant and Lavellan flashing behind her eyes and thrusting her regularly back into wakefulness. She stretched, curling onto her side so she could face into the sunlight, twigs crackling underneath her like little mounds of bone. She inhaled the scent of pine and the light air of morning and looked around her. Just beyond the remnants of the fire they had laid, Elva and Brodie were sleeping, their shoulders rising in time with the small rhythms of their breath.

Sysa propped herself up on her elbows and took in the scene around the clearing. She had always loved trees, perhaps because there were so few of them where she had grown up in Caithness. She loved the way light scattered through their branches, and larger shafts spread out in the spaces between the tree trunks. Perhaps that was why at first she wondered if she was dreaming when she saw him emerging from the trees.

Framed between two large tree trunks was a creature of such beauty that Sysa let out a momentary gasp of wonder.

*Perhaps I'm still sleeping,* she thought vaguely, gazing at the perfect horse-like animal, with sky-blue eyes and a horn protruding from its head. It was a unicorn, Sysa knew without hesitation. But more than that, through every inch of her body and the soul that lay beneath it she recognised him. It was her Grandfather. He had died, he was gone, and yet he was here now, somehow, his spirit existing within this creature. She knew it as well as she knew the sky was still above her. She felt hot tears flow suddenly, without warning, down her cheeks and into the corners of her mouth.

Sysa clasped her hand to her lips and cried out involuntarily.

'I knew you wouldn't leave me,' she sobbed, her voice emerging ragged and breathless through a curtain of unabated tears. She also knew, with a devastating sense of clarity, that this meant the Grey she had known in the human world was gone, had died alone there, back in the cottage, in the glen where it had always been just the two of them. She felt a piece of the child inside her step out of her body then, pulled by some invisible force towards him. She watched the child walk across the clearing; a living, moving memory in the sun. Finally, the child disappeared, swallowed in a shaft of light that fell in front of the unicorn like a blanket. Sysa blinked, clearing the haze that had clung to her eyes, framing the world in its watery, soft roundness. She nodded, she understood now.

The child was gone – that part of her was never to return.

Sysa rose to her feet, and stretching an arm out, stumbled towards the creature whose eyes had never moved from her. With one hand still covering her mouth she moved towards him as he lowered his head to meet her touch. She ran her fingers through his mane, feeling the soft hair, the firm body beneath it. When the unicorn moved in closer she bent her forehead to meet him, inhaling his scent – warm, just like she'd imagined it to be. He made the smallest of sounds, snuffling in the space between their foreheads and releasing something between a whinny and a sigh that felt damp and hot against her cheekbone. They stayed like that, each inhaling the other's breath, each content to absorb every tiny sound or movement or thought the other made.

In her peripheral vision then, Sysa saw it – the pure light that wrapped around them and flooded through her being. It moved over and around her, falling and pooling at her feet like a waterfall flowing downwards to a burn. She knew in that instant that wherever she was, she would hold onto it – it would always be with her. She lifted her head and stroked the face of the unicorn, her cheeks gleaming with life and joy and tears. He had to go now; she could feel it in the fur that rippled underneath her fingertips.

But in that instant, she felt a surge of understanding. Her Grandfather had told her everything she would ever need to know.

# CHAPTER TWELVE

'I know how we're going to find Krystan,' Sysa said, looking down on the two sleeping bodies beneath her.

'What?' Elva replied, poking one eye open, her voice thick with the remnants of sleep. 'Good morning to you too.'

Brodie looked up with a half-cocked eyebrow, stretching and yawning noisily. Twigs crackled and crushed as Elva pulled herself up, hair poking out in wild angles and directions. She dragged at the wayward strands with her fingers, drawing out tiny pieces of bark and moss as she pulled.

'I said, I know how to find Krystan,' Sysa repeated, ignoring the half-conscious grumbles coming from the others. 'We're going to follow the sound of Peter's pipes; they'll lead us straight to where she is. Think about it – Peter's doomed to entertain her now forever. We listen for his music, we find the way to her.'

'That sounds great,' Brodie replied, splashing water over his face and chest as he washed himself in the burn that flowed not far from where they had been lying. Sysa turned away as he looked over his shoulder towards her, apparently oblivious to her unease as he'd pulled the jacket he'd been wearing over his head and slung it to the ground.

'I don't know about you two – but I haven't heard any music since we got here. Not since the ceilidh in fact. So I'm wondering how that helps us.' Brodie walked towards her, his dark hair dripping over the pale skin beneath his shoulders. Sysa flashed a glance towards Elva, whose smile indicated she was rather enjoying the advancing scene.

'Good grief, put some clothes on,' Sysa said, grabbing the jacket and swinging it towards him. Brodie grasped it against his stomach, making a mock exclamation of being winded as it slapped against his dampened skin.

'We just haven't been listening in the right way, in the right places,' Sysa continued, ignoring him.

'O-kay,' Brodie replied, stretching out the vowel sounds as he looked back at her, bemused. 'So how do we listen in the right way?'

Sysa looked away again as he pulled the jacket over his head, his torso lengthening before his milky skin was finally covered up again.

'Well for a start, we need to actually be quiet,' Sysa snapped, inwardly chastising herself as soon as the words escaped. She couldn't seem to stop herself snapping at him, although she knew he was only trying to help her. There was something about him she found infuriating. All these magical Fae powers and she was bamboozled by strange emotions she couldn't even begin to understand.

'My lips are sealed,' Brodie answered, widening his eyes and planting two fingers over his lips, covering a twitching smile beneath them.

'Look up,' Sysa said, lifting her head and watching the treetops as they gently swayed above. They stood there for a while, as the crowns of the trees swished and swayed, their outermost leaves occasionally touching. The sounds they made as they rustled and rushed against each other reminded Sysa of the sea. She thought of the sea then, and the long stretches of beach back in Caithness as she closed her eyes and let the sounds wash over her. The sound of waves that carried all the secrets of the ocean as they curled and lipped towards the coast. As she opened her eyes, she knew she understood now.

'It's in the leaves,' she whispered, puncturing the silence. 'They're carrying the sounds of the forest. We just have to listen to the leaves.'

'The leaves?' Elva said, jolting out of the half-asleep state she had been languishing in.

'Yes, the leaves,' Sysa replied. 'I understand it now. They hold onto the sounds.'

Sysa thought for a moment about telling them of her visit from the unicorn, the touch and the light that had transferred some sort of ancient wisdom from its spirit into her. Just as Grey had told her the stories, transferring all that knowledge and magic that could be unlocked when she most needed it, unfurling like a carpet beneath the trees.

But for now, she wanted to keep the unicorn to herself, just for a little longer. He was the only thing she had that connected her to a time when the world was just she and Grey. She moved to the nearest tree and stretched a hand up, lowering down one of its branches, her fingers rubbing an oval shaped leaf that protruded from a knotty piece of bark. She held it to her ear and listened, thinking of a time when Grey had handed her a seashell and the sounds of swirling and swishing ocean had crashed and thrummed against her ear. And then she heard it, the sounds of a distant lament, the rising, almost metallic sound of the bagpipes.

'Here,' she gestured to the others as they angled their heads towards the leafy offshoot, smiles of recognition spreading across their faces. Sysa pulled the leaf gently from its knotty cradle.

'Let's go,' she said, placing the leaf carefully in her cloak pocket. 'Let's go and find Krystan and see if we can turn her to the light.'

'What about Rogart? What if he knows we're coming again?' Elva asked as they made their way back to the place where the light met with the darkness.

Sysa held the leaf to her ear, checking for the ebb and flow of the sounds that would direct them on their path.

'That's a chance we're just going to have to take, Elva,' Sysa said, looking around instinctively for any sign of the Giant – or more likely, she thought, Lavellan, who could have wheedled his way into the light forest to follow them by now.

'We're never going to be able to do this without some risk of Rogart finding us. Don't worry, I'll take care of you,' Sysa continued, the words springing from her with more confidence than she felt. Elva nodded and looked away for a fraction longer than felt comfortable.

'We'll take care of each other,' Brodie said, eyeing the pair of them as they walked beside him towards the gloom.

Together, they crossed into the dark side of the forest, feeling the wind and rain and misery descend around them. The air was thick, like wading through dark treacle, Sysa thought. She felt her heart grow heavy as they trudged their way through the bleakness, as if all the hope and happiness in the world could be sucked away just by being there. One of Rogart's tricks, a glamour, no doubt useful in the converting of Seelie faeries, she assumed. The forest wasn't just alive, just reaching its dark fingers further into the light forest daily – it had the power to change them.

'Do you feel it? The darkness?' she said to the others. They both nodded.

'We don't have much time then.' Sysa clutched the leaf to her ear again, and the sound of the pipes grew louder, humming and ringing against her ear.

'Not much further to go now. This way.' She gestured towards a clearing between some thorny branches that poked out of the ground not far away from them. As they turned into the place, the sound of the leaf rung out against her skin. A moment later it had been enveloped by a lament that spread out around them and carried its way forward on the wind.

They twisted and turned through ragged, bare branches as the sounds became more urgent. Pushing their way through the spiked maze, they finally burst out into a clearing where a man sat, slumped against the remnants of a tree. Sysa looked into the face of the long-lost piper – a face that was gaunt and exhausted-looking, framed by an unkempt beard. Slumped across his chest were his pipes, the silken bag ragged and filthy from lack of care. The tip of the pipe hung from his mouth loosely and his eyes stayed half-shut, as he tried to form his lips around the stem. He looked up at Sysa and the others, glazed and weary, too exhausted to even speak. The pipe fell from his mouth, dropping onto his chest, which was streaked with dirt and sweat above the trim of the kilt which hung loosely around his waistline.

'For the love of Fae,' Sysa said, using one of her Father's expressions. 'What has she done to him? We need to get him out of here.'

She turned to face the others, but from somewhere behind them a looming figure stopped her in her tracks.

At the other side of the clearing stood a Fae woman who could only be Krystan. Unlike Peter, she looked vibrant, dressed in robes of green silk with gold ringlets tumbling around her neck. Her face glowed, as dewy as if she had washed it in the lush green grass of May Day.

'Who are you and what is your business here?' she said, harsh green eyes flashing anger, her beauty instantly dispelled.

'I am Sysa Steel,' said Sysa, 'and this is my sister Elva, and this is Brodie. We are here to send Peter home to Caithness, Krystan. It's been wrong of you to keep him here like this.'

'Oh, you think you know me?' Krystan said, one eyebrow arching. 'And you think you're going to take my dear Peter back to the human world? Well, we'll see about that, won't we? Peter has no wish to return to Caithness, nor I to the other side of the forest. I've heard about you. We all know what you're planning. And for your information, *dearest*, Peter has been entertaining me quite happily here in the darkness for some time.'

Sysa glanced at the dishevelled-looking man slumped against the tree and sighed loudly. It was quite apparent that he was here not of his own choosing, but rather to satisfy every one of Krystan's unfortunate demands. His silence, coupled with the look of desperate anticipation on his face confirmed that he was terrified. Whatever his own personal failings, Sysa needed to get him out of here and return him back home where he belonged.

'Look at him, Krystan!' Sysa made a hurried gesture towards Peter. 'He's filthy, he's exhausted – does that look like a happy man to you?'

'It's not how I'd choose to spend my days. Whatever the company,' murmured Brodie, from somewhere in the background.

Krystan glared at him. 'How dare you!' She flicked one arm towards him, sending him crumpling in agony towards the ground.

Sysa looked back at Brodie, who lay doubled up in pain, Elva prodding him in a vague attempt at comfort.

'I'm fine,' he shouted over to Sysa, embarrassment blooming on his features as he raised an arm to indicate she should continue with the task in hand.

Sysa seethed, anger bubbling up inside her.

'No, how dare *you,*' she answered, feeling nerves flicker like liquid steel across her body. They prickled down her arms, reaching to her fingertips. Sysa smelled something like peat, crackling and tingling at her extremities. As she raised her hands towards Krystan, the crackling exploded, pushing a bright light searing towards the Fae woman. Sysa jumped back, looking down at her hands in wonder for a moment.

'Oh, this looks fun,' Krystan said from across the clearing, a wolfish smile across her face.

Instantly, Krystan raised her arms, pushing her own crackle of green towards Sysa. Sysa felt herself tumble backwards, hearing the sound of Krystan's laughter as she fell awkwardly against the forest floor. Brodie and Elva gathered as Sysa sprang up, raising her arms again and pushing her palms outwards, ignoring the pain that seared along her forearm. She squeezed her eyes shut, trying to connect with the energy she'd felt in her fingers just seconds before her fall. In answer, a stream of silvered light emerged from Sysa's fingers and locked with the green torrent Krystan had unleashed on her. She saw Krystan's eyes widen in anger and disbelief as she strained against the force.

For a few moments the two streams locked against each other until Sysa saw Krystan's face contort in an expression of horror as silver light flooded green lightning before rushing through Krystan's hands, her limbs and her body. Suddenly, Krystan was enveloped in a light so bright that it flashed against the darkness of the forest, before disappearing so quickly that Sysa wondered if she had imagined the whole thing. The sight of the golden-haired Fae woman thudding to the ground assured her she had not though. Sysa trembled, looking over at the crumpled pile of silk in front of her. She looked down again at her hands, the light in her fingertips crackling and fading away like sparks flicking from a stone. She looked around at the others, sensing their heavy breaths in the atmosphere around her. In the distance, still slumped against the tree, was Peter, trembling and muttering wildly to himself.

'What did you do to her?' Elva asked, wide-eyed, moving slowly towards the curled-up figure who lay unmoving in the clearing.

'I have no idea,' Sysa answered as she crept towards

Elva and Brodie who were peering over Krystan as she lay in a crumpled, silken heap. Sysa wondered for a horrible moment if she had killed her, if that flash of anger and darkness she'd felt had led her to destroy another living being. Just as that awful thought washed over her, Krystan's eyelids fluttered and she slowly began to open up her eyes.

For what felt like an age, Krystan stared up at her, the deep pools of her eyes conveying something that hadn't been there in their previous encounter. *Was it surprise?* Sysa wondered. *Gratitude?* Whatever it was, the steely look of just a few moments earlier was gone. Sysa found herself looking into the face of an entirely new faerie, just as beautiful as the one before but wiped clean of the anger that had glazed her looks with its severity. Under Sysa's gaze, Krystan's eyes bloomed like a green flower opening up to the sunshine. Her hard features softened and her mouth curved to a smile as she pulled herself up onto her feet.

'Sysa,' she said, reaching out both arms towards Sysa, who stumbled backwards, confused by the sudden turn of events unfolding in front of her. 'Sysa, it's all right. You saved me. You saved me, Sysa. I'm me again. You have brought me back to life.'

'I have?' Sysa answered, still wondering how she had managed it. The light which had flown from her fingers a few moments ago had come instinctively from a place buried deep within her. The sight of Brodie harmed – that anger – she knew that had triggered it, had awoken it somewhere in the depths down in her soul. She looked around at the others, who were nodding back at her in agreement.

117

'You have,' Krystan confirmed, placing a hand gratefully across Sysa's forearm. Sysa looked down at the hand that lay on her, resisting the sudden urge to flinch at Krystan's touch.

'I'm sorry if I hurt you,' Krystan murmured at the sight of Sysa's arm, which was blooming with a purple bruise – albeit one that would disappear quickly.

'I'm sorry if I hurt any of you.' She looked shamefully around the group, stopping at Peter and dropping her gaze down to the ground.

Looking at Krystan's face now, Sysa knew she no longer needed to question whether the faerie had really changed or not, and felt guilty for hesitating.

'It's okay,' said Sysa, encircling her other arm around Krystan's. 'It's okay,' she repeated, holding her in a quick embrace before pulling away and allowing the faerie to go on.

'For so long I've been trapped in this darkness, Sysa,' Krystan began, pain etched across her features. 'I hated myself for what I was doing but the longer it went on the more difficult it seemed to be to change. The forest seemed to be feeding me, sending me further and further into this' – Krystan looked around, almost spitting the words out – 'into this pit I had created. I felt like I was in a hole that I couldn't climb out of. Believe it or not, I was once a good person like you all.'

Sysa nodded, thinking of the darkness that had enveloped her when she stepped into this side of the forest, the air that was so thick with its misery. How could she blame Krystan for not being able to resist it?

'I know you were. And you still can be,' Sysa replied,

watching the flicker of hope that lit up across Krystan's face.

'But how did you end up here in the first place?' Sysa asked, looking at the bleakness that surrounded them. She felt the sharp, stinging air poke at her skin as if in answer, and with a wary glance around herself, pulled her cloak a little tighter to her chest.

'I was just another one of the Fae folk who stumbled into the darkness,' Krystan answered, her eyes drifting away into an oblivion of shame and sorrow. 'My family – I lost them all, you see, when Rogart started to wreak his vengeance. He did horrible things to them. Horrible, horrible things.'

'It's okay,' Sysa said gently, 'you don't have to tell us,' and Krystan looked back at her gratefully. The darkness that had flashed across Krystan's eyes had told Sysa enough of the pain and misery she and her family had endured.

'But how did you end up with him – after all that I mean?' Sysa tried to keep her tone even, keeping the horror that was rising up like bile in her throat hidden from her question. *How could she have ended up colluding with this man after he killed her family? Is that what he had done?*

Sysa chastised herself. How could she know what anyone was capable of when their very existence was at stake?

'Rogart chose some of those in our village to *save.'* Krystan's lips curled as she tried to form the words around them. 'He told us we were special, that we were the chosen few he'd bring to his kingdom to live protected by his rule. He told us the – *sacrifices'* – again she curled her lips like sour milk around the word – 'were necessary, a punishment to your Father for his dishonour. He said your Father's actions had forced him to do it. And he actually looked sorry, Sysa – he really did.' Krystan looked up, her eyes pleading for understanding. Sysa nodded, encouraging her to go on, the bile and horror now mingling and burning against her throat.

'And he was kind. He was actually kind to us. That day, after he had stormed our village – after everything that happened' – she stepped over the words like cracks in a pavement – 'I remember he put a blanket around us, the young ones, the ones he was saving. He didn't harm any children,' she added quickly, looking up at Sysa, her eyes flashing. Sysa nodded again, unable to say anything in reply.

'I was so young, and I had no family. What could I have done but go with him?' Krystan pleaded. 'Your family couldn't do anything to help us,' she added blankly. Sysa's skin crawled, prickling against the anger and shame that were buried underneath.

'You had no choice. You were no more than a child,' Elva said, from somewhere in the distance. Sysa turned, catching Elva's eyes – was that a challenge than flickered within them?

'Of course you had no choice,' Sysa said, turning back towards Krystan, not sure if she even believed herself.

She thought of Grey, how she would have fought and railed against anyone, even as a child, if they had so much as taken a step towards hurting him. Then she thought of Lavellan, and that day so many years ago by the river, a picture of herself standing alone on the hillside, powerless and vulnerable. She pushed the thought away quickly.

'You had no choice,' she repeated, more to herself than anyone else.

'I grew up after that, here in the dark forest,' Krystan continued, scanning the gloomy place, eager now to absolve herself of the rest of her story.

'I was weak, I had no family, and without Rogart I was all alone. He chipped away at me, at everything inside me,' she said, as if realising for the first time what he had done to her. 'He made me hate you all, made me hate everyone. Made me blame your family for everything. But all the time he was so' – she shook her head in disbelief and wonder – 'so very, very kind. Eventually I forgot how it felt to be good and all I felt was anger and resentment. I was so scared when I first came here, Sysa, and so very, very young. He made me believe that the only way to stop those feelings was to feel hate and anger so that I never had to be afraid again. When your light entered me just now it brought back all those feelings – all the feelings I used to have when I was young. But now I'm afraid again – I'm afraid that you won't forgive me.' Her eyes were deep pools of anxiety.

'Will you forgive me Sysa?' Krystan looked up at Sysa, her face open and pleading.

'Now that you have recovered me, I'm begging you, will you take me home?'

'What about the piper?' Brodie interjected, stepping forward. 'Krystan, that's the forgiveness you need to worry about the most.'

Sysa and Krystan turned, surveying the piper, who was now huddled in a blanket that Elva had offered him. Elva sat aside him, her arms around his shoulders as he continued to tremble. His eyes cast around, finally allowing himself a sliver of hope that his nightmare might be close to being done.

'Peter,' Brodie said slowly, walking towards him, as Peter helplessly pushed himself back against the ragged tree stump. Brodie stopped a few feet away from him, sensing his distrust.

'Will you forgive this faerie for what she's done to you and allow us to take her back to the light forest? You've been through a lot here Peter. Once we get the two of you out of here, we can send you back home where you belong.'

Krystan turned slowly to look at Peter, who remained silent. For a moment, he looked like he was opening his mouth to say something, but thinking better of it, pursed his lips and looked down at his feet. Krystan made a slight move towards him, her arm outstretched in sympathy and penance. Peter flinched, edging ever backwards, evidently hoping to be consumed wholly by the tree stump behind him. Krystan stopped where she stood, lowered her arm and shook her head in shame.

'Oh Peter,' she said, lifting her face towards him. 'I'm so sorry – so very sorry – for everything I've done. I had no right to take you from your home and I should never have kept you here. I can only beg that one day you'll forgive me. But if you can't then I will have to understand.'

Sysa watched as Peter painfully pulled his gaze up towards the faerie who had imprisoned him. For a long time they stared at each other like that, as if a cord ran the length of the distance between their eyes.

'I forgive you, Krystan.' Peter's stammering voice was barely louder than a whisper. Krystan looked back at him, her cheeks wet with slippery tears as she nodded her thanks. Sysa watched, wondering if Peter's statement was real, or just something he had offered up to speed his exit from Krystan and this dark and awful forest. If forgiving her was the quickest way to do that, she couldn't blame him for being eager to oblige.

'Well then,' said Brodie, who had been observing the scene alongside Sysa. 'If that's settled, then we really should be off.' He looked up at the inky sky, heaving with the weight of rain that was falling like flags cascading from a banner.

'Sysa,' he whispered, pulling Sysa away from the others out of earshot. 'Do you really think we should believe her? What if this whole thing is just a trick?'

'Brodie.' Sysa stared back at him, incredulous. 'Look at her.' She gestured towards Krystan who was standing with her arms folded, hugging herself, apparently too nervous to approach the piper yet.

'She's changed. I can feel it in my bones.'

Sysa felt her body echo her reply in a wave of light that spread through the depths of her, making her shiver.

'If you believe that, it's good enough for me,' Brodie said, staring back at her for a little longer than Sysa thought he should.

'We haven't yet had cause here to believe much that comes from the depths of the dark forest, that's all,' he said, pivoting towards Peter who was being dragged gently onto his feet by Elva. Sysa sighed and turned back towards Krystan, her curiosity piqued. Though she wouldn't admit it to Brodie, she couldn't help but wonder over Krystan's motivations in taking Peter away from his own world.

'Why did you take him?' she found herself asking as she drew close to Krystan's shoulder. Krystan flashed a look towards Peter, who was finally accepting water from a canteen Brodie was holding out.

'I had no family here. Not really. They had all been taken from me,' Krystan said, wet eyes flashing and gleaming against the darkness. Yes, Rogart looked after me, but I had no one who was really *mine*. Is that something you could ever understand?'

'More than you know,' Sysa replied, thinking of Grey, and how for so many years they had belonged to only one another. Yet when they'd parted, she'd had another family waiting for her. Krystan hadn't had that chance.

'So you took him, so that you'd have someone? Someone who belonged to you?' Sysa asked, looking over at the ragged man still half-cowering under the heavy blanket.

'Yes! Yes, I did and it was awful!' Krystan replied, barely concealed anger cracking and spitting in her voice, as she buried her face into her hands.

'Rogart was pleased with me, he said I had done well, he *wanted* us to steal people from the human world,' she continued, her voice muffled both by her palms and the pain that thudded through the words as they escaped.

'Us?' Sysa said, leaning in closer to Krystan's heaving shoulder. 'You said there were others Rogart saved that day. Who were they, Krystan, are they here too? Maybe we can help them – like we've helped you,' she continued when Krystan gave no answer to her question.

Krystan looked up, eyes brimming, rimmed red with pain and sorrow. As she opened her mouth to speak, the sky shook and thudded in reply.

'He's coming!' Krystan whispered, her face changed; a picture of fear and horror.

'It's Rogart!' Brodie shouted from the other side of

the clearing. 'Let's get out of here,' he ordered, heaving a terrified Peter heavily across the ground.

Sysa squeezed at the leaf in her pocket, willing it to guide them on the quickest route back to the sounds of the light forest. She held it to her ear, just as she had done earlier.

'This way!' she called, gesturing towards a gap in some thorned branches a little further to their right.

Sysa heard the spotters at their backs as they scrambled through wet branches, tearing skin and ripping clothes as they pushed their way through the thorny maze of undergrowth. In a couple of booming wing beats the spotters had caught up with them. Sysa looked over her shoulder, seeing them hovering vertically, great black wings spread beautifully in the dark. All around them lightning flashed and cracked across an ebony mirror, the sky growing darker in the moments between flashes, as if someone had tipped an ink pot on the universe. After the next flash, Sysa saw the Giant, walking almost gracefully through the dark forest behind them, raising his arms to his sides and slicing the air around him, raising trees to the sky where before there had been only stumps. In the next flash, he lowered his arms, razing them again to the ground as they fell around him. Sysa stole breathless backward glances, watching him disappear into the dark and then reappear against the lightning in a thundering, rhythmic beat. The trees were falling ever closer to them, bouncing off the ground and sending mud and stagnant water flying into their faces.

'Which way?' shouted Elva, looking round for an exit. 'He's trapping us here Sysa. I can't see a way out past all the falling trees.'

Sysa held the leaf to her ear, silently pleading for it to find escape for them. But it just rang loudly back at her, a piercing wail that couldn't seem to penetrate the cacophony of noise. She looked around wildly, Brodie's eyes flashing back at her in understanding. She couldn't save them – she couldn't find a way out through the thorny tangles and the trees. At the front, they were surrounded by branches, closing in on them like merciless warriors, while at their rear Rogart was advancing ever closer, sweeping along in long, unhurried strides. Sysa hated him in that moment – that look of cool, clear precision on his face – safe in the knowledge he had them surrounded like trapped animals. She placed her feet a little wider on the ground, steadying herself, feeling the tingle of power in her fingers – she was ready to unleash some of that new-found power right now. She raised her arms as Rogart curled his lip just slightly – was he laughing at her? Brodie and Elva flanked her, pushing Krystan and Peter behind them in an awkward huddle before Krystan stepped out alongside Brodie, her chin aloft, her eyes fixed on Rogart's face.

'Well, well, well,' the Giant drawled in answer, rolling his shoulders lazily, his muscled arms flexing under the down that covered them.

'Leaving so soon Krystan? I should have guessed as much. You always were the least promising of the three. Still, a disappointment, though.' He raised one eyebrow, goading her to answer. Krystan just stared back at him, the old severity resurfacing across her features as anger flashed white-hot across her eyes.

'Yes, she's leaving. With us,' Sysa said, darting a look at Krystan for confirmation. Who were the three Rogart was

126

talking about? She'd have to think about that later, she told herself, for now, she could only stall Rogart and keep him talking while she tried to formulate a plan.

'We'll see about that,' Rogart said, his face like stone now, evidently not wishing to engage in further conversation.

He raised his arms up, holding them aloft to the dark sky that hung above. Suddenly something was right in front of Sysa's face, its edges flicking against her skin, something strong and solid and moving. Had Rogart brought down the sky on her? she wondered, blinded by the commotion and the murk. Then she saw it – Arno's face in the darkness, his amber eyes peering out a few inches from her. And not just Arno either – he'd brought others, four matching sets of eyes behind him, the outlines of heads and feathers and wings whipping and booming in the sky.

'Good boy!' shouted Brodie, grinning towards the chief eagle, whose size had increased tenfold since the last time they'd encountered him.

'They're going to take us back with them,' Brodie called to the group in general, apparently unruffled by the sudden change.

'Quickly, get on everyone!' He moved his arm in a sweeping motion towards the eagles, whose huge claws hovered a few inches above ground level. Sysa glanced at Peter, who looked as terrified as ever, but evidently finding the prospect of winged flight more appealing than a Giant, was scrambling with the others in a race towards the birds.

In a wing beat, they had clambered onto the eagles and were rising, rising, crashing through branches and careering into the open darkness. Sysa looked down to see

Rogart staring back at them, something like a smile flitting across his face.

*He's enjoying this*, Sysa thought to herself, as she clung on to Arno, and watched the Giant turn and sweep back in the direction he had come from.

She looked over her shoulder towards his castle, which seemed to vibrate, absorbing and expelling the thunder and the lighting that crashed and boomed around its towers and peaks. The wind whipped Sysa's face, slashing streaks of hair like gaping wounds across her cheekbones.

'Just hang on,' she called to the others, and to Peter, who was clinging onto his eagle with white-boned fingers, slipping and sliding over its body.

'Dig in with your knees and your heels,' she shouted to him over the commotion. Peter looked back at her, nodding like a terrified animal, gripping on tighter, pieces of feather protruding from the spaces between his fingers and underneath his hands.

'We're nearly there,' shouted Brodie as the light side of the forest became visible. 'Hang on,' he screamed towards Peter who was panting and clutching at his side.

'I can't hold on much longer,' gasped Peter, 'I'm going to fall off this thing.'

Sysa glanced over, surprised to hear him uttering more than two words. From the corner of her eye though, she saw them: dark outlines approaching somewhere behind them, the thudding vibrations of wing beats, rising cries that pierced and stung at the dark sky.

'The spotters aren't far behind us!' she called out to the others. 'We have to hurry!'

She dug her knees tighter into Arno's solid body. 'Please

Arno, get us home now,' she whispered, as the huge bird soared downwards, the others following fast behind.

Sysa felt the air rush behind her, felt the spotters' cries drum against her back as they careered towards the light forest. It was right ahead of them. She heard the snap of teeth behind them, perilously close now. And then light – golden and bright and illuminating. They crashed into the woodland, landing roughly, tumbling off their eagles and onto the familiar forest floor.

As they looked back the spotters were flailing and bashing and cawing at some invisible force that hardened the air like glass, preventing their entrance. *Dark hearts*, Sysa thought, looking towards Brodie, who confirmed by nodding once. Finally, the spotters reared back, their plaintive cries ringing out and then disappearing into the distance. The group looked on, panting and gasping as they lay there, mesmerised by the retreating scene.

'Is everyone okay?' Sysa managed, looking round at the others who were nursing a few bumps and bruises.

'Nothing that won't be gone in a few minutes,' Krystan replied, standing up and stretching out her arms, skin suddenly glowing against the sun. Sysa looked over at Peter, who was cradling one arm painfully, beads of sweat glistening across his forehead.

'He's hurt,' Sysa said, making to move in his direction, before she met with Krystan's arm gently blocking her, the faerie's fingers circling lightly over Sysa's outstretched hand.

'Let me – please,' Krystan said, guilt still tracking her features as she glanced towards Peter, who still looked for all the world like a hunted – and now an injured – animal.

'It's the least I can do for him.'

Sysa nodded, letting Krystan move towards the piper, watching as the faerie placed long fingers on his arm before he had a chance to back away.

'What about you?' Are you okay? I mean, do you have magic to…' Sysa said, swinging round towards Brodie and gesturing at his hand as he rubbed at the muscles on his forearm, the site of some insignificant injury.

'This?' Brodie looked down at the purplish bruise that was blooming there. 'That's nothing. No need for magic. Not that I have any anyway,' he continued, flashing her a grin.

'And you? Are you okay?' His eyes suddenly clouded with concern as they flicked over her.

'I'm fine. Just glad we got everyone back safely,' she answered, watching as the eagles retreated back into the sky, the beat of their wings echoing as they left.

'Thanks Arno,' she whispered, touching the solid mass of the bird's wings as he began to lift himself to follow his companions.

'Yes, thankyou,' Brodie said, raking a hand over the hard sheet of Arno's feathers. 'You always manage to be in just the right place at the right time don't you, old friend? Off you go now.' He slapped the bird's wing in a companionable address.

'Elva? Everything okay?' he continued, turning to look towards Elva who was crouched over, deep in concentration, contemplating something on the ground as Krystan busied herself with tending to Peter's arm.

'I'm fine. It's just. This,' Elva answered, her voice trailing off as she furrowed her brows over whatever was taking her attention on the floor beneath her.

'What is it?' Sysa asked, moving closer. 'A plant?' All Sysa could see were a few violet petals that were poking uncertainly through the soil below.

'It's growing,' Elva answered, pointing towards it and then scanning the clearing around them. 'Everything is. Look.'

Sysa looked round and saw it: the ragged tree stumps that were slowly rising, the withered branches that were arcing twigged fingers to the light. The petals that were blooming infinitesimally, bursting to life in tiny colours, like rainbows all around them.

'This was part of the dark forest,' Sysa said, realisation washing over her like the sun.

'Yes. We moved it. We pushed the dark backwards when we took Krystan over here.' Elva grinned, looking around towards Krystan, who had stopped what she was doing and was holding Peter's arm against her side.

'You can turn it back? The darkness I mean?' Krystan said, her face warming with understanding.

'It certainly looks that way.' Sysa grinned back, looking around at leaves sprouting and unfurling from somewhere within branches, colours that were once dark turned again to greens and golds under the bright illumination of the sun.

Sysa spun round, inhaling scents of pine and lavender, the air bursting into life around her and once more laden with the treasures of awakening. In the distance, she heard the rustle of the tall trees, their leaves spreading the news like batons handed in a race. Sysa smiled, first to herself and then back towards the others: they had done it. Krystan was here again and they had moved the darkness back.

In the next breath, she felt a sudden, strange sense of belonging.

And not just for herself, she realised, as arms and hands enveloped her in celebration. From now on, this part of the forest belonged to them.

# CHAPTER THIRTEEN

'Are you okay Sysa?' Brodie asked, as they stood at the edge of the stream beside the clearing. Sysa looked around at the place which was scarred on her memory like the remnants of a burn.

'I'm fine,' she said, waving her hand in a throwaway gesture, dismissing the uneasy feeling that fell over her.

'It's just a little strange, that's all.' Had it really been just a few days since she had arrived into Fyrish through this grassy portal herself? How little she had known then, she reflected, and yet how much knowledge had existed within her. How could she have ever imagined that she'd be standing here again now, having pushed back a dark curse and turned a wayward faerie to the light? For a split second she wished she could return to Caithness through this grassy gateway, and then she felt the howling and the jarring and the pain – the physical pain – of leaving Grey there. She shuddered, pushing the memory away from herself like the closing of a door, behind which the contents of a room were overflowing.

'I'm fine,' she repeated, pivoting on her heel and turning towards Krystan, Elva and Peter. 'Come on, let's see about getting this boy home.'

The burn ran clear beside them, silver strands of

rushing water bubbling over smooth rock, as Brodie and Sysa picked their way over grass that sprung back up the moment their heels had lifted.

'It's time to send you back to Caithness Peter,' Krystan said from ahead of them, looking at her departing charge before her, his eyes wide as Krystan made her final address.

'A lot will have changed since you left and time will have moved on a lot faster than it's appeared to. But after all I have done to you I'm going to send you back to your birthplace with a blessing. One that I hope will go some way to repairing the damage that I've done.' Peter bit his lip, no doubt, Sysa thought, nervous of the newest fate to be doled out from Krystan's magic. It did little to lessen the streak of panic that rushed across his features. After all he had been through, Sysa couldn't blame him for wondering if this blessing would lead to a happier future than the last.

'I promise that no matter what happens,' Krystan continued, 'you will have a long and happy life in Caithness. I no longer offer fame and fortune but I promise you a family and a home filled with laughter and most importantly, love. These are the only gifts I can offer you after everything I've done to you.' Krystan bowed her head, everything about her scented with the shame which would cling to her, Sysa knew, far beyond this day. After a long moment, Krystan finally lifted her chin, raising an arm towards Peter in a gesture that instantly made the human man step backwards. She shook her head, her eyes glassy against the sunlight.

'All I ask of you now is that you return me the gift which has brought you nothing but despair.'

Krystan reached her arm out again and Peter hurried

forward in a couple of scurried steps, jabbing the pipes – which had miraculously clung around his waist during their avian voyage – towards her.

He puffed a long exhale out through his lips, finally able to breathe again as he croaked:

'Take them. I never want to see those pipes again.'

Krystan cradled the bag against her chest, tendrils of material running down her stomach like ragged silken rays. She nodded, clutching the bag which had made him a prisoner a little tighter.

'In a moment I'm going to ask you to close your eyes Peter. When I do, you must shut them and don't open them until you feel the sun on your face again. When you open them you'll find yourself back at the place where we first met. The place where I...' Her voice trailed off, and she looked down at the ground again.

'You'll be back in Olrig then, and you probably won't remember much about all this. Move over here,' she directed, gesturing towards a grassy mound that rose up a few feet to the left of them. Peter sidestepped towards it, his eyes never leaving Krystan, who held her hands up, a silent promise not to make any further contact with his skin.

'Now close your eyes,' she said, lowering her hands to her sides again, the world seeming to stop turning as she furrowed her brow, engulfed in thought. Sysa looked around, as for a moment the very air was suspended, the trickle of the stream beside them halted and the birds stopped flying in the sky like tiny frozen statues.

It was as if the world had held its breath for a second.

They didn't have long to wait for the exhale.

Sysa looked over to see Krystan's arms aloft, pulling some invisible force out of the earth and up towards the sky above them. Leaves and petals rose, magnetised against whatever tugged them, and the stream lifted upwards, pulled in watery threads like arrows pointing to the sky. In the centre of it all, Sysa saw Peter, his whole body tightly pressed against the force that engulfed him. Sysa heard the faint burr, then the whirring that rang against her ears.

*No*, she thought, as it pierced against her memory, as she saw Grey's face contorted in the screaming and the rushing. *No, I can't bear to feel it all again.*

But the storm and the chaos that rang around her paid no heed to her silent pleading. Through a patch of blurred-out air, she saw Elva's face, etched lines of concern around her eyes.

'Just hold on. It'll be over soon,' Brodie grimaced beside her, pulling her in towards his shoulder. She dug her face into the crook of it, unable to breathe against the wild reckoning, unable to move against the force that tugged to what once had also been her home.

Around her head she felt the wind crash into her, turning and twisting, making its final course into a column. Its pace quickened, unrelenting and fierce against her face. As the whirring moved ever upwards, she felt that sensation again, like its pressure was going to burst the sky above them. And then silence. She opened one eye, peering out from under the warmth of Brodie's armpit. The sky had calmed, and the world was falling back to earth.

Sysa looked around. Peter was gone, of that she was certain. Just like the circling chaos, he had disappeared into the air. Krystan stood, looking at the grassy mound that held such magic. Her eyes, Sysa thought for a moment, looked as vacant as the place that Peter had just left.

'He's gone,' Krystan said unnecessarily, staring into the grass before her. 'It's done.' She turned and moved to leave. Sysa realised that despite everything, Krystan was going to miss him. She shivered.

'Are you okay?' Brodie said, for the second time that morning. Sysa felt his breath on the curve of her neck, warming the skin.

'I'm all right... that was just – hard for me,' she answered, this time meaning it. 'The last time I felt that – well, it was the last time I saw my Grandfather alive.' Brodie nodded, his face a tight line as she tugged away from him. She had forgotten while she'd looked on at Krystan that she was still nestled into his shoulder. As soon as she moved away, she felt suddenly, inexplicably unhinged.

'I felt like it was pulling me – the wind, all that, I mean,' Sysa continued, sweeping her hand in a gesture to encompass the chaos she had no name for.

'I would imagine that's normal,' Brodie answered, looking towards the grassy peak.

'It was your home for such a long time, and as Fae you'd need no external magic like Krystan's to get you back there. That pull will probably always be there. Hopefully in time, you'll come to see this place as home.'

Sysa nodded, feeling the look he gave her burn across her features. There was something hidden in his statement, some other kind of hope that darted fleetingly behind his eyes. For a moment, she wanted to tell him about the unicorn, to tell him every thought she'd ever had in life. Her mouth rounded to an 'o' as Elva appeared in the passageway her words were meant to fill.

'Sysa, I was worried about you,' she said, looking between the pair of them. 'Your face when the wind started… you looked afraid, are you all right?'

'I'm fine,' Sysa answered, shaking her head, dismissing the split second of whatever had passed with Brodie and accepting the arm that Elva looped in hers, guiding her away from him.

'Let's get home, Mother and Father will be worried about us.' Sysa looked to the distant towers of the castle, peaked like snow-tipped mountains against a frame of pale blue sky. From somewhere deep in her stomach she felt the tug of an invisible line, coaxing her gently backwards. She looked over her shoulder – only the mound and Brodie lay behind. She railed against the feeling, pushing herself forwards. Her feet were leaden as heavy blocks of ice as she trudged on towards the trees.

★

'I have something I need to tell you all,' said Sysa, looking around the table of the dining hall later, the faces of her family, Brodie and Krystan blooming with warmth from the glow of the fire that flickered and cracked behind them.

Telon, who as far as Sysa could tell, either did not possess magic or kept his talents well hidden, flicked his head up from in front of the hearth, before surrendering to languor and flopping himself down with a weary sigh against the rug.

The afternoon had passed in a series of pleasant, if slightly awkward, introductions between the members of the household and Krystan, and although Elise and Bruan had spent most of the time absorbed in hand-wringing and worried exclamations over their encounter with Rogart, a sort of congenial ambience had finally settled over them. Sysa knew she needed to tell her parents about Grey and her meeting with the unicorn before too much more time passed, though, and she fixed her gaze on her Father who looked up from his conversation with Brodie and eyed her expectantly over the spoon he had been raising to his mouth.

'Go on,' he said, wiping over his beard with a napkin that sat on the table in front of him. He placed it down and nodded at her, his green eyes flickering with warmth.

'It's Grandfather,' said Sysa, holding her Father's eyes across the table. 'He's died, just like you said he would.' Her words spilled out in an avalanche of responsibility and regret.

'He's died and left the human world. And he came to me in the shape of a unicorn when I was in the forest. It's just as you said it would be. Now that he's given his powers to me, he can no longer exist in human form.'

Sysa spluttered out the words, finally holding her breath as she waited for the onslaught.

*They should hate me*, she thought. *I killed him. All this happened because of me.* Her mind swept back to Peter, to the noise and confusion as the world had reeled on its axis in front of her. She wanted to cover her ears, do something to shut out the din that threatened to tear her brain to shreds. Instead, she sat on her hands and looked down at the table, waiting for someone to say something. It was her Father who spoke first, his voice like a hand tracing a path across soft fur.

'It's all right Sysa, we felt it,' he said, standing up and moving around the table before dropping to his haunches beside her. He picked up her hand, his palm rough against the smooth skin of her grasp.

'We felt it, but I didn't want to mention it until the time for all this' – he gestured around the table – 'had passed us. We knew he'd come to you Sysa. You were always going to be the first one he'd seek out.'

'Your Grandfather was a great man,' said Elise, who had appeared beside Bruan, her eyes misted with understanding. 'He will be so proud of you and everything you've done.'

Sysa sobbed, a great gulp of gratitude and relief that jumped loudly into the air between them.

'If anyone's to blame for all this it's us Sysa,' her Mother said, reading her expression and somehow managing to decipher the thoughts behind her eyes.

'You should have told us.'

The voice came from the other side of the table. Bruan and Elise looked round, the softness of their features suddenly sharpened by the brittle edge of Elva's voice.

Across the table, Elva had risen, her hands bunched at her sides, her body stiffened in a manner Sysa had never seen before. Elva's eyes flashed dark against the firelight, her face flushed with an emotion entirely unrelated to the flames.

'Although I never met him, he was my Grandfather too,' she said, in a voice that spat like the burning embers. 'You should have told us Sysa. You should have told us in the forest yesterday. Brodie and I were right there with you. You should have told us as soon as we woke up, you should have woken us to tell us. We're supposed to be doing this together.'

Elva sat again, her challenge now thrown across the table, her words flying like rocks that clattered and crashed across the wood.

'I'm sorry,' Sysa said, reaching a hand along the table towards her sister. 'I'm so sorry Elva. I just wanted to focus on getting to Peter and Krystan and bringing them back. It didn't seem the right time to bring it up, but I was wrong, I should have told you. Forgive me, sister. I made the wrong decision.'

And when Elva didn't answer: 'I made a mistake. That's all.'

'All right,' said Elva finally, anger rolling off her shoulders like steam from a boiling copperpot. 'But in future there must be no secrets between us, do you understand?'

'I promise.' Sysa tightened her grasp around the hand she'd found across the table.

'I know how much you loved him,' said Elva, looking down at Sysa's fingers, a lingering edge to her voice despite the gentle words. 'He obviously loved you very much as well.'

'You have us now to watch over you, as well as your Grandfather,' said Bruan, his own pain and grief stabbing at his words and clawing over his features.

'All of us,' said Brodie, who until then had been watching silently with Krystan.

From across the room, Sysa saw something in his eyes that had not been there when she'd looked into his face before.

141

PART FOUR

# THE MERMAID

# CHAPTER FOURTEEN

Grey sat on his wooden chair in the centre of the cottage. At his feet, Sysa looked up from the rug which lay beneath them on the floor. She wrapped her arms around her knees and pulled them to her chest, rocking with excitement. She bobbed her head in encouragement at Grey, who responded by inhaling loudly through his nose. It seemed to Sysa that her Grandfather was absorbing his whole story from the air somehow, as if preparing to splutter the entire thing out in one huge exhalation. She glanced around quickly, as if she might catch some lingering tendrils of the story hanging around like dust motes. Grey's voice soon brought her back to the present, though, the illusion forgotten as her attention snapped back towards his words.

'Tonight, Sysa, I'm going to tell you a story about a mermaid – that is, a woman who is only part human.' Grey paused so Sysa could absorb this information.

'Their top halves are the same as any other woman's, but the rest of their bodies, when they are near water at least, are contained in the scaly tail of a fish. Can you picture it?' Grey nodded without waiting for Sysa to answer, the movement encompassing his categoric faith in Sysa's thoughts.

'Mermaids are the most beautiful of creatures and are often seen on the shores of Caithness floating on the water or sitting on rocks combing their long tresses. Many men have been bewitched by their stunning beauty. But this is a story about what happened when a man made a mermaid very, very sad.'

Sysa's eyes grew wide as Grey nodded again, pausing for a moment to prod the fire with the poker. He hung it back against the hearth, each passing second peaking Sysa's excitement like the stretching ribbons of the flames.

'Go on, Grandfather, I want to hear the story!' she cried out, unable to resist any longer as Grey folded himself back into the chair, long forearms stretched out, fine fingers reaching over the curved ends of the armrests. He settled himself again, pressing firmly against the slats, rocking the chair gently as he smiled that familiar peaceful smile.

'There was a young man who came upon a mermaid bathing in a shallow pool between Murkle and Castletown,' Grey began, the tang of peat caressing the air around him.

'The mermaid was startled upon seeing him, but the man, who was called William, told her not to be afraid. He was most taken with her appearance and the way she frolicked in the water. He was entranced by the way her long golden hair gleamed in the sunlight and her tail shone like silver as it flicked and twirled around the pool.'

'William asked the mermaid her name,' Grey continued, his eyes fixed on Sysa who sat still and rapt on the rug beneath him.

'And the mermaid told him her name was Luna. That's a beautiful name, isn't it Sysa?'

Sysa nodded back at him, and raised herself up a little higher on her knees.

'Anyway, the young man moved closer to the mermaid,' Grey continued, 'and she wrapped a lock of hair around her hand, and fluttered her eyelids – two simple gestures that had him quickly smitten. He realised he could no sooner leave this woman alone than stop himself from breathing. So he sat down on a rock at the edge of the pool she was bathing in and just stared at her, perfectly content to spend the rest of his life looking into the deep pools of her eyes.

The two began to talk, though, and found that despite their differences, they had a lot in common,' Grey continued, clearing his throat, as if he for a moment had also been bewitched by the mermaid. 'Luna laughed at all of William's jokes and looked at him in a way that made him feel like the handsomest man in all the world. As the sun set they agreed to meet again at the same spot the very next morning. And as William left his new love he felt like he was floating all the way back to his home.

The next day the two met, and again the day after,' Grey continued, as Sysa remained in earnest concentration. 'The pair would sit on the rocks talking, holding hands and doing all the things that people who are young and in love will tend to do. Sometimes, they would leave the water and Luna would walk on two legs just like a normal girl. On these occasions William would wrap a blanket around her shoulders and put his arm around her as they wandered through the fields and marsh. William told Luna that when the time was right he would take her to his parents and tell them he wished to marry her. Luna would smile and laugh and imagine herself as the happy wife of a handsome human man.

Luna was so in love with William that she started to shower many gifts upon him,' Grey continued, his expression suddenly darkening. 'Soon, every time they met she would bequeath him with all manner of jewels, hauls of gold and silver brought back from the faerie lands. William was astounded at the gifts and took them from her gladly. But before too much time passed, a difference in William started to emerge.

Instead of looking forward to seeing his lover, William started to feel that her growing affections were getting a little too much to bear for him. Now that she was his, he seemed to find her less appealing. Often a weakness of human men, Sysa,' Grey added as an afterthought, before shaking his head, his white hair streaked orange by the flames.

'Anyway,' said Grey, continuing, 'William started to miss some of his meetings with Luna as he became more and more detached from her. Back in his own life, he was growing in popularity due to his increasing and unexpected wealth. He was quite a feature on the local social scene and had found a lot of favour with the lassies. Yet, in an effort to hang on to her lover, Luna would give him more and more riches when he did turn up to their trysts. William began to pressure Luna to bring him ever better and more lavish jewellery. William had become greedy and had forgotten the feelings he'd had for Luna when they'd met all those months ago.

One day, when William again failed to turn up to one of their meetings, Luna followed the path she had seen him take into his village. There she hid and looked on as he bestowed her jewels, and his own affections, on other women in the town. Once she was sure William wouldn't see her, she pulled up the hood of her cloak and slipped back to her pool where she waited for their next meeting.

Of course, she was furious,' Grey added, after a moment. 'And woe betide the man who makes a mermaid angry.' He made a small whistling noise, the sound escaping in an ominous peep through the gaps between his teeth.

'What happened when they met again?' Sysa asked, leaning forward, the heat of the fire dancing across her cheeks and temples.

'Well,' answered Grey, 'when William did eventually turn up to one of their meetings, Luna showered him with affection, not letting on that anything was the matter. In addition to that, she gave him the best and most lavish jewellery she had ever brought.

*William, so sure of her affections, enjoyed the attention and fought away any guilt about the promises he'd made her. He no longer held any desire to take her to his parents or to take her as his wife. But when Luna told him she wanted to take him to a place where he'd find riches beyond imagination, he was eager to go there with her. For all William could now think of was how he could use the riches to further his own personal popularity, his grand lifestyle and his wealth.*

*What he didn't realise was that Luna, so enraged about the gifts he'd bestowed on earthly rivals, had tricked him. Legend has it that she lured him to a cave filled with riches where she tied him to a rock secured by a chain of gold. To this day William remains tied up in the cave where he's watched over by his mistress Luna.' Grey turned to the fire again, his words addressed to the orange fingers.*

*'And never since has a man in Caithness ever betrayed a mermaid in matters of the heart again.'*

★

'How do you always seem to know where we should go next, Sysa?' asked Brodie, smiling down at her as she lay on a grassy mound, her arms resting behind her head, face tilted up towards the sun that winked through the trees of the light forest.

They had laid down to rest on their way to the jagged edge of the coast which rimmed one side of the dark forest, Elva and Krystan staying behind at Bruan's insistence, so that Krystan could rest and reacquaint herself with light magic after her long absence from the Steel side of the woods.

Sysa remembered Elva's pinched face as her Father had asked her to tend to Krystan until she was fully recovered.

Despite pretending it had nothing to do with the perilous experience they had all been party to, Sysa wasn't fooled by Bruan's assurances that Elva was needed at home for some sort of lofty goal. He lacked confidence in Elva's powers, he was afraid that she would be harmed, he doubted her. Sysa could see this, and so, she knew, could Elva. Her sister's sharp inhale and swift retreat to her bedroom on hearing her Father's decision confirmed to Sysa that her sister knew exactly why she was being left behind.

'Mmm?' Sysa murmured, returning to the moment and looking up into Brodie's question.

'Well, I know because Grey told me all these things years ago, before I knew what his stories even meant. Grey told me about a mermaid called Luna who had fallen in love with a human man and who took revenge on him when he wronged her. He told me she had taken him to a cave and tied him up there and he has remained there ever since. The story came back to me in a dream last night, just the way the story about Krystan came to me. I knew when I woke up this morning that Luna was the next one we had to find.'

'I bet that poor young man's in need of finding too, you know,' Brodie said, nudging her, and Sysa couldn't help but smile as she looked up at his grinning face above her. He was propped up on one arm, his dark hair flopping gently on his forehead. Sysa squinted into his blue eyes and noticed that the irises were rimmed with grey.

'Well then, we'd better get on with it if you're so concerned about him,' Sysa said, rising to her feet abruptly.

'Enough resting now, it's time to move.' She brushed the flecks of bark and grass from her robe and arranged herself into what she hoped presented an authoritative stance.

'Yes, Ma'am,' Brodie said, bowing and swaying his arm across his body in a flourish. 'You're in charge here, oh long lost Fae Queen. Whatever you desire, my wish is your command.'

Sysa laughed, shaking her head as she strode off, Brodie hurrying in behind her.

'So, tell me more about yourself,' she said, her eyes kept forward, hoping to conceal the curiosity that was no doubt scrawled across her face. Instead, she made the words sound like a command, like she was doling out orders to a younger subordinate. Checking herself, she stopped, pausing so he could level up.

Brodie smiled at her, a strange sort of understanding behind his features, his dark hair tipped with the light that fell in the space between them. For a moment, Sysa saw something familiar in him, something she had seen before, a flicker that was gone almost as soon as it appeared. It had left so quickly that she felt it almost unseen, scuttling away into the tiniest of holes, retreating to an echo within her memory. Still it thrummed away though, drumming like raindrops on a window. Whatever it was, it had suddenly lost its language, and as quickly as morning dew is lost to the garden, the feeling disappeared.

'There's not much to tell, really,' Brodie began, oblivious to the shiver that had run the length of Sysa's spine during the pause in conversation.

'Your Mother found me on the shore when I was a baby and she and Bruan took me in. I sometimes live with them, I sometimes do my own thing; I like my freedom. But your family mean so much to me – without them I doubt that I'd be here today.'

'And your own parents? You know nothing of them?' Sysa asked, her thoughts stirring again towards this boy, who was once again new and unfamiliar.

'No,' Brodie replied, his face suddenly darkening over like a clouded, heavy sky. 'I remember nothing of them at all. I suppose they didn't want me and that's why I ended up on the beach that day. I don't think about it,' he muttered, looking away in a manner that indicated the conversation was now over.

Something in the mist that covered Brodie's eyes told Sysa that he thought about his parents more, perhaps, than he was willing to admit.

'And Elva? You two are close, aren't you?' Sysa asked, her voice spilling out an octave or two higher than she'd intended. The question struggled to find the pitch she had wanted; unimportant, carefree, a matter of no significance to her.

Brodie glanced back quickly, his face still etched in shadow.

'We're close,' he said, 'in the way a sister is to a brother. We grew up together. Elva has always been my friend.'

'But you're my best pal, aren't you boy?' Brodie turned towards Arno, who had appeared behind them, diverting any further need for discussion.

'Did you think I didn't see you there, Arno? Come here, now, come and say hello.'

Sysa watched as Arno gently rested himself on Brodie's outstretched fingers. She flinched, still marvelling at what Brodie had told her after their flight away from Rogart: that

Arno could make himself smaller when he chose to rest on the hand of one he was willing to obey. In the same manner, Brodie had explained, Arno could change his size in order for someone to fly him. As Brodie nuzzled into Arno's stiff feathers, Sysa observed the easy friendship between them and considered what he'd said about Elva: like sister and brother. She thought about the way Elva looked at Brodie and wondered if her sister felt the same way about him.

'So what about you?' said Brodie, releasing Arno so that he soared up and into the spaces between the treetops, his size increasing as he flew over them. 'How are you adjusting to life with super powers? I have to say, based on what I've seen so far, I'm suitably impressed.'

'It's been... interesting,' said Sysa, embarrassed now. 'It's wonderful being back with my family – even just finding out they actually exist has been a shock to me. But just a few days ago I was with Grandfather and knew nothing of this place. It's been a lot to take in, these powers, all this...' she waved a hand around, a gesture that encompassed the forest, the magic, Rogart's dark powers.

'But now knowing that Grandfather was dying, that he died for me, that he knew he would all that time...' Sysa's voice trailed off and she bit her lip, attempting to hold in the tears that threatened to spill onto her face.

'Hey, I'm sorry, I didn't mean to upset you,' said Brodie, rushing forwards and taking one of her hands, cupping his own hands around it. The tenderness of it unblocked something in Sysa's throat then, and a solitary tear trickled a path across her cheek. His skin was warm, softer than she remembered from their brief contact at the ceilidh. Or maybe she herself had softened, she thought strangely, dampened eyes lifting towards those dark ringed pools that refused to look away.

'You're doing amazing,' Brodie continued, his thumb tracing the silvered path that the tear had left, wiping away more, Sysa realised, than the sadness that had passed there. With it he took something else, a shield she had been holding against herself since the first day they had met. Suddenly she was exposed, laid bare against the sunlight. She could no more return the tears to her eyes than step back behind it now.

'What I mean is, you're amazing, and so is everything that you're doing here,' Brodie continued, apparently unaware of the shift that had taken place within her.

'To take all this on with everything else that must be going through your mind right now – I don't know how you do it,' he said, shaking his head, tipped ends of his hair swishing gently in the sun.

'Your Grandfather was right about you, you are special, you know that? He saw that in you Sysa. He saw that you were going to be the one to change it all.'

Sysa looked up at him and saw again the look she had seen at the dining table. A moment that might have been a second or an hour passed, in which she felt his face edge closer, before they were startled by a rustle of leaves and the beat of Arno's wings. She jumped away, glancing behind her, before turning back to Brodie, only to find the space between them now filled with something else, a sense of awkwardness and embarrassment that clung to the air around them. Brodie stood, looking down at the grass, running a hand quickly through the dark mop of his hair.

'Well, I suppose we'd better get a move on,' he said,

nudging a piece of moss with his foot as he continued looking downwards.

'Yes, we should,' said Sysa, turning and moving onwards into the dark forest as Brodie and Arno fell in quietly behind.

She felt angry, for some reason that she couldn't quite understand, any less feel able to articulate. And so they trudged on, in silence, as they advanced towards the thundering dark of the forest that lay ahead. Sysa pulled up the hood of her cloak as she walked, pulling and looping the cords under her chin; pinching the skin there. She glanced towards Brodie, his face as shadowed as the gloomy sky they met.

The darkness of the other side of the forest still surprised Sysa despite her previous visits. It was a mean and miserable place where nothing seemed to grow. The sky was filled with bruises, remnants of a hundred wounds that spat out rain and misery like arrows. In the distance, she saw the outline of Rogart's castle, surrounded by the usual boom of thunder and lightning, cracking out of the sky like the loosing of a white, atrocious whip. Her Mother had told her of the Fae Lines, invisible markers that traced an edge beside the borders of the Fae Courts. Court castles were built across the lines, allowing them to harness the power that lay within the unseen tracks. The Castle of Steel had the power to unleash light, a force that was becoming weaker as it butted up against Rogart's growing darkness. The thought stopped Sysa for a moment, marvelling at the power unleashed by the castle that lay ahead. Even from this distance, she could feel the anger of the thunder vibrating round them, lightning scorching through the sky, scarring anything that dared to live there. Sysa fingered the glass jar her Mother had given her, lying hidden in her pocket, a small comfort that might shine against the dark. The jar was filled with starlight, pulled from the highest peaks atop Steel Castle. The unusual thing about this, Elise had said, was that these were actual stars, fuelled by the power of her family home. They were obedient, listening and ready. Stars which bent to Sysa – starlight she could switch on and off at will.

She turned to look at Brodie who was trudging along beside her. He had said nothing since the conversation on the other side of the woods. In the shadows, though, she had sensed him sneaking glances towards her. She wondered what he had been thinking before Arno had disturbed them. She wondered what she herself had been thinking, and swallowed, clearing the tightness that still lingered in her throat.

The far edge of the coast reared up towards them. The earth was grey and brooding, mirroring, she thought darkly, the emotions she and Brodie breathed out into the air. Looking towards cliffs which rose up like great granite statues she pictured the darkness of this place seeping into her very being. Like a ribbon of black shadow, twisting and melting against her skin.

'Let's get this over with,' she shouted, the wind whipping around her face, slashing streaks of wet hair across her cheekbones. Brodie nodded, his eyes lowered to her cloak which flapped ceaselessly against the onslaught, clapping out a melody, fierce and relentless against the din.

'Over there, look, there's a place where we can climb down safely.' Sysa pointed to a piece of coastline in the distance where the cliffs lowered towards a tiny beach, sand tracing a small arc along the coastline. A bleak sea broke furiously against it and waves edged with white clamoured and leapt against peaked rocks. The crash of sea against stone repeated like some ancient punishment, a whip of waves lashing out against the landscape.

'Okay,' said Brodie, peering over the steep ledge beside them and into a deep and rocky chasm that ended only with an angry-looking sea.

'Watch your step,' he shouted to Sysa, as he lowered himself slowly onto the first stony ledge over the cliff edge.

'There are hidden drops all over the place, we'll need to take our time.' He reached out a hand towards Sysa and she made to grab it, anticipating his soft skin, tender aside the unyielding stone around them. But as she reached for him, all she felt in response was the biting emptiness of a cold expanse of air.

She heard the sound first, and then saw the blackness. A huge, winged cackling thing reared above her, shrieking out horror to the sky. Below it, hung Brodie, suspended on a grotesquely clawed foot, the fabric around his collar straining where it had been pierced by the spotter.

'Brodie!' shouted Sysa, feeling her head spinning, looking around wildly for something – anything – to grab onto in the dark.

Then she called for Arno, sensing the sky seer beating a path towards them, amber eyes burning.

'Arno! Help him!' she pleaded, screaming towards the eagle as she stood, watching Brodie's face bloom against suffocation, his eyes flashing like a cornered animal who had been lured into a trap.

Arno flew towards the spotter, fighting and flapping in a flash of fur and feather. The spotter turned and hissed as Brodie, his face red, flailed around, trying to find release.

'No Arno, he'll drop him!' Sysa called, watching as the spotter flew on and upland, circling perilously close to a pointed edge of the cliff that jutted out like a marker, steep and looming over the circling sea below. Sysa's eyes flickered to the beach, lying shrouded by jagged, dark rocks in the space directly below the cliff. *If Brodie falls there*, she thought, *the rocks will kill him*. An image of Brodie splayed out over the rock face jumped without warning into her mind's eye. She remembered something Grey had once said about drownings – that the sea might now and again show mercy but the rocks forgave no one. She had to do something, and quickly. She raced through the corners of her mind trying to come up with something – *anything* – that might help.

'Has your friend got himself into a spot of bother?' a familiar voice said, as if in answer to her thoughts.

Sysa wheeled, wind lashing dark hair across her cheeks as she looked into the icy face of Lavellan. Despite the storm that raged across the landscape, his features remained untouched by the wind and chaos, his expression marked only by a hint of amusement that twinkled in the corners of his eyes. Those blue eyes flickered quickly towards the cliff edge, where Brodie still hung, suspended by the hooked claw of the spotter, before settling again on Sysa, perfect arched eyebrows goading her in response.

'You!' Sysa bellowed into the space between them in answer. 'Did you do this? Get it to put him down, make it put him down right now.'

'My, my, such a temper,' Lavellan said, inspecting something under one of his fingernails.

'How little you think of me. What would your Grandfather think if he heard you being so demanding? So very, very rude?'

'Don't you ever speak about my Grandfather!' Sysa screamed, fighting to hold her voice over the layers of wind and rain that pushed against her.

'Just put him down.' Sysa's voice was slow, defiant. She looked over her shoulder again at Brodie, still flailing, Arno now helpless, only the black wings of the spotter looming large above his head.

Lavellan continued looking at his fingernails, flicking each finger out against his thumb as the horror and rain and wind battered the earth around him.

'Please,' Sysa said eventually, the word almost disappearing with the wind as soon as she said it, her fists clenched as they hung against her thighs, her nails pressed hard into the soft skin of her palms.

'Ah!' Lavellan said, flicking his head up and grinning towards her, his teeth white against the dim of the surroundings. 'Manners at last. Why of course my dear.'

Lavellan jutted his chin towards the spotter, clicking his fingers, the sound lost amongst the icy blasts.

Sysa turned, watching as Brodie fell through the air and disappeared beyond the cliff on the far side of the upland. The spotter, released from obligation, reared up and retreated, large black wings beating a dark path above the foaming sea.

Sysa turned back towards where Lavellan had stood, finding instead an empty space where only darkness hovered. She cried out, running towards the cliff edge, the sound of her scream stolen quickly by the outstretched fingers of the wind.

# CHAPTER FIFTEEN

'Go, Arno, go and get help!' Sysa's cries hit dark air as she ran towards the upland, hearing the faint rhythm of the bird beat behind her with a call that sounded like a human scream of horror. She reached the edge of the cliff and dropped to her knees, her knuckles white over the rough edge, her fingers curving over the unforgiving stone. Below, waves crashed into rocks like thunder, wicked and inviting, as spray leapt into the air and formed a thousand tiny teardrops. Sysa dropped her head, feeling her sorrow dripping down towards the surging water. Brodie was gone; stolen by the rocks that guarded that cruel, dark, furious-looking sea.

The voice that spoke to her seemed to come out of that sea, like a wave whispering and rising.

'Sysa, help me,' it croaked out, until Sysa lifted her head and saw the arc of Brodie's fingers curled over a ledge she hadn't seen before. Beneath it, was the rest of him, swinging in the wind, face turned upwards, one arm clinging to the ledge, the other seeking purchase alongside it.

'Sysa, help me!' he said again, no longer whispering. Sysa exhaled, the wind carrying her relief off and over the cliff edge and towards the water, taking with it the sense of another feeling she didn't yet fully understand.

'Don't worry, I'll get you,' called Sysa, desperately trying to think how she could get him out of this situation. 'Just hang on and I'll think of something.'

'Don't think about it for too long,' shouted Brodie, managing a nervous smile that flickered across the dim as he swung beneath her, finally gripping the rock with his seeking hand. Sysa noticed the sparkle of his teeth, and an idea began to take shape in her mind, arriving in pictures and piecing itself together like a pathway. In a second, the path was in front of her; opening up like a clearing emerging through the trees.

She thrust her hand into her pocket, pulling out the jar of starlights that nestled there inside the fabric. As she began to spool them out of the jar and over the cliff edge, they lit up, bending to the silent commands she uttered inside her head. Within seconds, they formed a staircase of stars cascading down the cliff face, bound together by some invisible thread, twinkling and glinting against the dark. Sysa looked down at Brodie's face, lit up by the radiance of starlight, white rays flooding his features against the black sea which now seemed to disappear into the distance. As the last star tumbled in front of him, his eyes widened, looking up at her in shock.

'Just grab on to them and pull yourself up,' she shouted, throwing her words into the wind and over the cliff edge. The stars railed against the force, bending this way and that, before steadying themselves, as if they were rooted by some anchor that went unseen.

'Are you serious?' Brodie asked, his dark eyes flashing up the passageway towards her.

'Just do it!' Sysa commanded, fingers gripped around the star closest to her at the top.

'What other choice do you have?'

Brodie nodded, suddenly bending to her will as quickly as the stars had. He grabbed the bottom rung of the makeshift ladder and began to climb, stars twinkling below him as each foot raised a little closer to the top. He kept his eyes on Sysa, until with the final step she could hardly discern what was starlight and what was the light behind his features. Finally, he pulled himself over the edge of the cliff in an explosion of light that left him panting, rolling onto his back as the staircase retracted like a door closing into darkness against the palm of Sysa's hand.

'You saved me,' Brodie managed breathlessly after a long moment in which they'd done nothing but look at each other, sprawled out on their backs across the barren grass they'd collapsed onto.

'You seem to be making a habit of it,' he said, smiling slightly and holding onto his chest, his breath still coming in ragged, gasping breaths.

Sysa had no answer but to rise to her knees in the same instant he did. She felt a quick moment of longing, before the air between them was swallowed entirely by his kiss. She felt her face in his hands, his mouth pressed soundlessly on her own, her whole body alive like the wind and the sea that howled around them. The warmth of his lips made her stomach rise and fall like it was lurching somewhere in the upper regions of her chest. Her head filled with air so light that she could see only a clear glaze behind her eyes, now closed and shuttered to the darkness. She was suddenly no one, nowhere, yet at the same time exactly herself, exactly where she needed to be. His kiss felt like walking through a door, heading over an unseen boundary that had changed her very being. Her shield was not just lowered, but cast away now, flung over the edge of the cliff like the starlight she had thrown. In the warmth that lingered between their bodies she could feel it; like a fire calling to her, the pressure of his lips pushing the words into her being. It spoke to something deep inside her.

*I am yours only, I love you, I will love you forever. I am your home.*

But like the starlight retracting to her fingers, the shield pushed itself upwards, calling to her in the darkness. Its thoughts stabbed behind her eyes, pricking at her with a hundred voices, all chorusing out: *your sister loves this boy.*

As the thought pressed deeper, burrowing into her, Sysa pulled herself away, turning her face from Brodie's, and the eyes that suddenly opened into deep pools of yearning and enquiry.

'We can't do this,' she protested, wiping a hand over her lips to erase the need that throbbed there, his eyes burning against her cheek, his hands still crushed around her face.

'Why not?' Brodie answered, turning her face to look back at him, demanding she see the pain she'd left there.

'Don't you know by now the way I feel about you? I knew it from the first moment I saw you. Please don't say you don't feel the same way, Sysa. Please don't say you don't feel the same way I do.'

'It doesn't matter what I do or don't feel for you Brodie,' said Sysa, picturing that shield, firm and steadfast again, hiding away the feelings she couldn't find a place for. 'My sister… I think my sister loves you. How could I do that to her? What sort of sister would I be?'

'But I don't love Elva in that way, Sysa,' said Brodie,

almost shouting out the words now. 'She's like a sister to me. I don't love her like that and I never, ever will. I don't even know that she loves me as you say she does. All I know is that I want to be with you. Tell me you don't feel the same, you don't kiss someone like that and then tell them you don't want them.' His voice was almost breaking now, his hands sliding from her face in a final acceptance of defeat. He swiped his sleeve quickly over the corner of his eye and swore, turning his head away. His words were quickly lost; banished into the darkness of the barren, broken land below.

Sysa looked down at him, his dark hair cloaking the shadows across his features. She wondered how she could ever find a way to refuse him, after feeling what she'd felt there, after learning all the ways this boy could speak directly to her soul. And yet there, between his voice and her stood her sister, her only sister.

*How could I do it?* she wondered, her heart thrumming in heavy beats now. *How could I take the thing that Elva seems to love?*

A thunder of feet, wings, hooves and shouts roared out in answer to her question. She heard her Father's voice then, calling out to both of them as the group emerged over a craggy, windswept peak. Sysa watched as her parents, Elva and Krystan appeared atop white and grey horses, flecks of mud and dirt flying into the air as they reared up towards them, the horses braying and puffing in noisy outburst. Arno hovered in the sky above them, wings tipped in their direction, doing everything, Sysa thought miserably, she had asked of him. Arno, the faithful messenger, unwittingly laying bare the secrets that were strewn across her face.

*And my sister*, she thought, watching as Elva looked between she and Brodie, searching their expressions and finding everything the kiss had left there. When Elva's gaze landed on her face again Sysa held it, trying to convey everything she felt across the icy air that lay in the space between their eyes. But it was futile, she could see that, as she stared up at her sister, Elva's long hair flying out against the wind, robes thrashing and beating against the darkness. She had seen it – nothing and everything. Sysa dropped her head, the wind raging around like the storm that grew inside her, ravaging gently, raking its fingers through her heart.

*

'What happened?' Bruan called, rushing towards them, his face tight, his eyes darting between them, apparently oblivious to the undertone. 'Arno told us you were in danger, are you all right? What on earth's been going on?'

'We're fine, Father, I'm sorry, I panicked,' said Sysa, rising to her feet, moving away from Brodie and towards her Father. 'A spotter took Brodie and dropped him over the edge of that cliff.' Sysa gestured towards the rock, jutting ominously out over the sea which seemed to rear up in a fury, raging against the opportunity now lost.

'Good grief, are you hurt Brodie?' Bruan looked Brodie up and down, raking him with flashing eyes that finally found no need for alarm and relaxed to a gentle enquiry. 'How did you manage to get out of that?' he asked finally, satisfied that neither his daughter or Brodie were in immediate danger of any harm.

Brodie shrugged, a gesture that stabbed at Sysa's chest as she watched his shoulders rise and fall, weighted by a burden that only she, and perhaps Elva, could decipher. She looked away, unable to bear the weight of his hurt any longer, casting her eyes to the sea, hating it, hating Lavellan for starting the chain of events that had led them to this place. Her hate sang loud and cold in her chest now, rising up like the waves beneath them, crashing against the shield that she kept still against her heart.

'I'm fine, Bruan, I managed to cling on to a ledge,' Brodie said, his words puncturing the swirling air around them. 'Sysa saved me, she used the starlights to make a rope and pulled me up.' Brodie ruffled his hair, shaking away whatever words might allude to their fleeting kiss.

There was a pause for a moment, where no one said anything, a ribbon of expectation left fluttering around them. Sysa looked down at her feet, feeling her face glow like a beacon in answer to Elva's scrutiny. Even without looking up at her sister, Sysa felt her attention still fixed on her; landing heavily, silently ordering her to confess.

'Thank goodness you're both all right,' Bruan said, piercing the moment, pulling Sysa and Brodie towards him and kissing the tops of their heads in an embrace laden with relief and realisation.

'Elise,' he said turning to his wife, who stood a few steps behind him, 'this is just too dangerous. We need to stop this now.'

Elise stepped forward, taking the two of them from Bruan's embrace and into her own, peppering them with concern and soft, darting kisses.

'Your Father might be right,' she said, gently pushing

Sysa away from her and placing her hands on her shoulders, trying to convey some sense of honourable surrender across the gap. All she found there was Sysa's steady resolve, as unyielding as the barren land beneath them. Elise stepped back, raising her palms in understanding. This was a battle neither Bruan or Sysa would be willing to concede.

'No, it's not too dangerous. I just panicked that's all,' Sysa said, her words coming quickly, hurried by the confusion that lingered within her. On this, she saw clearly though – 'I shouldn't have sent for you. I managed to fix it by myself and Brodie is absolutely fine. Please don't say we can't do this because that's not going to stop me. I know what I'm here to do and nothing anybody says is going to change that. I'm sorry Father,' she said, glancing towards Bruan, who stood looking back at her, a mixture of anger and pride flashing across his features. She surveyed him with a cool green stare in answer.

'Not even if that person happens to be you.'

Bruan closed his eyes and sighed, and Sysa recognised the inevitable veil of acceptance fall over him, that same look she had seen back when Elva had defied him over going into the dark forest. Eventually, he moved towards her, taking her hands in his, all trace of anger disappeared.

'My daughter, you're such a very brave girl,' he said, his eyes gleaming, 'but I insist on us joining you and Brodie until you find Luna. My powers may not be as great as yours, Sysa, but humour your old Father and let me keep an eye on you for now.'

'Of course, Father,' said Sysa, hugging him, feeling the weight of responsibility across his broad shoulders. There was something else that lingered there, deep within the fabric of his muscles. Shame, perhaps, Sysa thought – shame that he couldn't protect her, shame that she was already so much more powerful than he was. She could almost smell it on him, that sense of the world being somehow misaligned, the relationship between them upside down, topsy turvy. But in his arms was also a sense of gratitude, of understanding – he was relying on her, just like the others were. Sysa knew he would take her place a hundred times over, if he had only been given the destiny she had.

'We were heading towards the place where the mermaid's cave is just before the spotter came,' Sysa continued, wiping her eyes and returning to thoughts of her mission.

'I think it's over there in the distance, you see that little beach?' Sysa pointed to the sandy cove that lay underneath the cliff.

'Come, there's a way down over here,' she said, motioning to her Mother and Krystan, who fell in behind Brodie and Bruan.

'Elva?' she questioned, looking towards her sister, who hung back silently. 'Are you coming Elva?' Sysa reached a hand out for her sister, a brief look passing between them; a sudden, silent acknowledgment of what the gesture really meant.

Elva looked back at Sysa's hand as if seeing nothing, nothing where the fingers and the pale skin met with the dark fabric of the cloak that brushed Sysa's knuckles. Elva raised her eyes to meet Sysa's and stared at her blankly, ignoring the proffered hand and the apology contained within its grasp. As Sysa looked into her sister's eyes she saw a sudden flash of cold, icy steel, something she had only seen once, back at the castle, and had hoped not to see again. She thought quickly, sifting through explanations, apologies. She felt traitorous, wanting to tell Elva everything, yet finding there were not enough words in the world to convey the sense that she and Brodie were somehow *necessary,* somehow one. Instead, she let the words that slipped from her mouth come from somewhere else – and found she hated herself. As she threw them out into the air, she had the sudden, crushing sense that her sister already hated her even more.

'Elva, what's wrong?' she heard herself say, conscious of a backwards glance from Brodie as he walked ahead with Bruan in the distance.

Her kiss with him now felt so long ago, left in a place where the thin membrane between life and death had been almost visible, curving around them, goading them like a chant. The only way through it had been to cry out that they were alive, reaching out to each other to claim their own existence. But where the world seemed to have shrunk to her and Brodie a few moments ago, reality now stung at her, searing at the inside of her chest.

'What's wrong?' said Elva, spitting out the words, her hair clamped in long strands against her cheeks, rain dripping from her chin like tears that blistered the ground they fell on.

'We said no secrets, that's what's wrong,' she continued, her voice rising on the wind, words clinging to the storm like a reproach sent directly from the skies.

'And that was quite a secret.' The arch of her eyebrows disturbed the air, suddenly still despite the wind that waged war around it. 'So tell me dearest sister, when did you and Brodie decide that you were a pair?'

'We're not a *pair* Elva,' said Sysa, all thoughts of trying to explain what had passed between she and Brodie forgotten.

That small word, *pair*, the way it had fallen like ice from Elva's mouth, didn't even start to convey what she had felt when she kissed Brodie, the sure knowledge that they were somehow bound together, like a key seeking out a lock. She saw the hurt in Elva's eyes, flashing there deeper than the anger, though, and knew she would have to lie, to forget, to pretend that none of it had ever happened.

'I don't know what you thought you saw but it wasn't anything at all.'

'Oh come on. He kissed you, didn't he? Do you think I'm stupid?' Elva's eyes bored into her like daggers. Some way up ahead the others looked back, sensing disagreement. Sysa dropped her voice to a whisper and looked back at her sister, her gaze soft, an antidote to ice.

She heard herself offer up an explanation, while inside, every part of her shouted *liar, liar.* Every part of her being railed and fought against the words as she spoke them. They came out in a hurry, her voice much lighter than she felt.

'Brodie had a shock, that's all, and he kissed me,' she said. 'I didn't kiss him back because I know about how you feel. You're my sister, Elva, I wouldn't do anything to hurt you. I choose you, always, Elva. I choose you, and I always will.'

'Oh, forgive me if I don't seem grateful,' said Elva, bitterness seeping through her voice, the ice unmelted.

'And don't tell me you know how I feel because you don't. You don't know anything about me and Brodie, you don't know anything at all. You only just got here, you don't know about my life, or how I feel, or how everyone has just been waiting here for you to get back so you can *save us*. How does it feel to be their perfect saviour? Oh, and on top of all that you get Brodie to fall in love with you aswell. And by the way, don't tell me that you don't feel anything for him, because I saw the look on your face when we came over that hill and saw you there,' Elva continued, the words gushing out like a dam had been breached within her.

'And it doesn't matter that you *choose me*, as you put it, because Brodie has already chosen *you*. Just the same way that everyone else has.' Elva flung her arms up, encompassing what seemed like the whole world, apparently laid at Sysa's feet before her.

'So don't patronise me with your lies, sister,' she continued, in a voice like cut silver. 'Because the truth is written all over your face.' She jabbed her chin towards Brodie. 'And his.'

Sysa stood, stunned at the force of Elva's vitriol. *Of course*, she thought miserably, *this isn't just about Brodie, this is about everything I am*. Elva's words had opened up an understanding, the image of a young girl forever in the shadow of her sister carried on the edges of her diatribe. Sysa knew her parents would never purposely have done it, but somehow, at least in Elva's eyes, they had favoured her, even through the separation of years and realms and magic. How could she not have noticed how Elva must have felt?

Sysa's reappearance after all these years must have been as strange to Elva as it was to herself. She had been so busy thinking about how her new life was affecting her, that she hadn't thought to consider how it was affecting Elva. And perhaps Elva could have coped – but *this*, this thing with Brodie had undone her, like a thin layer of material being ripped from her body, leaving only hurt there, naked and exposed. Remorse cut through Sysa like a blade, as Elva's eyes burned into her; a sheet of thin, icy thunder. They stood there for a moment, staring at each other, Elva burning like a beacon, Sysa hiding behind the shield that had returned to keep her feelings locked up from the world.

'Girls, are you coming?' Sysa heard their Mother's voice as she opened her mouth to formulate some words of comfort, of apology.

'Elva, I'm so sorry,' was all that she could offer, her words lost to the wind that seemed to know they were as futile as she did herself.

Elva ignored her, running towards the rest of the group, who waited in a dark, expectant huddle. Sysa could do nothing but follow, her cloak battering the angry gusts as she advanced forwards in the gloom.

# CHAPTER SIXTEEN

'Is everything all right girls?' asked Elise, looking between her daughters as they caught up with the others.

'Everything's fine, Mother,' said Elva, her cool voice doing little to break the tension that surrounded them like an arc. Elise opened her mouth and then closed it again, settling on a quick nod that sliced the air, dispatching any need for further discussion. Up ahead, Brodie glanced round and met Sysa's eyes in enquiry. Unable to provide the answer he was seeking, Sysa looked away.

Elva remained cold, haughty almost, her chin aloft, her stare as purposeful as her strides as they ventured towards the cliff edge. Sysa stole small glances towards her but all she could really think about were Brodie's eyes, his lips, his presence in the distance pressing hard on her like the wind upon her chest.

What he had said about his feelings for her: *from the first moment I saw you.*

She wanted to be beside him, to wrap her arms around him – all of a sudden, walking without him made her body ache. For she knew she had felt it too, when they met that first time, that connection, that sense of finding something lost to her. And yet she was going to have to bury this, lock these feelings away inside her. She looked again at her sister and knew she was going to have to put these feelings somewhere they could not be seen.

'Here it is,' called Krystan, as they reached the area where the cliff face lowered, sprawling out in jagged steps that reached downwards.

'Help me down, Brodie.' Sysa watched as Brodie took Krystan's arm and she clambered down the sloping, jutting rocks. As Bruan and Elise passed him, Brodie's eyes remained on Sysa, his hand stretched out to her in silent offering.

'I can manage,' she said, waving away his gesture and clambering over the edge herself. She kept her attention on the rough stone below, conscious not to look at his face as Elva's eyes bored into her back, drilling the same question over and over. In her head, Sysa replayed her own answer, recalibrating her feelings into something hard and unyielding, like the stubborn rock that lay beneath her feet.

Finally descended, the group looked round and surveyed the tiny beach around them. Flanked by rocks it curved into the battering, ramming waves. To one side, a waterfall plummeted downwards, splattering and gushing onto the rocks beneath it. Sysa wiped soaked lengths of hair from her face, a graze of spray touching her cheeks with the cold, damp fingers of the sea. At least, she thought, pushing her hair behind her ears, the location of the beach afforded some shelter from the torrents of the exposed cliff edge. She could see why Luna might have taken William here, to this hideaway that escaped the worst of the dark forest's angry outbursts, the worst excesses of its sky. In this land, here was a perfect place to take a man who would be a prisoner, to exact some sort of solitary vengeance. A perfect hideaway, she thought, glancing at Brodie, who stood scanning the rocks around him, for a mermaid who wanted a man completely to herself.

'There it is!' said Sysa, her gaze stopping at a small opening in the rocks slightly to the left of them. She scrambled towards it, a sense of focus suddenly giving refuge to her feelings and replacing them with an urgent need to move. As the others surged forward, she felt a hand grab her, unnoticed in the commotion. She swung round, finding herself looking straight into Brodie's face.

'Sysa,' he breathed, his eyes a dark misery of longing, the simple sound of her name weighted with a hundred questions.

'Brodie,' she whispered, 'there's no time for this. Let go of me.' She peeled her hand away, and turned.

She realised then that letting go of him was like ripping flesh away from bones, like turning herself inside out, the pain so seething, so unnatural. What hold did this boy have over her? she wondered, eyes stinging with emotion. Even worse, what hold did she have over him?

She felt Elva's eyes again, drifting over her, seeking out the same answers. Catching up with the others, she moved ahead of them into the rocky opening, unspooling the starlights as their familiar glow lit up the entrance to the cave.

They looked around the cavern, half-lit and silent save for the thrum of splashing drips that pooled on the rocks beneath them.

'Let's go further in,' she said, snaking through the narrow corridor and peering into the open round beyond.

At first she didn't see him there in the starlight, the

kilted, bare-chested young man who looked almost like a painting. And then as her eyes focused she took in the details – his pained expression, slick skin, the pile of jewels that lay around him – and the gold chain that secured his arms to the rock above his head.

'For the love of Fae,' said Bruan, coming up behind Sysa, 'we must help him.'

Bruan pushed past Sysa, moving towards the man, who shrunk even further back into the rock in answer. Sysa raised her arm, blocking her Father's passage.

'He's frightened.'

'Of course.' Bruan raised his arms in surrender. As her Father stepped back, Sysa took a step ahead.

'William, it's you William, isn't it? I'm Sysa,' she said, remembering for a moment that day Bruan had approached her like a wounded animal.

'I know you've been kept here for a long time, and I'm sure this must be frightening for you but we're here to help. We're going to get you out of here. I'm just going to come a bit closer, okay?' She edged forwards. 'Just a little bit closer so that I can untie that chain.'

William looked at Sysa, his face etched with confusion and fear, lines of sweat trickling down to his chin and settling in the beard there. He offered no answer to her request but taking his silence as encouragement, Sysa seized the opportunity to move forward a few quick steps. She thought of the lover who had wronged Luna, the brash young man who had cheated, and lied, and meddled with her affections. What a shadow of that man, she thought to herself.

*I'm saving shadows who lie and cheat and fritter love away.*

Thinking of Grey, she batted the thought away and studied the chain, wrapped around the man's arms at the wrists, lines of muscle and sinew stretching out against the rock face. She searched her mind, seeking out something within her new arsenal that might release him.

'Hold on,' she said after a moment. 'You might want to close your eyes.' She lifted her hands above her head and exhaled loudly through her mouth.

'Hurry, she'll be back soon,' said the man, suddenly finding his voice, his eyes gripping at Sysa's in terror. 'She's gone to the water, but she never stays away for long. You have to get me out of here. You have to free me, before she gets back.' His eyes scanned beyond Sysa, darting around the cave like a ball careering in a room, constantly bouncing off its target.

'That's just what I'm going to do,' Sysa said, nodding at William to follow her instructions. He closed his eyes, and the flash of silver light that escaped as she lowered her arms broke the chain, which slithered in a golden heap, chinking against stone as it met with the rocky floor.

'Thankyou,' breathed William, his relief filling the cave as he rubbed the angry welts that streaked his forearms.

'Come now, let's get you out of here,' said Sysa, pulling him upwards and onto his feet, his legs wavering and unsteady from lack of use.

Brodie and Bruan stepped forward, each hauling one of William's arms over their shoulders and flanking him as a cry from outside pierced the air, weaving its way through the narrow corridor of the rocky walls around them.

'Arno,' Sysa said, looking to the others. 'He's warning us. Luna's back.'

'Go!' Sysa's voice boomed out, echoing around the cave, bouncing off the rocky walls like Rogart's thunder. As they scrambled out onto the beach Sysa saw something above the patch of water Arno was circling – a head floating on the water's surface, a beautiful vision of gold hair, smooth tanned skin, and bright green eyes. Luna stared at them, her steely look doing little to diminish the beauty that still lurked behind her features. She stayed like that for a moment before drawing her hands back over her hair, smoothing dark strands over her head in a casual, lazy gesture that momentarily held her audience enthralled. Behind her, Sysa saw for the briefest moment a flash of silver, flicking out of the water and slicing through the sudden silence.

'Going somewhere?' Luna finally drawled, looking pointedly at William, who stood agape in the space between Brodie and Bruan, his features slack, his mouth open in an expression of sudden, silent shock.

'I... I...' William's chin bobbed up and down as he stammered uselessly.

Sysa stepped in front of him, drawing herself up to her full height and meeting Luna's stare with her own, steel meeting steel across the water and the waves.

'He's coming with us,' she said. 'We're leaving now.'

Luna smiled back, the lines of her lips meeting somewhere between cruelty and amusement as they twitched upwards at the corners of her mouth.

'Really?' she replied, one eyebrow reaching skyward. 'My fiancé? And, why, do tell me, Sysa isn't it?' – she looked around the group for confirmation, stretching out every word like a cat loosing a mouse and then reclaiming it – 'why on earth would he want to do a thing like that?'

'Because this isn't love!' Sysa's words spat like the spray that hurled itself against the rocks, finally finding release for her own frustration.

'You can't keep him here like this. You can't lock him away.' She sliced her arm through the air as she spoke, anger rising up within her like a blade.

She felt Brodie's eyes on her, burning her as she cried out her challenge to Luna. Her anger repeated inwards.

*I am choosing to lock my own love away at the same time as freeing it for someone else.*

She ignored the thought, pressing it, turning it, pushing the force of it out into the air around her. Behind her, Bruan, Elise and the others stood ready, poised for Luna's retort, the wind around them suddenly dropping, an uneasy still descending as if the sky had held its breath.

'Don't tell me what I can and can't do!' Luna's call bellowed as the waves around her rose skyward, forming a solid liquid wall in front of her.

Sysa saw the mermaid's watery form behind it, sneering her challenge as if through shards of broken glass. Luna held her arms aloft, ready to let the wall of liquid fall, her fingertips twitching with a question.

Sysa answered it with a wall of light from her own fingers.

In the distance, another thunder advanced towards them, cleaving the sky as it raced towards the shore.

# CHAPTER SEVENTEEN

'Get William off the beach!' Sysa cried out to Elva as the others joined with her force and turned their light and magic towards Luna. Brodie, devoid of magic, vaulted over the rocks towards William, grabbing and pushing he and Elva as far as possible from what was happening and towards the ragged perimeter of the beach. Throwing a look over her shoulder, Sysa saw something like hesitation in Elva's eyes before Brodie yelled at her to go and she stepped backwards, finally taking William and running with him, Arno following behind them. Sysa risked another glance a second later, and saw her sister clambering the rocks to the ragged cliff edge. Elva was safe. William was going to be all right.

'This is not how it has to be,' Sysa called, returning her attention to Luna through the wall of light-infused water.

Straining against the opposing powers that pressed together she saw Luna mirror-like, beyond the light and the foam and the relentless swell. The wall rose up between them, shrieking and ringing, Sysa realised, like metal against metal.

'You can come back with us, you can join us,' Sysa called out, trying to push her voice through, or over, the barrier that existed between them in the water.

'We can free you too Luna,' she said, her anger dissipating, her hold over the wall of light that held the wave from them slipping away from her as she cried out every word.

*I have to get this right*, she thought to herself wildly. *I can't win this fight full of anger and hatred.*

The words that slipped from her mouth came from somewhere else though, bolstering her anger like a weapon in her fingers. Her hold tightened on the wall in front of her.

'Luna, your life does not have to end out here in the dark.'

'She's right, Luna, I know it,' called Krystan, her voice carrying over the grating thunder where the wall of water met its opponent.

'I was where you are, in the darkness, and Sysa turned me back to the light. You can come back too, Luna. I know you.'

Sysa flashed Krystan a look, her eyebrows raised skywards. Krystan shook her head in answer – an explanation would have to wait.

'Luna, look around you.' Krystan held tight to the bond of light that intersected with Sysa's and her parents'. She gestured with her head, encompassing the beach, the dark, the cruelty.

'This isn't really you Luna. This thing you have here isn't love.'

'Love.' A voice echoed around the beach, casting the whole place into even darker shadow.

The voice was cruel and ancient, rumbling off the cliff like a mound of falling rocks. The darkness descended further, like a cloud pressing down on the beach around them. Rogart stood on the cliff edge, looking down towards Sysa and the others, a small smile playing across the sharp planes of his face. Behind him, the spotters hovered in the air, framing his bulk against ink-stained sheets of darkness. To his side stood Lavellan, his face glowing and silent like a slender, wicked moon.

As if in response, Sysa felt her grip on the wall of light loosen, falling away to nothing as it simpered away, flickering and darting into the darkness. At the same time, Luna's wave fell, like a shutter quickly closing, suddenly enveloped by a hungry, growling sea. In the Giant's presence, it seemed that neither of them had any answer to the hold he had over the land around them. As their grips loosened, his twisted, tightening the air around them, squeezing like a vice.

'Love! We know all about that don't we?' he finally called out, his words unhurried, tone perfectly measured.

'Love is what got this place to what it is today. Any fool who thinks that love can save them is mistaken. Love is weakness, Luna,' he cocked his head towards the mermaid.

'I thought you'd know that. Haven't you learned anything by now?'

The mermaid opened her mouth to speak, but it was Elise's voice that answered.

'Rogart, you don't really believe that,' she called out, the wind carrying her words up the cliff edge. 'There is still good in you Rogart, I know it. The boy we knew cannot be so lost as that.'

'Silence!' Rogart boomed, his tone suddenly changed, his voice for the first time risen. 'You do not speak here!'

183

Sysa noted that the Giant did not look down towards her Mother. He kept his eyes on the distance, a place level with the cliff. But he had known her voice immediately as it curved and rose towards him. Sysa noticed him flinching; the tiniest of flickers around the edges of his mouth.

'Rogart, we don't want this,' called Bruan, stepping in front of his wife and raising one hand up. 'Things do not have to be this way, we can live in peace again.'

At the edge of the cliff, Rogart shook his head, Lavellan expressionless beside him. Sysa heard the rumble of a growl falling quickly towards them. Whether it came from Rogart, or somewhere inside the rocks, she couldn't tell.

There was a second, a moment of silence, before Sysa realised what was happening. Rogart said nothing, but the cliffs around him started to shake and crumble, the sound of scuffing and vibrating resounding in her ears. Tiny rocks began to splinter from the rock face, spitting out in response to Bruan's statement. Sysa turned, seeking out the faces of her family. She saw instead a flash of silver: Luna had disappeared into the sea.

As larger and larger rocks spilled onto the beach, flinging up arcs of sand like sea spray, Sysa and the others scrambled towards the cliff edge. She searched her powers for answers, but realised quickly none were going to come.

'Let's get out of here!' she called to the others as they clambered up rocky edges, dodging falling rocks and grabbing onto whatever they could find to haul themselves up and over the ledge above them.

Sysa gripped and pulled herself over, feeling brittle grass under her palm as the other side of the cliff crumbled into the dark sand of the beach. She lay panting on her back, so close, she realised, to where she had fallen a few minutes ago with Brodie. She scanned the faces around her: Krystan, her Mother, her Father, who was lain next to her, stretching his arm towards her across the grass.

Where was Brodie? She drew up on her elbows, squinting around amongst the dust that had filled the air and thrown it into even more impenetrable darkness. She knew even as she looked for him, though, that he was there, back on the beach, looking up into Rogart's face.

What happened next unfolded to Sysa as if in slow motion. Rogart atop the cliff, his face like stone, as hard and unforgiving as the rock. The slight tip of his head that sent the last of the cliff falling towards Brodie who stood frozen, waiting beneath him. And then Brodie was gone, in a roar of wind and wave and rock, hurtling away, effortlessly swallowed by the sea.

Rogart and Lavellan turned as the last of the cliff fell before them, their figures disappearing soundlessly into darkness. As the earth around them crumbled, Sysa scrambled around frantically, her breath burning her in ragged, frenzied gulps.

'Come on, Sysa, we have to go!' she heard a voice cry out somewhere as she felt arms pull at her, dragging her away, heels scraping across land that splintered and shattered beneath then.

As they pulled, she felt herself scream, a sound that didn't belong to her, a sound that came from elsewhere, from fire and ice and steel. She heard and saw it around her, blinding her, burning her, crushing her with the force of its impact. It was a sound so full of sorrow that it echoed around the darkness and for a moment threatened to split the very sky.

★

'What now?' Sysa heard Elise say as she looked up numbly. She was laying on the grassy floor back in the light side of the forest and her recollection of getting there was nothing more than a hazy, misted blur. Images of roughly shouted orders, limbs moving and arms dragging her danced around the edges of her consciousness. All she knew for sure was that Brodie was lost to her; that he had been taken, swept away.

'Let me think,' her Father answered, rubbing his beard and pacing backwards and forwards.

'There must be something we can do, somehow we can get him back.'

At the sound of anything resembling hope Sysa sprung quickly upright.

'Yes, there must be some way we can find him. Let's start moving along the coastline and see if there's any sign of him on the waves.'

'Sysa,' Elise said, approaching her daughter slowly. 'Are you all right darling? We were so worried about you back there.'

Lines of concern etched across the normally smooth skin of Elise's face.

'It seemed that we lost you there for a moment, but I know that seeing Brodie disappear like that must have been very frightening for you. Try not to worry, sweetheart, we'll do whatever we can to get him back.'

Sysa slid a hand into Elise's palm, as much, she realised, a comfort to herself as to her Mother. Could Elise see the feelings she had for Brodie, Sysa wondered? Could she sense the things that were now written inside her, like indelible carvings on a rock? She opened her mouth, trying to summon the words that might explain it. Instead, she heard herself lying as she curled her pinkie around her Mother's trembling fingers.

'I'm all right now. Honestly Mother, truly I am. It was all just a terrible shock, that's all.'

'I know it was,' said Elise, drawing Sysa in and hugging her. 'It was an awful experience for us all. You know how much we all love Brodie, Sysa. And even though you haven't known him long I can see that you've grown to care for him very much aswell. We'll find him, don't worry. But first of all, we need to check where Elva has taken William. Elva!' Elise's voice rang around the forest as she quickly swung around.

*Elva*, thought Sysa, remembering her sister, and the look she'd given her when Sysa had told her to get William off the beach. Was it a look of challenge, defiance, or a question? Sysa had to admit that thoughts of Brodie had until now obliterated her concern for anyone but him.

'Elva!' she joined in with the others as they began to move through the forest in search of her sister.

'Elva!' the voices of Bruan, Elise and Krystan rang out around the trees.

As Sysa called with urgency, her panicked thoughts took over: *we don't have time for this.*

As that thought rose up and swelled within her she became aware of Arno flapping and cawing and hurtling towards them through the trees.

187

'Arno! What is it?' Elise asked as she turned to him. 'Is it Elva? Is it Brodie?' Her words spilled out with an urgent, uneasy edge.

'Easy, boy,' said Bruan, as he stretched out his arm for Arno to perch on.

Bruan curved his head to listen to the bird's cawed whisperings as Arno's talons hooked over the cloaked bed of his outstretched limb. Sysa watched as all expression vanished from her Father's face, colour dragging from him like liquid leaving a draining bottle. Arno flapped away, his steady wing beats resounding through the silence, Bruan standing pale and motionless, staring into the distance between them, apparently seeing nothing except an image harboured only behind his eyes.

'What is it?' Elise said, holding a hand to her mouth and moving towards her husband, putting herself in front of him. When he didn't answer, she grabbed at his arms and shook them, as if she were shaking snowfall from the branches of a tree.

'What is it, Bruan?' she said again, her voice strangled and rising, suddenly coated with a tang of desperation. When he didn't answer she shook him again, harder this time.

'Tell us, husband, for the love of all things good!'

'It's Elva.' Bruan seemed to come to life again, the light in his eyes flickering as he gazed at his wife with a mixture of sorrow, disbelief and wonder.

'She's left us and joined Rogart,' he said, wiping his mouth almost immediately as if he was trying to wipe his words away, to quickly dissolve them into the air and sky and trees. Elise stared back at him blankly.

'Left us? What do you mean, left us? She can't have!' Elise shook her head and held onto her husband's arm to steady herself, her breath coming ragged against his shoulder.

'It's true, Arno saw it,' said Bruan, his eyes rimmed and suddenly brimming.

'Arno saw her go to Rogart when she took William away. She's lost, Elise,' he said, holding his wife's shoulders and looking down at her.

'Elise, our little girl is gone.'

'No, no, this can't be happening,' Elise said, pressing her hands to her forehead and walking around in tiny, painful circles.

'Why would she do that? Why would she go to Rogart? She wouldn't have. Elva is ours – our daughter. Ours.'

'I know, I don't understand either,' Bruan said, pulling his wife once more towards him. Sysa watched as her Mother cried out and thumped angry fists into her Father's chest, as if punishing him for the words that had fallen from his mouth.

Krystan, who had been watching events unfold on the periphery, leaned in towards Sysa, placing an arm around her shoulder.

'Can it be true, Sysa?' she whispered. 'Could Elva really have joined forces with Rogart?'

'I don't know,' said Sysa, although somewhere inside herself she knew that Elva had done exactly that.

*How can this be happening?* Sysa thought, the question drumming against her, sending waves of shock through her body, stoking her guilt like a poker.

*How could I have brought nothing here but pain?* she

wondered, trying to make sense of what her parents were saying across the gap.

Had she caused so much suffering to Elva that she had turned her sister's heart to darkness? How could she be the one to save Fyrish if all she had done was tear her own family apart?

'Mother, Father,' she said, moving towards her parents, blinking away the thoughts that burned against her.

'If it's true and Elva has turned to darkness, I can save her, I can turn her back to the light. It's my fault, you see, none of this would have happened if I hadn't come here. It's my fault and I'll fix it, I promise I'll fix it,' she said, the words tumbling out of her like the upturned contents of a jar.

Her parents, who had been clinging to each other in disbelief finally turned to her. Sysa's voice brought them back to the present and out of the half-living state they had been in.

'No Sysa,' Elise said, moving towards her daughter, the softness in her face returning. 'No, you must never think that, my darling. How could any of this possibly have been because of you?'

Elise reached out a hand to Sysa's wet cheek and Sysa clasped her own hand against it. She could literally feel her Mother's pain coursing like a river through her veins.

*I can't hurt her further*, Sysa thought to herself, pushing away all thoughts of divulging what had happened earlier with Brodie.

'I don't know Mother, it's just that my coming here seems to have set all this trouble off.'

'This is not you, it's Rogart, do you hear me?' Elise said, placing both hands on Sysa's face and pulling her closer.

'What's happened here has had nothing to do with you.' Elise's face was only inches from Sysa's now.

'You're the one who's been trying to help us out of this,' she continued, looking into Sysa's eyes so deeply that Sysa thought for a moment she would see what raged beneath them. But just as she felt the lock of realisation turning, her Mother released her.

'Don't ever think that any of this could have been caused by you.'

'Your Mother's right,' Bruan interjected, moving towards the pair and wrapping his arms around them.

'However Rogart's managed to turn Elva has not been down to you. Elva has always had a mind that's been her own in making. She was an independent spirit from the moment she was born.' Bruan managed a wry smile, a glimmer of something like pride flashing momentarily across his face.

Sysa pressed into her Father's embrace, salty tears dripping down her cheeks and curling against the corners of her lips, and nodded. She knew she had to focus. The priority was getting Brodie and Elva back, all the rest of it would have to wait. She felt Bruan reach out his arm to Krystan who moved towards them.

'I too was in the darkness, Sysa, and I know it's possible to come back from that. If you can bring me back you can bring back Elva too.'

'I can,' said Sysa, rubbing at her cheeks and turning. 'But first we have to find Brodie before it's too late. We'll need Brodie to get through to Elva, she'll listen to him, I'm sure of it. We need to go now. We need to set off along the coast.'

'You're right,' said Bruan, his expression filled with such weariness that Sysa felt her heart bloom against her chest, a surge of such love and empathy that for second it felt like all the air had been pushed right out of her body and into the sky around them.

'Brodie and Elva have always been very close,' Bruan continued, finally regaining composure, finding refuge in the call to action; a focus that could shield his thoughts from this too-familiar loss.

'Let's go now and find him,' he said, the strength in his voice restored, resolve surging through every inch of his being.

'Then we come back for Elva. Then we take her home.'

Bruan cast a look over his shoulder, lingering for a moment, instinct pulling him in the direction of his erstwhile daughter. Elise, who seemed to sense his hesitation, took his hand, raised it towards her lips and pressed it softly to her mouth.

'We'll be back for her,' she whispered, nodding at him, as if the two of them were for a moment the only faeries who ever existed under the tree-dappled sunlight of the light forest. Bruan nodded back at her, something quiet passing between them, as Sysa and Krystan curved in silently behind.

As the light pooled in the spaces they had left, they departed the clearing, heading towards the coastline. The trees shimmied in the breeze that followed, caressing them with a whisper that buzzed like hope between the flowers.

# CHAPTER EIGHTEEN

'You knew her. Luna I mean,' Sysa said later, turning towards Krystan as they moved towards the coastline.

The horses the group had taken to the cliff edge had scattered amidst the chaos, leaving them to make the journey to find Brodie on foot, heels squashing against the grass. Sysa felt the sun on her face and the promise of the coast on the salt-tinged air that hung around them. Up ahead, her parents paced through the long grass, peppered with wildflowers, their colour doing little to ease the tension that weighted their heavy strides. The sky was the palest blue, filmed with light clouds that gave the impression of white paint bled into a delicate azure palette. Sysa's mind felt restless, swimming with thoughts of Brodie and Elva, and she needed a diversion. Now was as good a time as any, she thought numbly, to find out what had passed between Luna and Krystan back among the rocks.

'I did… I do,' Krystan began, her eyes flashing towards Sysa as she walked along beside her.

'Luna was another of the children Rogart took from the village. Lavellan too,' she continued, gauging Sysa's reaction with a sideways glance, to which Sysa just nodded in response.

'Later, as he got to know us all better, he came to

believe that the three of us were somehow linked to a sort of ancient wisdom he believed in about a "Young Trinity". Some sort of prophecy,' she shook her head and waved her hand around dismissively.

'He believed that there were three who could together become all-powerful, and that with us in his Court, he could never be defeated by anyone at all. That's why he singled us out to go into the human world and cause problems – he was trying to strengthen our powers and to test us, to test if the prophecy was right – if *he* was right – about us. But I guess he was wrong about me, at least.' She shrugged quickly, her shoulders dropping into place as if some sort of weight was slipping off them as she spoke.

'So why didn't Luna go back to him, back on the cliff there?' Sysa asked, questions rolling through her mind like a pebble picking up grains of sand on the seashore. Finally she felt she was starting to piece her thoughts together, to get a handle on this man who'd thrown such a dark shadow across her life.

'Because she's scared,' Krystan said simply. 'She let William get away from her, didn't she? Rogart won't take kindly to that sort of weakness. Plus, it doesn't say a lot about her strength or her place in the Trinity if she can't stand up to you. If she went back to Rogart after that he'd probably kill her. He'd probably think she was useless to him now.'

Sysa swallowed, digesting the information. Her throat felt tight, scratching and burning against her breath.

'And Lavellan?' she said, 'he was there you know, on the cliff – before I mean. It was him who ordered the spotter to drop Brodie over the cliff edge. It was him who started this whole thing off.'

Krystan looked back, a silent question wrinkling across her forehead. When Sysa didn't answer, she pursed her lips, puffing a deep exhale out through her nose.

'Lavellan is the favourite,' she said finally. 'He's like a son to Rogart. You know, I think he might even love him, if that beast is capable of that.'

'So now Rogart has lost you, and probably Luna,' Sysa murmured, 'what happens to his precious Trinity?'

'I suppose he tries to replace us, to find out where the other parts of the jigsaw are,' Krystan said, her eyes drifting towards the approaching coast.

'Yes,' Sysa said, her own eyes reaching out to the horizon.

*Elva*, she thought, a shiver of realisation prickling through her. They walked onwards, thoughts of her sister hanging silently in the air around them like a noose.

★

'*Tell me about the water kelpies again please Grandfather,*' Sysa pleaded, climbing onto Grey's lap for her story. Beneath her, Grey shuffled, wrapping his long arms around her waist and folding his hands across her lap. Sysa wriggled around until she was satisfied in the arrangement of overlapping bones and knees and elbows, then looked up at her Grandfather and nodded.

'*The dreaded kelpie,*' Grey said in answer, a flicker of amusement spreading across his features. '*A much-maligned character indeed.*

*Kelpies are shape shifters,*' he continued, settling into his story with an expression more suited to the sombre nature of his explanation.

'*That is, Sysa, they are creatures who can assume completely* different forms. They sometimes appear as humans with hooves but most often they appear as horses. They are usually found by the edges of lochs and burns waiting to entice their unsuspecting victims to their doom.'

'Their doom?' Sysa replied, her eyes widening in anticipation.

'Yes, their doom,' said Grey, tapping a finger on Sysa's nose, 'well at least that's how all the stories go. You see, a fellow might find himself chatting to a man at the lochside and the next thing he's getting pulled under the water and drowned by a magnificent stallion. Or he might come upon a lovely horse at the water's edge and feel compelled to get on and ride him along the moor. The next thing he knows he's on the horse's back getting pulled underneath the water and drowning. Not a pleasant way to die Sysa. Not a pleasant way indeed.' Grey shook his head, looking towards the window with his usual faraway expression.

Instinctively, Sysa snapped her head round in the same direction, and sighed, disappointed. There was nothing there but the window, the hanging drape staring back at her, as familiar as the odd look on her Grandfather's face.

'There was a story of a young man here in Caithness, who had an encounter with a kelpie you know,' Grey continued, his words diverting Sysa's attention back to him, and the glow of the peat fire that simmered alongside them.

'This man unknowingly bathed in a kelpie's pool after a long day of working in the fields. Before he knew it, he was being dragged down by a force like a magnet.' Sysa's eyes popped again, all traces of her earlier disappointment forgotten. Grey nodded down at her.

'It's true, you know, there was simply nothing he could do to get himself back up to the top. So he kept going down and down, until he finally reached the bottom of the pool and saw an open door leading to a large hall decorated with gemstones. He walked

196

through the door – he could walk around again normally now – and found himself in awe of all the wealth and beauty on display. For this was a hall that glittered with the rays of a thousand gems, in every colour of the rainbow, all twinkling back at him. The man stood there looking up and around, craning his neck just to take it all in. But then he was struck by an even more powerful sense for a hardworking man – the scent of a salmon being cooked, the smell of it wafting through the hall and making his mouth water.' Grey mimicked the man's pose, nose upwards, sniffing deeply.

'After a day's work he was ravenous of course. So he went to investigate, and through another open door he saw a kitchen where a woman was bent over a stove cooking the salmon. By now, the man was ravenous with hunger, so he ran into the room, grabbed the fish and took off with it. And this time, he managed to swim his way right back up to the top of the pool he'd been bathing in before.'

'What happened then?' Sysa asked, her upturned face shining in the fire-glow.

'Well,' said Grey, 'the man took off with his prize and ran back to the fields where he had been working earlier that day. The other workers, though, on hearing of his adventure, warned him that the kelpies would now be looking for him and advised him to get as far away from the place as possible. And just as they predicted, shortly after that, a herd of stallions arrived at the field with a hooved man who threatened to flood the field if the workers did not tell them where the thief had gone. The workers were terrified, of course, and pointed the kelpies in the direction the man had run off in. The kelpies soon found him and galloped along beside him, the hooved man swinging the thief onto the back of one of the stallions in one great swoop. The man was carried away by the herd screaming and wailing.' Grey shook his head and made a sort of clicking noise.

'The very next morning, his body was found floating in the dark water of the pool he had been bathing in the very day before.'

'My goodness!' said Sysa, wrapping her arms around her Grandfather and shuddering against the fabric of his nightshirt.

'That poor man, there was nothing he could have done to save himself.'

'Well, perhaps he shouldn't have stolen, Sysa, but yes, the kelpies' punishment was harsh, as punishments go,' Grey conceded, his eyes watery and rimmed from the tang of the peat fire. 'But there might have been something he could have done to save himself if he'd known of it you know – he could have got hold of a bridle and put it over one of the kelpies' heads. Folk say you can gain control of a kelpie by putting a bridle on it,' he continued, raising his arms over Sysa's head as if he were placing a winter hat there.

'And once you have that bridle on its head, it must obey every single one of your commands.'

'Imagine that, in control of a kelpie,' Sysa said, eyes shining as she swished her arms around in a display of mock commands, leaving Grey to dodge her flailing hands and elbows.

'I don't know, Sysa,' Grey said, ducking underneath a flying knuckle, 'maybe one day you'll find yourself in command of one. I wouldn't be surprised.

I have no doubt that kelpie would be compelled to listen to every order to leave your mouth,' he said, lifting her up and off his lap and making his way towards the hearth, where he stoked the embers with the poker.

Sysa watched her Grandfather, bent over the fireplace, the outline of his body rimmed orange like some sort of fiery echo. Beneath him, sparks rose up and arced down again, falling back to the embers like the tiny golden fragments of a star.

PART FIVE

# SELKIE ISLAND

# CHAPTER NINETEEN

'What's that over there by the water?' Krystan asked, jolting Sysa out of her thoughts and pointing towards a burn that bisected the land ahead, snaking its way towards the coastline over rocks that glistened in the sunlight.

Sysa held a hand to her forehead, shading her eyes from the light and looking out at the view ahead. The last few hours had been tiring, they had found no trace of Brodie and despite their collective magic, the events of the day had drained their reserves of energy.

'It looks like a man,' Sysa said eventually as the figure Krystan had pointed at came into focus. A man, with his back to them, standing by the burn's edge and looking out to sea.

'Let's go and see if he can help us,' said Bruan, 'he may have seen something of Brodie. Elise, who is that man?'

'I don't recognise him,' said Elise, squinting. 'Come,' she gestured, arcing her arm in the man's direction. 'Let's go and find out.'

'Excuse me!' called Bruan as they drew nearer, the tone of his voice closer, Sysa thought, to that of a question than a greeting.

The man turned and smiled broadly, looking at the

group, his eyes flashing between them like small dark beads that had been polished by the sun.

'King Bruan!' he exclaimed, extending his arms in an exaggerated greeting, as if he had been waiting for them, the planes of his long angular face betraying little of his feelings.

Sysa glanced at her parents, who responded by saying nothing, and then stared back at the man, who arced one eyebrow at her in response. She let her eyes fall over him, lingering for a moment as her gaze lowered to the reeds and grass beneath him. She swallowed, understanding the sudden lack of conversation. The man had hooves instead of feet.

'I wonder if you can help us,' said Bruan, reaching a steadying arm in Sysa's direction.

He had seen the hooves too, she thought, but evidently thought their current cause was more pressing than the matter of the kelpie's feet.

'We are looking for a young man – Brodie – who may have come past here,' Bruan continued, adopting a tone well used to matters of diplomacy. Sysa stepped back a fraction, letting her Father continue.

'He was forced into the water by Rogart some way back, and we had hoped he may have washed up here, somewhere along the coast.'

The man surveyed Bruan, a mixture of curiosity and amusement flickering over his features.

'Well, let me think,' he said finally, fingering the tendrils of a thin, curled beard that fell just below his chin.

'It would be my honour if I could help the true King of all the land. I may indeed have some knowledge of your friend Brodie,' he said, the words dripping from his mouth like syrup.

'However, if I help you King Bruan,' he said, beady eyes suddenly darkening as his mouth formed a line, the smile that had been there vanishing. 'What will be your reward to me? What is finding this friend of yours – this Brodie – worth to you, I wonder.' He paused, rubbing the tendril of beard between his finger and his thumb.

'How dare you!' Sysa burst out, unable to contain herself any longer as she pushed herself forwards, darting looks between her Father and the sneering humanoid kelpie.

'How dare you address your King here with these disrespectful, selfish words! Tell the King where Brodie is and tell him now, I command you! Your reward will be the gratitude of your King, and absolutely nothing else.'

'Oh my!' said the man, clutching at his chest in mock terror as Sysa glared at him, fists balling at her sides as he spat back at her with his tinkling laughter.

'Is this the one I have heard of, the chosen one, Sysa, isn't it? Now tell me,' he said looking around the group, with that syrupy smile on his face, 'is it really she? My, what a ball of fire she is!' he said, looking her up and down, appraising her in a way that made Sysa's fingertips tingle with such desire that she had to dig her fingernails into her palms to stop her powers from literally exploding all over him.

*No*, she chastised herself. *He knows where Brodie is.* Instead, she stood statue-like as the man curved towards her, lifting his hooved feet carefully as if not to disturb something that was lingering beneath the earth.

'Come a little closer and let me see, you, my dear,' he said, his head tilted to one side, rapt in concentration and interest.

'I've heard so much about you Sysa, my dearest. Come here, and let me see you for myself.'

'I will not,' Sysa seethed through clenched teeth, tiny fragments of anger sparking and crackling against her fingertips. Bruan curved into her, pulling her away from the man while she struggled, flailing against the fire inside her hands.

'Please excuse me for a moment while I consider your request and talk to my daughter,' Bruan said over his shoulder. In answer, the man clutched a hand to his chest again, retreated backwards and floundered on the grass.

'Sysa! You must calm down,' Bruan whispered, his eyes bright with concern and urgency. 'This is not going to help us Sysa.' He flicked a glance over his shoulder at the kelpie. 'You know we need this man to cooperate with us.'

'He's a kelpie!' Sysa hissed, looking back at the man who now stood a little way from them, inspecting his fingernails and humming to himself.

'Grey told me about the kelpies. They drown people, don't you know? What is he even doing here, on the light side of the forest? I thought only good hearts could enter here. He's evil, Father, we can't trust him. Don't give him anything, we'll find Brodie by ourselves!'

'Sysa, I understand your concern but you need to calm down now,' Bruan repeated, rubbing his forefinger and thumb against his forehead and suddenly looking more tired than Sysa had ever seen him.

'And yes, I know all about kelpies and what they're

capable of but right now we don't have a lot of choice. And unfortunately, the rules about good hearts and the light forest, as you know, don't apply to shape shifters. The kelpies discovered that long ago. They don't belong to us and they don't belong to Rogart. But right now, we need this man, kelpie or not, Sysa. He seems to know where Brodie is, so for now, we must give him what he wants.'

'And what might that be?' said Sysa, pulling away from her Father and hugging at herself, defeated. Her Father was right of course but she didn't want to admit it, to herself or anyone else. She loosed a sigh, expelling the anger she felt bubbling up inside her. If this was what it was going to take to get Brodie back she knew she had no choice but to agree.

'Jewels, Sysa.' Elise's voice cut through the air between Bruan and Sysa, her green eyes darting back and forth between them.

'He wants jewels for their home under the water,' she said, casting a look towards Bruan, his face clouded with resignation as he nodded back at her, lips fixed in a small and understanding line.

Sysa thought of the story Grey had told her about the underwater room filled with glittering gemstones, and saw how the kelpie man's dark eyes settled on the string of green jewels collaring Elise's neckline. Her mother coughed, rubbing at the stones there.

'I'll give him my necklace,' she said, lowering her hand.

Bruan moved behind his wife, unlatching the necklace and pooling it in his palm, where it flickered, as if in bright protest. Sysa saw the look that passed between them then, the loss that was not of jewellery or riches but of everything that had been lost between them. Their powers, the might of their kingdom and now the loss of a second daughter. Sysa swallowed hard, feeling anger rising up again within her, unfurling like a flame.

'Wait. Is that the necklace Father gave you when you married?' Sysa asked, thinking back to that first day in the large hall of the castle when her Mother had told her about her wedding gift and the note from Bruan which had accompanied it in a green ribbonned box – for *the brightest jewel in the forest*.

Neither of them answered but the faint lines across their faces gave Sysa her response. Finally, Bruan strode towards the kelpie, his face brightening as if a shutter had been lifted. Pulling his large shoulders back, he extended an outstretched arm.

'I didn't catch your name.'

'Modan, at your service,' said the man with a flourish, his eyes darting towards the hand where the jewels were, a gleam of exposed gemstone flashing beneath the pink of the flesh there.

'So what have you decided to give me in return for news of your friend?' he asked innocently, although Sysa knew the man had been listening to every detail of her parents' previous exchange.

'My wife's jewels. The most precious gems in the land,' said Bruan in answer, unfurling his palm to display the necklace that lay there. Modan grinned and let out a small shrieking sound, the reflected green of the gemstones colouring his cheeks and dancing across the dark pools of his beady, piercing eyes.

'I see,' he said finally, grasping at the necklace and swaying it like a timepiece before him.

'Oh yes,' he said, 'that'll do nicely, yes that'll do nicely King Bruan.' His eyes shone with greed as he let out another strange shrieking sound, scraping against Sysa's senses until she curled her face up in disgust.

'And now you'll tell us about Brodie's whereabouts.'

Sysa's voice snapped Modan out of his trance-like state as his eyes drew up slowly in line with hers, recognition flickering across them as if he had already forgotten the terms of their bargain.

'Ah yes, your friend,' he said, rubbing at one of Elise's jewels between his thumb and forefinger, mimicking the movement Elise had made herself just a few moments before.

'I see that he is perhaps more than a friend to you, though, Sysa, and perhaps information about him deserves more than a few simple jewels,' he said at last, his eyes wide with realisation. Sysa stepped back, tiny pricks of indignation blooming in her cheeks as she opened her mouth to answer him.

*How does he know?* she wondered. *Is the truth written all across my face?*

'Enough!' Bruan called out, his eyes narrowing, his glare piercing the air around them. 'You told us you would tell us of Brodie if we gave you a reward. I warn you against making any more demands of us or talking in that manner to my daughter. You have received quite enough for one day, now tell us where Brodie is.' Bruan jutted his chin out, the white of his jaw just visible through the dark edge of his beard.

'Hmm,' Modan sneered, twirling a finger around a strand of his dark hair which hung in waves around his shoulders.

'I seem to have forgotten what I was going to tell you. Oops, how silly of me,' he trilled, raising a hand to cover his mouth, large white teeth still visible in the gaps. Sysa felt herself unfurl like a sail then, lunging towards him like an animal.

In the mist, she felt Krystan's arm on her, holding her back like a finger pressed against a wave.

She looked into Krystan's face, eyes burning, raking over her features. Krystan just nodded, stepping into the space between Sysa and Modan, eyes bright as she thrust her face in front of him, golden in the light of the midday sun. Sysa felt something escaping out of her body, like a valve had been opened and all the air released from inside her. She clenched her teeth shut, tasting the metallic tang of blood against her tongue.

Reaching her long fingers into the front of her dress, Krystan pulled out a golden timepiece.

*The golden timepiece she used when she met Peter*, Sysa thought to herself, *she's kept it there all this time*.

'Take this,' Krystan said, thrusting the hanging timepiece towards the kelpie. 'Take this and tell us where he is now. We have nothing else to give you. Modan, help us find our friend. Let this be enough.'

Modan grinned, snatching the timepiece from Krystan's hand in a deft movement.

'Very well then,' he beamed, with the air of the triumphant. 'I'll tell you. You see that island over there, the one I was looking at when you arrived?'

'That's where your friend is. Selkie Island. The selkies found him on the seas and took him there.'

Sysa looked out into the distance at the island which

edged the horizon, a small flat round peppered with the remains of crumbling ruins.

'Selkie Island,' she breathed, staring out at the expanse of brown and the waves that crashed and flailed against it, like a myriad of inviting, curling hands. Over that passage of water was Brodie, she could feel it, a small bud of knowledge that grew hard and true within her. Her heart lifted momentarily, rising up to welcome the stream of relief that trickled quickly through her veins.

'We need to go there,' she said, looking around at her parents and Krystan who were also transfixed on the island.

'How we will get over there, will we swim, will we need to find a boat?'

Bruan opened his mouth to speak, his lips forming a perfect 'o' just as Sysa noticed the shadow that crossed his eyes and spread across his face like a dark cloud had suddenly descended. She saw his head lift in recognition as she turned, knowing exactly what the shadow that fell over them was, knowing exactly what she would see even before the image was imprinted on her eyes. Modan, no longer a man, but a huge stallion, rearing up, shining and glistening in the sunlight. Every inch of his body was edged with muscle that swivelled and slipped under the silky coverage of his raven-coloured coat. Sysa stared up at him open-mouthed for a moment, listening to the sound that escaped from him as his hooves pounded, rising and falling next to the burn, sending the debris of stray stones and pebbles flying. The sound was unlike anything she had ever heard before but she recognised it instantly: a call to action. She turned back towards her parents and Krystan.

'Behind you!' Her voice was barely audible.

*I would not have imagined*, Sysa thought to herself vacantly, *that the sound of hooves on water would be so very, very loud.*

Behind them, coming in across the sea, was a whole herd of them. Sysa watched as they galloped across the water, huge waves rising around ebony with every thumping beat. Backs glistened as the water fell away, like servants bowing politely to a master.

*The kelpie tricked us*, Sysa thought to herself.

*Of course. I should have known.*

★

'Run!' shouted Bruan as the huge waves arced towards them, white-edged fury curving over the bodies of the stallions.

'No,' said Sysa, almost whispering, rooted to the spot where the land swayed beneath her feet.

'No more running.' She looked to her Father, his eyes searching her in question.

He nodded once, then turned back towards the horses. She wondered if he had felt her answer.

*I will not run away from Brodie yet again.*

Sysa reached into her pocket, feeling the hard stones of the starlights she had left there. She ran her fingers across them, feeling their muted vibrations as they woke. They were already responding, already tending to her request before she had asked it. She pulled them from the pocket, lashing them towards Modan in a flash of light that streaked across the sky. Modan reared up on his hind legs and bayed, the noise crashing through the air like the water that spat and flew as his hooves thumped against the ground and rose again.

He knew what was coming.

'A bridle!' Sysa cried out as the star-filled light poured from her open hand.

# CHAPTER TWENTY

The starlights fell towards the horse's head, arranging themselves in a pattern of twisted headgear. Sysa watched as Modan jerked his head about wildly as they reached him, a final flurry of defiance before his anger was tempered by the rope. As it floated down onto the horse's head, Sysa pulled on the remainder of the rope, testing it. In response, Modan lowered all four hooves to the ground, bending his head down towards her feet, dark eyes flickering behind his mane.

Sysa turned back toward her parents and Krystan, where the arced waves now stood frozen like blue and white statues. The rest of the herd, seeing they had a new master, stopped where they stood and bent their heads low, a row of glistening submission in the sea. The waves dropped back to the water around them, slumping down to where they had come from. Their power retracted, and they fell like defeated warriors sliding gently down a wall.

'Sysa!' her Father boomed out, coming towards her with the two women, placing two large hands on her shoulders.

'You saved us. You're the kelpies' master now and they'll follow you anywhere, of that I'm sure.' He looked around the scene, as if seeking confirmation from the stallions, who stared back at him in dark-eyed unison.

'Your powers are magnificent, Sysa, quite unlike anything I've ever seen before.'

'It was nothing, Father,' Sysa shrugged, the slight tremble of her hand on the rope betraying her. 'All I did was draw from the stories Grey told me. Any powers I have are down to him.'

Her Father nodded once, eyes glistening in the sunlight. Her Mother draped an arm around her, Krystan following closely at her back.

'Your Father's right. And we're so proud of you,' Elise said, turning back towards the row of bowing kelpies. Sysa felt a sudden sense of urgency at the sight of the distant island, ragged edges peeking alluringly over the band of horses' heads.

'Come now, everyone, we must go to this Selkie Island and find Brodie,' she said, pulling a little on the rope she clutched in her fist, the line of stars now transformed and yielding.

'Kelpies, I command you, take us to Selkie Island!' she said in a low voice, looking up at Modan who watched her intently through dark, enquiring eyes.

She watched as he bent lower, her thoughts interrupted by a flicker of gold and gemstones. On the ground lay the timepiece and the necklace, tiny in comparison to Modan's large frame, and the dark shadow it cast across the grass. Still holding the rope, Sysa bent down and picked them up, slipping the spoils of Modan's bargain into her pocket. She looked back up at the horse and jutted her chin towards him, feeling the puff of his exhale on her cheek as she swung herself up and onto the silky firmness of his back.

Sysa watched as the other kelpies also bent low, her

parents and Krystan mounting them without difficulty. Holding the ropes of Modan's bridle, Sysa rode ahead of the group to the edge of the water, leading them out towards Selkie Island, waves foaming against the stallions' hooves. The herd cut through the waves with ease, like blades of grass parted by children running. Sysa tasted salt against her lips and felt the rhythmic breath of the island curve and sting against her throat.

Sea spray danced against her face as Modan surged onwards. She looked up and saw that Arno had rejoined them, circling and cawing in the azure skies above. She looked forward to the island and imagined a rope, like the starlights, pulling her towards it; every tug dragging her closer to Brodie. What would she say to him when she found him? How would she find a way to make this situation right?

The streak of the island suddenly loomed larger as if in answer. There was no more time to think, no more time to wonder what to say. The green and brown stained land of Selkie Island was upon them.

Sysa's thoughts were stolen by the waves that curled around them, their voices indistinguishable from the winds that eddied gently in the sky.

*

'Selkie Island,' said Bruan as the group dismounted onto a small beach, feet crunching as they landed against rough shingle.

'It's such a long time since I've even thought of this place,' he said, looking around, a faraway look in his eyes, a strange, lilting melody humming through the breeze.

'What even *is* this place?' Krystan said, following Bruan's gaze as Sysa settled the horses next to the water, the thrum of the song ringing through the shells and the pebbles that lay beneath them.

'And what's that noise?' she continued, looking around for the source of the melody that seemed to be coming from the heart of the island itself.

'Ah, that's the selkie song,' Bruan answered, looking towards Elise, who smiled back at him, the same faraway look washing over her features, the lines of concern that had lain there suddenly softened.

'The selkies set themselves up here to find refuge from Rogart and his evil many years ago. This place is their home now, and we leave them in peace. But it seems that Brodie has found his way here, and if he has, I know he'll have been taken care of. Let's hope we can find him. Come, let's go to the selkies over there by the rocks.'

Bruan indicated towards some seals basking on the rocks at the edge of the water. Sysa turned, Bruan's gesture exposing the silken bodies of six selkies, so closely matched to the mottled surface of the stone that she hadn't noticed them till now.

*Selkies*, she thought to herself – *those who are seals in water and shed their skins to take on human form*. Also, she realised quickly, the source of the lilting melody. Sysa watched as six pairs of dark eyes peered over at them, entirely unhurried, as if they had been expecting the arrival of she and her group for quite some time.

As she moved with the others towards them, Sysa looked around the small island, lying pale and lonely in the sunlight. The sandy beach on which they'd landed led to a flat expanse above them, the well-preserved remains of a ruined castle the only habitable accommodation that appeared to exist on the tiny scrap of land. Elsewhere, in the distance, she saw other ruined places, crumbling slowly into the earth beneath them, like they had given up all hope in the world. There was something beautiful about the place, though, something queer and desolate. Wildflowers pricked through rugged spaces where the sand met the dampened grasses, peeking out like colourful reminders, tiny fragments offering cheerful slivers of renewal.

As the group moved closer, the seals plopped into the water, swimming around and curving behind a rocky outcrop. When they emerged from behind the rock Sysa saw that they were all now human, their seal skins discarded as they moved fluidly across the shingled sand. Three women and three men, all beautiful – and also strangely familiar. Their taut skin shimmered and glistened as they moved, droplets of water clinging to long limbs, tracing watery paths on flesh illuminated by the sun.

The dark-haired man at the front strode out from the group and extended his hand towards Bruan.

'King Bruan,' he said, shaking Bruan's hand and nodding to the others. Sysa noticed a long scar running along the length of the man's bare chest. He observed her Father for a moment, his gaze filled with warmth and familiarity. Bruan slapped the man's shoulder and they briefly touched foreheads. The selkie's dark silky hair and olive skin shimmered in the light as he bent towards the King.

'Frode, how are you my friend?' Bruan said to the selkie. Sysa remembered – this was the man she had seen Brodie talking to at the ceilidh before they danced. How long ago that now seemed, she thought, as a surge of longing rose up inside her, quickly quelled by a surge of hope that met with it in equal measure. This man knew Brodie. He was his friend, and perhaps his confidant. If Brodie was to be found anywhere, she knew it would be here.

'It's good to see you, Bruan, it's been a long time,' replied the man, looking Bruan up and down approvingly.

'We didn't get a chance to talk to you at the ceilidh, but I welcome you to Selkie Island as your loyal servant and your friend. Queen Elise,' he continued, turning his attention towards Sysa's Mother. 'What a pleasure.' He kissed her hand lightly.

'It is we who are grateful to see you this day, Frode,' Elise replied, smiling back at him. 'Let us introduce Sysa, our daughter, and Krystan, our very good friend.'

'Ah, so this is Sysa,' said the man, taking Sysa's hand in his and pressing his lips against the skin there.

'It's a pleasure to meet you, Sysa – and you too Krystan,' he added, greeting the other woman, his eyes resting on her for just a second longer, Sysa thought, than he had intended that they would. If he recognised her from her previous life, he didn't show it. Sysa felt a sudden surge of gratitude towards him as he turned, sweeping his arm in the direction of his companions. 'And these are my friends,' he said, 'Roman, Dursten, Lilia, Rose and Emile.'

Sysa nodded at the selkies, who observed her with the same dark eyes she'd seen as they'd watched her on the rocks earlier. They were tinged with a mixture of curiosity and, she noted as an afterthought, a sense of wariness, perhaps. She returned her attention to Frode, who was looking back at her expectantly.

'It's nice to meet you, Frode,' she said, extending a hand and breaking the trance which seemed to hold him there. 'We are here in search of our friend Brodie, and we believe he may be here with you.'

'I see you brought the kelpies with you,' Frode murmured, ignoring the question and gesturing towards the horses who were standing dutifully at the shore where Sysa had left them. Sysa glanced back at his questioning expression – he wanted to know first if the kelpies had led them to this place.

'Yes,' she answered, looking over her shoulder at the stallions who stood peacefully by the water, one or two thrumming hooves lightly on the shingle.

'They took us here. I am in command of them now. It was their leader, Modan, who told us Brodie was here.'

'Brodie is indeed here.' Frode looked Sysa over, as if waiting for her to say something else on the matter. When she didn't, he inhaled loudly, a sort of distracted brightening as he gestured towards the ruined castle above the beach.

'Let me take you to him,' he said, striding over the roughened grass that edged the shingle and making his way in the direction of the castle. Sysa felt something grip and lurch in her stomach then, as she tucked in behind Frode while he called over his shoulder to the others.

'Come, my friends, this way.'

'Is he all right? Is he well?' Elise asked as she fell in behind the others, her face etched with the worry that had now become familiar to her features.

'Yes, he is perfectly well,' Frode answered, looking back encouragingly, his smile as easy as the sun. Sysa found that she could say nothing, her fear of betraying her emotions heightened, like the air around her was laced with tiny arrows, pricking at her. All she knew was that this man was leading her back to Brodie. She just had to concentrate on putting one foot in front of the other until he did.

As they neared the castle, Sysa saw a figure step out from behind it. It was Brodie, his tall frame silhouetted against the light, his presence looming over them like a cloud. Forgetting herself, she ran forward, reaching towards him, her hands grappling for him, suddenly shaking and disorientated.

'Brodie,' she gasped, her breath coming ragged, her voice an octave higher than normal, pinched and squeezed by her emotions.

'We thought you were dead. Oh, Brodie, we thought that you were drowned!'

'Sysa,' Brodie said, staring down at her, his voice flat, his body unresponsive. Sysa looked into his blue eyes and saw that they were darker somehow, the rim of grey around them strangely grown, like a new order had established its presence across his face.

'Brodie,' Sysa repeated, her voice a whisper now as she lifted his hands up, trying to force some kind of physical contact. All she felt in return was silence, Brodie dropping his arms to his sides again, dead weights that recoiled away from her, like leaden springs retreating from her touch.

Pulling away she looked up into his face to find only emptiness staring back at her. His eyes now fixed somewhere in the distance, somewhere out beyond the deep blue brushstrokes of the sea. She tugged at his hands, trying to shake him back to life again.

*Where has he gone?* she thought to herself, anger and

disappointment stinging at her throat now. *How could he want me so much one minute and now this?*

Bewildered, Sysa backed away as her parents and Krystan caught up and huddled around, Bruan extending his hand towards Brodie in greeting and Elise covering his cheek in kisses. All the while Brodie stood there smiling like an echo, a faded remnant of the boy she had kissed earlier – could that really, Sysa wondered to herself, have actually all happened just a few short hours before? All that passion, all that emotion, just gone, like cotton floating off somewhere distant and forgotten. Sysa brushed away a tear that etched a path along her cheekbone and dripped to the ground, defeated. She inhaled, pulling her inner shield up again, sealing it over herself, tighter and tighter.

*Why*, she thought to herself, *did I ever let it down?*

'Come, let us go and discuss things,' Frode said, interrupting, his eyes flickering back and forth between Brodie and Sysa. He gestured towards the castle, the group following behind him, Bruan and Elise's arms wrapped around Brodie as they flanked him for the walk.

Sysa listened to the hum of Elise's steady stream of questions as she walked ahead with Krystan.

'What happened Brodie? How did you get here? What happened after you went into the water?' Sysa looked over her shoulder and saw Brodie staring back at her, looking right through her as if he saw everything and at the same time absolutely nothing at all.

'The selkies found me in the water and took me here,' he replied.

'I'm fine Elise, honestly. All back to normal.' He

shrugged at her. Elise squeezed him a little tighter, smiling at him.

*Normal*, thought Sysa blankly. *Nothing could be further from the truth.*

# CHAPTER TWENTY-ONE

They rounded the corner to the castle, where birds, startled by the sudden arrival of visitors, darted from gaps in the stone like small, winged arrows. Frode motioned for the group to be seated, directing them into a circle. Sysa watched as his selkie companions dropped, cross-legged, in that easy, silken motion of theirs, tufts of grass peeking up in the triangled gaps between their limbs.

'We have some bad news, I'm afraid Brodie,' Bruan began, settling into the circle and turning towards Brodie, whose eyes flickered in response for the first time since they had found him.

'It's Elva – my daughter,' Bruan continued, looking back at the others, who watched him intently, dark pooled eyes absorbing every word.

'I'm afraid when she left us on the beach earlier – when she left to take William away to safety I mean – after what happened to you Brodie – she went with Rogart.'

Bruan inhaled a gulp of air, the words tumbling out of him, while Brodie hung his head, pinching the skin between his eyebrows with his finger and his thumb. Sysa heard his long exhale across the circle, a breath of pain that seemed to curl under her nose and penetrate deep within her flesh, scraping and hurting her. When Brodie said nothing in reply, Bruan continued.

'For some reason Rogart has bewitched our daughter, and she has joined him. Arno told us.' The final words escaped Bruan with a gasp.

'Forgive me,' he said, composing himself once again, 'this is a difficult time for my wife and I.' Elise, sitting on his other side, squeezed his hand, her thumb kneading gently at his skin.

'We need your help. Brodie?' he said, looking at Brodie, who was staring down towards his hands, appearing to be in another world entirely.

'We need you to help us. Sysa believes you are the only one who can persuade Elva to come back to us. Friend, will you help us get our daughter back?'

Hearing the catch in Bruan's voice the rest of the group murmured collective words of sympathy and encouragement. Sysa looked round at the group, their luminous faces radiating empathy – all except Brodie who was staring back at her, his face tight, his expression a wordless, empty void. There was a long pause while he kept staring at her, as if he expected her to say something, to divulge some sort of insight that would bridge the gap between them. Finally, when she said nothing, he gave a tight laugh, shaking his head, his dark hair falling in a wave across his forehead.

'Of course I will help you Bruan. Of course I will. I knew of Elva before you came here. Arno told me. He arrived here just before you.'

'Of course, and thank you, Brodie, this means so much to us,' Elise said, moving behind him and placing her hand on his shoulder in gratitude. Brodie reached up to touch her fingers, his eyes closing for a moment as his pinkie wrapped around hers, a seal on their agreement, an evocation of the years of care that had been given and received. Just as quickly, though, he pulled his hand away, eyes opening back to that hard, grey place they had come from. Sysa watched as his gaze dropped to the ground beneath him.

'And we will help you too, King Bruan.' She heard Frode's voice somewhere amongst the bustle that had begun around them.

The rest was lost in the throng as the group members rose and started to discuss a myriad of plans.

'How did Frode get the scar?' Sysa heard Krystan whisper to Brodie, her voice breaking his concentration across the departing circle.

'What?' said Brodie, blinking as if he had been woken out of slumber by an unexpected light.

'The scar, how did he get it?' Krystan did her best to discreetly indicate the long dark welt covering almost the whole length of Frode's chest.

'Oh that,' Brodie said, glancing over towards Frode, who was talking animatedly to Bruan, his scar catching the light as if it were somehow aware of the attention.

'It was given to him by a hunter who drove a knife into Frode's chest when he was in seal form in the human world. Frode managed to escape and some of the selkies captured the hunter on land and dragged him here. When he saw Frode, in his human form with the hunting knife still in his chest he begged forgiveness and withdrew the weapon. The selkies returned the hunter to the human world and made him promise that he and his kind would never again hunt the seal folk. Ever since then, Frode has been the selkie leader. He wears that scar with pride as a reminder of the promise made by man.'

'Oh,' said Krystan. 'My goodness.' Slightly flushed now, she looked again at Frode, who was still deep in conversation with Bruan and the group.

Sysa kept her eyes on Brodie. That little speech was the most he'd spoken since they'd found him here, she thought. Krystan, as if picking up on the tension, flicked a look between them. Her voice rang with forced brightness as she swivelled on her heel, turning from them.

'Oh, well, I better go and see what they're all talking about. I'll leave you two to catch up.'

'I know that story, Grey told me of it,' Sysa said, scuffing her foot along the gravelly floor beneath her as Krystan hurried away to join the others.

'Grey told you a lot of things,' Brodie said, looking away into the space that Krystan had just left.

'Brodie... I need to talk to you about what happened before the beach, before Luna and William,' Sysa rushed out quickly, piercing the air that now seemed to press back in on her, threatening to crush her.

'The things you said, the things I said to you...' She drifted off, trying to catch his eyes, which still looked through her, staring back blankly when she finally ensnared them with her own.

'It doesn't matter,' Brodie said, his words slicing the air like a blunt knife, dull and unwieldy.

'I didn't mean the things I said, and it was silly of me to say them. It must have been the excitement of kissing you.' He paused for a moment, letting the knife go deeper. 'I'm sorry I said those things and I'm sorry if they upset you.' His neck tightened. Sysa saw his fists clench, his nails digging into the skin of his palms as he turned his face away.

'I see.'

The two words did not convey the way Sysa's world was spinning all around her. She swallowed down hard, pushing air into lungs which seemed to have shrunk and constricted with every word that Brodie spoke. She was afraid that any further sound she made would come out of her mouth as a half-strangled, tiny squeak, weak and pathetic. And yet as Brodie moved to walk away her voice sounded braver than she felt as she called out to him.

'Are you all right Brodie? I mean, you just don't seem to be yourself.'

Brodie turned back to look at her, his darkened eyes meeting hers – actually seeming to *see* her – for the first time since the beach, since Rogart. Sysa saw something wash over his face before his eyes flickered and once again hardened over – a shield, she realised with an ache, that was not dissimilar to her own.

'You have no idea what I am Sysa, no idea at all,' he said, shaking his head and turning.

And with that he walked away and left Sysa shivering in the air that now felt as if it had turned completely into ice.

★

'Sysa?' Elise's concerned face came slowly into focus. Sysa had no idea how long she had been standing there, frozen in the aftermath of her conversation with Brodie. Her eyes had misted over until the world in front of her had become nothing but a blurred-out scene, her senses dulled as if she were listening in from underneath the sea. Her heart seemed to have dropped in her chest and the space it left pushed upwards, narrowing her airways. She had been ready to tell Brodie everything. Knowing that he really cared so little about her carved out a deep wound inside her, like someone scraping out the core of her, leaving behind an empty shell.

'Sysa, are you all right?' Elise repeated, green eyes raking over her.

'Yes, I'm fine Mother,' Sysa replied flatly, slowly letting all the air inside her escape. She hadn't realised she had been holding her breath since Brodie walked away, as if letting it out would lend some sort of agreement to his dismissal.

'I saw you talking to Brodie,' Elise said, looking back at the group Brodie had rejoined over her shoulder, her face full of empathy.

'I understand Sysa, really I do.'

Sysa looked into her Mother's eyes and put her arms around her. From the vantage point of Elise's shoulder she saw Brodie glance across, just as quickly resuming his conversation with Frode and the others in the group.

'It's nothing Mother, I'm fine now,' Sysa said, as if saying the words aloud could make any difference to her feelings.

'I just thought for a while…' her words trailed off as her Mother pulled back and pressed her mouth to Sysa's ear.

'I can see things, you know Sysa. I was young like you once too, with all the same feelings and emotions.' She glanced quickly over her shoulder.

'Once this is all over there is so much that can come to pass. Things will be as they should one day. If he's meant for you, like Bruan and I were, then the two of you will find a way to be together. Try not to worry, Sysa. Things will turn out as they should do in the end.'

Sysa opened her mouth to tell her Mother everything, about Brodie and Elva and the kiss, all of it, but her words were swallowed by a sudden commotion, like a foot stamping them back into the ground. She looked towards the others, whose circle had now widened, opening up a space filled by something that Sysa couldn't yet see.

'Elise, Sysa, we have a visitor,' Bruan called out to them, a questioning look on his face as he approached the two of them, someone following closely behind him.

'It's Luna, she has come to join us.'

The golden-haired mermaid, now wholly female, stepped out from behind him and moved towards Sysa.

'Hello again Sysa,' she said, a half-smile on her face, her body glistening with the jewelled remnants of the ocean.

'I've come to join you in your quest.'

*

'Well. This is a surprise,' said Sysa, feeling strangely glad of a distraction from thoughts of Brodie and Elva.

'I'm very glad to hear it, but do tell me, Luna, whatever has happened to make you change your mind? When we saw you on the beach you were firmly set against us.' Sysa looked round at her friends, who stood, arms tight across their chests, nodding their agreement.

'So tell me, mermaid, what could have happened to make you want to join us now?'

'Rogart happened, Sysa,' said Luna, her green eyes flashing. 'Rogart took William along with your sister – don't you see that? He took the man I loved away from me. And yes, maybe I was wrong in what I was doing.' Luna rolled her eyes as if she didn't really believe what she was saying. 'But I was in love Sysa, and love makes you do strange things sometimes. Do you understand Sysa? Tell me, have you ever been in love?'

Sysa looked around, startled by the question and the burn of a prickling heat that now rose up across her features. All eyes were focused on her, seeking out her answer. All but Krystan, who cast her gaze downwards, shamed at the thought of what 'love' had once made her do. Like the pull of a magnet, though, Sysa found herself staring at Brodie, who stared right back at her, arms still folded, that muscle in his neck still twitching.

'No, Luna, I don't think I have,' Sysa said finally, setting her jaw as she clenched her teeth, holding tight the words she knew she could now never let escape.

'Then it will be hard for you to sympathise with me,' Luna said, shaking her head, golden hair bobbing on her shoulders.

*I know more than you realise*, Sysa thought to herself. *Look what love has done to each one of us here. Maybe Rogart is right. Maybe love really does cause us all nothing but a life of misery and pain.*

Instead she heard her voice answer with a note of irritation.

'Not hard. I have an imagination. Tell me, Luna, are you here to help us or are you here to get revenge?'

When Luna didn't answer, Sysa continued.

'If we find William and my sister, do you plan to imprison him in a cave again? Because if that is your plan I have to tell you that's something I won't allow.'

Luna stood, hands on hips, staring at Sysa with raised eyebrows. After a long pause, she smiled, as if she'd come to some sort of amusing conclusion.

*She's enjoying this*, Sysa thought, feeling her fingers twitch, the pulse of her powers snagging at the inside of her skin.

'Aren't we all here for revenge to some extent?' Luna finally said, eyes twinkling. 'Come on, Sysa, there is none of us that is either fully only good or only bad. But to answer your question, no, I don't plan to imprison William in a cave again. I've had time to think since he was taken. I shall let him choose whether he wishes to be with me again or not.'

Thinking back to the fear etched on William's face when they had found him, Sysa couldn't imagine that a chance to be with Luna again would hold very much attraction.

'Very well,' she said. 'And if he chooses not to be with you, we offer him the chance to return to his own world again.' She felt the pulse which had been throbbing at her fingers ebb away – for now at least, Luna was co-operating.

'But there will be no argument on this Luna. If you cannot agree to these terms then you can leave this place right now.'

Luna nodded and smiled, offering Sysa a deep curtsey. Sysa flinched, digging her nails into her palms. It was obvious Luna did not believe their agreement would ever stand.

*She thinks William will be seduced by her again*, Sysa thought, thinking of the man who had run off with Elva only to end up running to Rogart and Lavellan.

'You have my word,' Luna said, interrupting the flash of memory. Sysa nodded back, dismissing Luna into the circle of onlookers. Whatever her reservations, right now they needed all the help they could get.

Sysa looked around the assembled group, feeling their energy vibrate in the air around her, rolling away in a hum of anticipation. Faeries, selkies and a mermaid, a group of kelpies at the water's edge and an eagle circling in the sky above. Some here because they wanted or needed to be, others coerced – others thinking only of themselves. Through her haze, Sysa now saw that light and dark existed in the same space, brushing up against each other and blurring the overlapping edges. And at the edge of the group she saw Brodie, who had carried the lightest part of her heart and now reached into its very darkest place. She watched as he stared into the distance and felt the sting of it all again, the pain of a loss that she hadn't had time to comprehend or fully analyse. His eyes met hers briefly, almost in question. Before she could answer, he turned his face away, his dark hair flying like a flag against the wind.

Amongst it all, she heard Bruan's voice cry out 'onwards!' – his command ballooning into the sky as the group surged to the shore, clambering onto the backs of the kelpies and away from Selkie Island.

Sysa heard other voices call out around her, in a throng of agreement and unison, and she looked ahead to the coast and the dark forest, rearing up in the distance like a grim blanket as she rode. She felt Modan shift beneath her, sweeping through the current like a blade, his silky mane slick against her legs as she squeezed her thighs against him. She looked over her shoulder to the retreating shape of the island which now stood empty, save for the crumbling ruins and the birds that circled the castle. Sysa could hear their plaintive cries, calling out to them across the ocean. She fixed her gaze ahead, steadied on that blanket that was opening up in front of them, dark and heavy like a cloud.

To each side of her, her companions also sought out the coastline. Eyes brightened in the face of looming darkness; hopeful, she thought, of seeking a prize that had eluded them too long. Sysa surveyed her small army, watching as the kelpies crashed through the curling, biting waters. She felt the tang of sea spray on her lips, sharp and salty, refreshing her dulled senses as the wind whipped her hair across her face.

In the sky above, Arno was in flight and soaring, guiding them towards the darkness. To Sysa's left her Father rode, while on her right, her Mother advanced, resplendent against the glassy mane of her kelpie's polished coat. Just behind, Brodie rode, moving onwards yet somehow retreating away from her. Sysa did not turn to look at him. She was afraid she'd find him diminishing as quickly as the island they had left.

Sysa thought back to her journey towards that island, and the hope she'd felt as she reached it. Had she known what had awaited her, would she have still gone there, she wondered, if only to help seek her sister out? She knew she would have, yet somehow couldn't shake the feeling that a piece of herself was left there, hidden beneath the shingle. A tiny piece of that hope, alone and stranded and without protection from the whims of passing tides.

Sysa shuddered back into the moment as the coastline reared up on them, dark cliffs looming like angry faces. Beneath the stone that edged the dark land the group circled, kelpies baying as they flitted around, hooves pounding at the edge of foaming waves. Sysa dismounted, keeping her grip on Modan's bridle, and looked round at the others, nodding her encouragement.

'Here we are, friends,' she said, drawing every eye to her, as she stood with them on the shingle. They nodded back at her, grim and resolute and hopeful.

'The time to defeat Rogart comes now.'

The sound of cheering voices echoed around the coastline, seeping and curling into the dark and listening stone.

# PART SIX

# THE GIANT AND THE UNICORN

# CHAPTER TWENTY-TWO

Sysa looked up at the cliff wall which stood staring back at her, a linear darkness reaching high up to the sky above them. Still holding Modan's bridle, she heard words spoken in anger from behind her, recognising the speaker as Brodie, who was talking to Frode in a quiet, urgent tone. Though her senses had dulled these last days, his lowered voice was still no match for her keen Fae hearing. She fiddled with Modan's bridle, catching the last of their conversation.

'All right then. But after this I leave for good.'

Sysa felt her breath catch in her throat, pinching the flesh there, as she turned her head towards them. The conversation was over though, and she saw Brodie walk away, Frode looking after him with narrowed, troubled eyes. From behind Frode, Krystan appeared, placing one hand on the seal-man's shoulder in a display of consolation. Sysa had seen the looks between them since Selkie Island, the flush across Krystan's cheeks when Frode was around, and noted their entwining fingers now. The pounding in her chest softened for a moment: she was happy for them. Just as quickly, though, the echo of Brodie's words crept up behind her, thudding into her. He was leaving. After this battle Brodie would be gone.

Sysa turned away, the understanding of what they had almost had, and what she had lost, too much to bear now. The world seemed to suddenly spin all around her, darkness and blackness swirling relentlessly around her head. She felt like she was falling, falling deeper and deeper.

And then she felt the wing beat, the crack of dark, winged ebony all around her.

'Spotters!' A voice cried out from beneath the darkness.

It was Rogart's messengers, swooping and diving around the cliff.

Sysa raised her head, shielding her face against the descending, cawing creatures. Their cries rang through her, shrill and piercing like a knife. She felt the wind blast against her face, drumming at her in rhythm with their wing beats. In the gaps, she saw flashes of sky against the ragged length of the cliff edge. In between it all Rogart was there, looming over them, while Lavellan stood at his side, his face a pool of searching, milky ice.

'And so you come back for more!' Rogart boomed from above them, his voice echoing around the coastline. His roar reached out across the ocean, coming up behind the tiny army and thudding into them, as if the words had gathered momentum on the waves. Sysa saw Rogart's face, shadowed and contorted against the muddy sky around him, so dark in contrast to Lavellan's. And then she saw them – Elva and William, standing huddled and strangely fragile just behind the outline of them both.

Elva's face was blank, while William, Sysa thought, looked as terrified as ever. Beneath them, the cliff stood still and silent, observing like an ancient warrior standing guard. Elva's steely look from the beach was gone, replaced by an expression Sysa didn't recognise. Her robes were ragged, flapping in the wind, as she pulled back clumps of hair that streaked across her eyes. Her legs and arms looked dirty, her normally luminous skin made grey and sallow. Beside her, William stood, bare-chested, and even more dishevelled than he'd been back in the cave. His eyes bulged and flickered around the scene beneath them, trying to convey some sort of silent message as he stood shivering above them.

As Sysa traced the lines between them she saw it. Their hands entwined; the thing that made them vulnerable – Elva wanted her to see.

It was there in Elva's face too, the fear that held her, like an anchor that was frozen. From behind her, Sysa heard Luna breathe out a hiss of recognition, seeing exactly the same thing. Brodie had been right. Her sister hadn't really loved him. At least not in the way she thought she had. Sysa flicked a look towards him. He stared back at her, a strange sort of darkness in his eyes.

Behind her, Sysa's parents rushed forward.

'Elva!' Bruan called, 'Elva, are you all right?'

'He means to kill Brodie, and then you Father!' Elva blurted out, eyes suddenly flashing everywhere.

'It's a trap, Sysa, he knew you would come back here for me. I'm so sorry, I was angry, but then...' Her cries were swallowed as Rogart roared out to the sky.

There was a second, a moment that hung like an icicle before Sysa registered the movement that came with his roar, the single swipe of his arm that cut across the air around him. Sysa blinked, watching the hand that fell on her sister's, reaching out and batting she and William across the edge of the cliff, sending them tumbling like paper dolls careering in slow motion through the sky.

All at once Elise screamed, Bruan cried out, and the group behind Sysa rushed towards the staring cliff edge. But suddenly Sysa could see only her sister and William, cartwheeling like dancers in the air. For a moment, she remembered a table rising upwards, an evening spent in the dining room of the castle, laughter, a test of her new powers.

Flicking her arm out to the sea behind her she summoned that power now.

In response, the fingertips of a wave separated from the sea, stretching and reforming, and rolled towards her. The wave latched onto Sysa's fingers and stretched further out at her command. As it danced and curled around her, the selkies and the stallions moved forwards; Frode, Roman, Dursten, Lilia, Rose and Emile raising their arms up, the stallions aside them rearing up into a wall of hands and hooves. Sysa nodded in response, flicking up her hand, sending the wave skywards towards Elva and William. The wave rose up the side of the cliff like a swirling mirror and curled like a blanket under the falling pair.

Elva and William wobbled, steadying themselves on their watery mattress, looking at each other and the wave that wrapped around them, holding them as they floated back to the safety of the shingled beach below them. Through the carousel of white and blue Sysa saw her sister mouth a word: 'thankyou.'

The wave that had cradled them dropped to meet the sand like a ribbon, disappearing back into the sea.

'Elva! You're all right!' Elise rushed towards the pair, her voice splitting the sudden silence.

'I'm all right Mother, I'm just so sorry…' Elva's voice trailed off as she was crushed into the folds of her Mother's cloak.

Bruan and Elise wrapped round her as William clung to Elva's hand, looking around wildly. Sysa staggered across the shingle towards them, blinking and jolting herself back into life. The arm she had used to summon the wave felt deadened, heavy and leaden from its exertion. Her limbs felt weak, her senses dull and drained. She couldn't tell where the sound came from, the distant kind of thud that made the earth vibrate as she made her way towards her family. But she could see it in their faces; in the way the wind whipped around them in a torrent, the way their expressions clouded like the sky had fallen in.

'What is the meaning of this?' Rogart bellowed, the weight of his landing sending the shingle splintering and flying.

On the cliff edge above, Lavellan still stood, his face a mask of impenetrable white. Sysa looked down at her feet and the shifting of the sandy floor beneath her, a great dark chasm that had begun to open up between herself and her family. She saw the panic on their faces as they looked at something above her, knowing as she lifted her head that her whole body was shrouded in the shadow Rogart could cast without the sun. She turned around, looking up at his face, which contorted in a gargoyle snarl above her.

'How dare you take something else from me,' he said, his fur bristling and spiking, his whole body enlarged in anger and disgust.

Sysa watched, frozen, her arms hanging at her sides like useless weapons. As if in response, Rogart raised his own arms, fisting them into the air, holding them suspended in the sky.

'Stop! It's me you want.'

The voice that shattered the sudden silence was Brodie. He moved around between them, glancing towards Sysa and then back up into Rogart's twisted face.

'It's me you've wanted all along.' His voice was flat, devoid of all strength, like the fingers Sysa curled against her thigh, trying to spark her powers to life again.

'Sysa has nothing to do with it, Rogart. I'm here, take me and leave the girl alone.'

Sysa watched as Rogart's face emptied of emotion, a sudden mirror of Brodie's. He dropped the arms he had held aloft before her and pivoted, the energy burning in the flexed muscles drifting off somewhere as he turned. Sysa watched as he fixed his gaze on Brodie, looking him up and down as if he were making some sort of calculation.

'Perhaps you're right. It's you I want, well for starters anyway.'

He sighed, his eyes deepening into rounds of complete and sudden dark.

'You ruined my second chance in life. This time I finish you off properly. And once I'm done with you, I come back and finish off the rest.'

'No.' Sysa heard herself whisper, a word too small and desperate.

She looked at Brodie's face as Rogart stepped towards him, the Giant's arms outstretched like someone entering an embrace. But then his two huge hands were clasped around Brodie's chest, gripping and squeezing him. Sysa watched as Brodie kicked out, struggling to breathe, his hands pulling uselessly along the muscles of Rogart's bulging arms.

'Modan!' Sysa shouted, whipping her head around to the black stallion, her whole body suddenly alive and tingling with the waking heat that now curled and sparked inside her fingertips.

'Your bridle. Modan, I need it.'

Modan moved obediently towards her, Sysa looping her hands over his head and quickly pulling the bridle from his face.

'Thankyou,' Sysa whispered, nodding in understanding. If he wanted it, she knew the stallion could be free. Modan looked back at her, his eyes dark pools that stayed still and silent like a promise. He did not attempt to move or run away, only chafing a hoof along the shingle. He bowed his head towards her, the silk of his mane brushing in the wind against her jaw.

The power inside Sysa's fingers cracked and fizzed against its confines, and she flung the length of Modan's bridle up into the air, holding onto the end as it floated, bright and shining in the darkness.

'A rope!' she called out, commanding it, and before them the bridle transformed, looped at one end, the rest of it unfurling like a sail. Sysa watched as it soared through the blackened sky, hovering just above Rogart's head, which was now curved and bowed with the exertion of strangling Brodie. Sysa felt the force in her fingers expel suddenly, running its way along the rope and onwards, before finally reaching out, the looped end of the rope sneaking upwards and slipping over Rogart's head.

'Help me pull it!' she called out to Frode, Krystan and

the selkies, who were already scrambling forwards and starting to heave on the rope beside her.

Across the chasm, Bruan and the others looked on, clinging on to each other as if it that could somehow bind the growing gap that was cracking and splintering across the beach.

'Just hold on!' Sysa called to them, straining on the rope, which squeezed around Rogart's neck, puckering the skin under tufts of fur that spiked up over its edges.

Rogart spluttered, his eyes bulging and beaming, but if anything, his pain only seemed to incense him further, and he gritted his teeth and squeezed Brodie tighter. Their two faces once again mirrored each other as they twisted and contorted against the fires that were raging in their throats.

'This isn't working.' Sysa spoke almost to herself, her mind flailing as she watched them.

*Rogart is never going to give up*, she thought, the words hitting her, drumming against her as she felt them settle in a dark, empty space that suddenly grew inside her chest.

The earth seemed to spin underneath her feet, threatening to topple her, to plunge the whole world into that same empty darkness. She loosened her grip on the rope, looking around her.

'It isn't going to work. What do we do now?'

Her words hung in the dark as they entered the space between she and Brodie. Everything around them seemed to retreat away into the distance, the way they had back in the glen that day – Sysa an onlooker to her own life, the volume of the world around her suddenly muted low. She saw Rogart's beaming face, the strained faces of her friends, eyes lit up with determination. But despite it all, there was only the two of them who existed in that moment – only she and Brodie and the air and sea and sky.

Sysa watched Brodie's mouth open and form the words 'I love you.'

But she realised she had known that anyway, had known that even when his eyes had been dark and far away. She closed her own eyes and let her head fall back against the sky: he loved her and she wasn't going to be able to save him.

'I love you too,' she whispered, looking at him again, hoping the words would reach him before Rogart took so much of his breath that he could no longer hear, see or say anything at all.

All she could do was watch as the words found him, and his eyes answered. Where they once had been dark, she now saw a tiny sliver of light, like the sunrise nudging its way into the world. His face, despite the pain which lit up every part of him, softened and relaxed, stretching his lips to a tiny smile that carried within it both happiness and a strange, accepting sort of despair. He nodded slightly, a small movement containing everything that could and should have been between them. Sysa nodded back, tears streaming down her face. As Brodie's eyes closed she felt herself swallowed by a darkness that only seemed to get deeper, like a void that stretched out and up and sideways. She looked to the stony beach beneath her, trying to anchor herself to something: she could no longer bear to watch.

She fixed on the shingled beach, staring at the blur of small stones that came in and out of focus. She scraped at her cheeks, angry at the useless tears that ran down them, spilling under her chin and dropping to the pebbled floor below. As the tears fell, she saw it, though; a flicker of light within a stone beneath her. She watched as it spread and reached out, filling the dark and empty spaces. It lit up the beach, sending its warmth upwards to her face as it rolled its way across the sand.

She looked up, shielding her face against the sudden sunlight. The others looked on silently, stilled by the closing of Brodie's eyes. Even Rogart became quiet, looking skywards. Sysa peered up the cliff edge; something lingered there behind the streak of light. It was Lavellan, looking down at her, his mask unreadable as he turned and walked away from them. She watched as his outline faded, something else remaining in the space he'd left there: the unicorn.

The light was not the sun, it was Grey.

The unicorn was rearing up on its hind legs at the top of the cliff edge, baying and neighing as the light flashed all around him. Sysa whispered the words she had been holding inside her.

'Tell me.'

As her eyes closed, the light seared across her face.

# CHAPTER TWENTY-THREE

'It's here somewhere,' said Grey as he looked around the kirkyard. Sysa followed as her Grandfather frowned over another mottled stone.

'Not this one,' he said and turned the other way, the wind nipping at Sysa's body as she pulled her shawl a little closer. The shiver that bristled down her spine was less from the cold than the excitement of being here at Olrig. The graveyard was unnerving, though, and she shuddered at the thought of dead bodies lying all around their feet. She looked up at the trees, steadying herself as she watched their crowns swaying and colliding. If she closed her eyes they reminded her of the noise the sea made. She thought of the dead again, wondering if they spent forever listening to the sound.

'Here we are!' Grey called from some steps a little further through the graveyard, jolting Sysa back into the moment.

'It's just up here,' he said, as he climbed to a raised area at the back of the kirkyard and turned around.

'Coming, Grandfather!' Sysa hurried up the steps behind him and grabbed the hand he held out to her.

'Here it is, the selkie grave,' Grey said, pointing towards a small, unremarkable rectangular cavity within the earth.

Sysa peered into it, surveying its ordinary edges with disappointment. She didn't know what she had expected, but it had certainly been something more exceptional than this. It was just a hole in the ground, filled with water and framed with mossy dampness.

'Why is it full of water?' she asked, latching onto the only thing she thought might lead to a story. Grey's eyes brightened; her guess had obviously been correct.

'Well, that's the interesting thing about this grave, Sysa, it never goes dry, even in the height of summer. Come and sit by me and I'll tell you the whole story.' Grey patted the drystone wall by the side of him, shuffling up so Sysa could perch next to him on the stone.

Sysa curled her face into the crook of her Grandfather's neck, and draped her arms around him.

'Tell, me, please, I want to hear it.' She looked up into Grey's face, his gaze hovering on the trees ahead.

'They sound like the sea, don't they?' he said, a strange, watery smile washing over him.

Sysa nodded. 'I just thought that too.'

Grey breathed in, his chest rising as if he were inhaling his story from the air around him. When he spoke, his voice was quieter than normal. Sysa leaned in, determined not to miss a single word.

'There was once a couple in this parish who had been married for many years but had not been blessed with children,' Grey began, his eyes drifting off to the trees again.

'Each day the man would look upon his wife and see that sorrow etched into her – if only we could have a child, he thought to himself, my wife would be content.

And then the man went to bed one night and had a dream that seemed to give him an answer. In his dream, he was told by a lady dressed in green that if he walked the length of Dunnet beach each morning before sunrise for one year and one day, he and his wife would have a child. When the man awoke from his dream he was so sure that his wish would be granted he made off to complete his walk that very morning. He strode off and along that beach, reaching the end just as the sun was streaking its rays across the sky.

Every day, for the next year and a day he completed that walk along the golden sands no matter what the weather,' Grey continued, a solemn look on his face.

'He was happy to walk that beach in rain, hail, snow or howling wind. Can you imagine it Sysa, fighting against the wind, the sand blowing up and into your nostrils?' Sysa nodded, burrowing herself closer, shivering against Grey's chest in sympathy.

'Well, on the very last day, exactly one year and a day since his dream of the strange lady the man's wish came true. For there amongst the sand dunes he found a baby swaddled in a sealskin. He took the child home to his wife who was overjoyed, of course. From that day on, he would wake to find his wife happy again, cradling her baby and singing lullabies.'

Sysa swayed against Grey's body, feeling the warmth of him seep out and find its way underneath her skin.

'The child grew into a beautiful and intelligent young woman,' Grey continued, rocking Sysa gently.

'She was her parents' pride and joy and had the most captivating singing voice you've ever heard. But each year, on the anniversary of her arrival, something strange would happen. She would disappear with the sealskin she'd been wrapped in as a baby and would not return until the sun had rose again the following day.'

'Where was she going Grandfather? What was she doing?' Sysa interrupted, suddenly alert with the whiff of intrigue.

'Ah, the legends don't tell us where she was going or what she was doing Sysa,' replied Grey, 'but I have a mind that one day you might happen to find out. No, her parents knew nothing of where she had been or what she had done there, and every time she returned to them she just smiled and told them nothing of it. Her parents were so entranced with her that they never once pressed her on it, either. They were always just so glad to see her come back home again to fill the empty chair that she had left.

One year, though,' continued Grey, his face serious again, 'the girl came home from her annual disappearance feeling poorly, and this time did not smile at her parents, but staggered into their home looking pale and sickly. Her parents, fraught with worry, of course, asked her what was wrong. She just pointed at her belly, which had curved considerably since just the day before when she'd left them.'

'She was going to have a baby!' Sysa declared triumphantly.

'That's right,' said Grey, flashing Sysa the look of a proud teacher.

'She was going to have a baby. But this was not to be an ordinary baby, and she, as you might have guessed, was not an ordinary girl.'

Sysa nodded, puffing the air out through her nostrils. 'She was a selkie, Grandfather!' She looked up at Grey, and jabbed him with a reproachful hand.

'Did you think I didn't know that?'

Grey smiled back at her, brushing a strand of hair across her forehead.

'Oh no, of course I knew you'd know that. You're a clever girl, do I tell you that often enough?'

'You tell me that every day, Grandfather,' Sysa replied, wondering if he had forgotten.

Grey nodded, setting his gaze on the grave again, where ivy snaked around the moss and threatened to take hold.

'Anyway, the selkie begged her parents not to bring anyone into the home to tend to her, and refused to tell them anything about the baby's Father,' Grey continued, shaking his head in a way that gave Sysa a strange sense of foreboding.

'Her parents, fearing shame and persecution, vowed to keep her secret and kept her hidden from all the others in the parish until her baby was ready to be born. They told her they would pretend the baby was their own child, a sister or a brother to the girl, and that they would care for it and give it all the love it could ever wish for. But as the pregnancy progressed the girl became sicker and sicker and eventually died while the baby was being born. Her parents were distraught and she was buried here in the kirkyard,' Grey said, gesturing towards the small cavity that lay in front of them.

'From that day forward, it was said her grave here has never gone dry a single day.'

Sysa stared at the wet cavity, then up at Grey, who had paused and was looking up at the treetops. She pulled at his sleeve, suddenly wanting to find out more about this unassuming grave.

'But what about the selkie's baby Grandfather? What happened to her baby?'

'Ah the baby, Sysa. That poor baby.' Grey looked out across the graveyard with clouded, misty eyes.

'Well, the baby was indeed given all the love and care a child could wish for. The Grandparents did as they had promised and lavished on that baby all the love they had once given to their girl. They told their friends and neighbours that they had finally been blessed with another child, but that their daughter had taken ill and died most suddenly. Whether folk believed that or not was another story, but in the absence of any proof their gossip soon died out.

The husband and wife continued with their lives and tried to mend their broken hearts as best as they were able. But one morning, when the woman went to fetch the baby from the cradle the child was gone, it had vanished, disappeared into the night. The woman fell to the floor in anguish at losing another child and she and her husband never fully recovered. And that night – the night the baby disappeared – was the same date that their daughter had left her home every year before. Once again the disappearance was shrouded in mystery. But this time, the child never came back and that empty chair was never filled again.'

Sysa sighed and squeezed Grey's hand tightly.

'What a sad story,' she said, peering up into his face.

'Yes, it's a sad story indeed, isn't it Sysa?' said Grey.

'There are many sad stories in this world of ours.'

He rose from the wall, flicking a piece of moss from his thigh and turned to her.

'But you my dear, you'll write your own story.'

'With a happy ending,' Sysa declared, setting her mouth in a line of resolution.

'Let's hope so,' Grey answered, looking to the trees which railed and crashed as if in defiance of the wind.

★

The light crossed Sysa's eyes again, and she was back in the light forest, back to the first time she had seen the unicorn – the first time she had seen Grey as this other-worldly creature. She remembered her fingers resting on his horn as he had bowed his head towards her. He had told her everything that day, she realised, much more than where to find Krystan and Peter. She could see it all so clearly now. She was finally ready to understand.

Sysa closed her eyes again and inhaled deeply. Grey's light entered her, first a screaming, blinding light behind her eyelids, then a withdrawing frame around a scene. Sysa saw the baby in his cradle and Rogart stooped over him, huge arms folding around the child as the Giant lifted him. For a moment Rogart looked down at the baby, head cocked in wonder at the creature which wriggled and smiled beneath his gaze. A few seconds passed before Rogart's face settled like stone and he turned and rushed out of the house, stooping low beneath the door frame. Sysa watched as he sped away into the night, a gust of wind slamming the door behind him, the empty cradle left rocking, as if bewildered, in the breeze.

Next, Sysa saw the Giant at the edge of the water. He looked down at the babe in his arms before shaking his head and releasing one hand from behind the baby's head. With the other, he reared back and held the child aloft behind his shoulder, readying himself. Sysa felt her eyelids twitch as Rogart hurled the baby out and into the blackness of the water, his tiny body bobbing once on the waves before he disappeared, soundless, to the sea.

A moment later, Sysa saw the baby, somewhere else, where the sea was blue and the sky poured light across him. Six seals were there, forming a raft beneath him, their glistening backs arcing and shining, pulling him towards a familiar shore. It was Fyrish, Sysa could see now, and the seals were Frode, Roman, Dursten, Lilia, Rose and Emile. They had sheltered him then as they would one day shelter him again – his friends, his family. Sysa watched, her closed eyes stinging, as the seal folk pulled the baby onwards to the beach.

The light blazed again behind her eyes before Sysa saw another scene, on the beach to the rear of Steel Castle. She saw her Mother, walking along the beach there, laden with grief, as if she were pacing her sorrow into the sand. And then she saw Elise pick up a package – the baby, wrapped in a sealskin – Brodie. She saw the light that washed across her Mother's face, then, as if she were suddenly standing in the way of a sunrise. Sysa stayed with the scene as Elise murmured to the baby, raising him to her face, a fist of small fingers clinging tightly to her hand.

The next few scenes flashed across Sysa's consciousness quickly. Brodie, growing up as a young boy with her family in the castle, and then later, on Selkie Island with Frode and his selkie tribe. Then Frode, in human form, in the human world, looking for something, eyes pained and searching. And then in seal form in the water, a hunter's dagger above him; quivering, eager.

Ready to be driven deep into his chest.

The scenes cut off and Sysa shook herself back into the present moment. Whatever Brodie was or wasn't she couldn't understand. What she did know was that Rogart was his Father. Rogart had thrown Brodie into the sea as a baby and sent him back there when he became a man. And now, in a flurry of hatred, he had finally killed him. He had taken the thing she loved and snuffed it out like a light. As Sysa regained a sense of her surroundings she felt pain emanating from the deepest depths of her being. The light burned behind her eyes and threatened to scar her throat, her heart, and reach out to the edges of her soul.

# CHAPTER TWENTY-FOUR

'He's your son... you're his Father,' Sysa croaked into the air as her eyes once again opened.

'You're his Father!' she called out, louder this time, her voice returning as she looked up towards Rogart, where he stood motionless, still holding Brodie's limp body by the neck.

Rogart turned his face slowly, his jaw tight, a muscle twitching there under the soft bed of his fur, so at odds with the hardness of his expression. With one hand he pulled the rope over his head and discarded it, while the other released Brodie's lifeless body with a soft thump onto the shingled beach below. Sysa moved forward, fists clenched, eyes still streaming.

'How could you do it Rogart? How could you?' Her words flew at him, circling the beach like an echoing wall of pain.

'You think I didn't know that he was my son?' Rogart bellowed, his amber eyes wild with anger.

'You think I wasn't the one who took him as a babe from his cradle all those years ago? I spared him then, and I've spared him since, but no, he had to come before me, taunting me, reminding me of the pain every time I looked at him. He *took her from me,* took my second chance at happiness. Now I can no longer bear to look at him. I can no longer bear to look at any of you.'

He turned away, his face swallowed by a shadow of darkness and disgust.

'Don't you see? She loved him!' Sysa shouted to the Giant, forcing him to once again face her.

'She loved you, and she loved him, and you've taken away the last chance at happiness you could have had. What have you done, what have you done to him?…' Sysa rushed forwards, to where Brodie's body lay curled up on the beach like a silent question mark.

'Sysa!' Bruan's cry rang out across the chasm where Elise and Elva were wrapped around him, his robes flailing as he reached his arm across the gap.

'Be careful!'

Rogart looked at Bruan, shaking his head with a bitter laugh.

'I've done what I should have done years ago and now I finish it. First your sister, Sysa. Then you and the rest of them.' He flicked his head towards Frode and the others who were standing behind Sysa like furious statues, ready to uncurl at her command.

Rogart's lips twisted to a smile, fangs visible as he made his final judgement.

'Let your parents know what I've known. Let them see what it means to have the things they love stolen.'

Rogart lunged towards Bruan and the others, piles of sand and shingle blasting the air with every step.

Sysa knew it now, knew that the power of his hatred had finally overwhelmed her. As her parents formed a barrier in front of Elva and William, Sysa looked up into the sky and screamed.

★

The rain that answered fell onto her face as she clutched at Brodie's lifeless body. Warm, soft drops that felt like honey, clinging to her skin. Sysa touched a hand to her cheek and saw the red smear that streaked her palm, zig-zagging the lines there. She felt a trickle of realisation run down her spine as the blood tracked its way across her, tumbling over her curved edges and falling onto Brodie's waxen face.

'No! No Grey!' she cried out, jumping to her feet and looking up at the unicorn above them. He was lying now, his head slightly over the edge of the cliff, horn pointing outwards towards the sea, throat streaked with a line of red that juddered like an arrow across his coat.

'Lavellan,' Sysa whispered, feeling like the cliff wall itself had rushed towards her and slammed itself against her. *He did this.* She stood, frozen by grief and shock as the blood ran down under the unicorn's belly, finding a perfect sort of aim as it dropped onto Brodie, whose body lay curled and quiet against the sand.

'Please don't Grey, please don't leave me,' Sysa called into the sky above her. She knew what was happening, knew that in order to save Brodie, and the rest of them, the blood of the unicorn was flowing from the cliff. That blood was all-healing, all-powerful, able to mend the deepest, darkest wounds imaginable. Would it be able to heal the scar it would leave on her? she wondered, her head thudding with desperation.

Grey was giving up his life for her.

And this time, he would not be coming back.

*'After this I leave for good.'* Brodie's words swum between her ears and echoed in the air around her. But she knew now it would not be Brodie who would be gone for good, it would be Grey.

*'He believed that your love could save us,'* Bruan's words from so long ago reached her.

She saw it all so clearly now, like someone had wiped a misty screen. The only smear that remained there was Lavellan, Sysa thought, squeezing her eyes shut against the image of him, searing a blade across the unicorn. Had Grey asked him to? Had he known what her love for Brodie would do? Somewhere inside, she knew the answer to both these questions. But for now, all she could think about was how much her Grandfather had loved her. And that love for her was so big that right now it reached to every corner of the sky.

She felt that love push in from the air and move inside her, as she gulped down on it, swallowing hard on the breath it gave her. And she looked at Brodie and saw his eyelids flutter and knew that she could not live without him, any less than he could her. And she also knew that Grey knew all these things too, as he lay dripping from above, sending his life towards them.

'Thankyou,' she whispered, reaching her hand up towards the lifeless unicorn, fingers outstretched towards the cliff face.

'I love you,' she said finally, as the huge light seared from the unicorn and seemed to steal the very sky.

★

As the light faded, Sysa looked back again to the cliff edge. Her eyes adjusted, taking in the wash of pale grey filming the previously leaden sky. The space where Lavellan had stood seemed to mock her with its emptiness. The unicorn was gone, too, but the space he'd left behind was brighter.

In the world beneath the sky, Brodie was opening up his eyes.

Sysa looked down, watching those eyes open, seas of blue and grey swimming across her features.

'Sysa. I'm so sorry, I should have told you...' Brodie's voice trailed off as Sysa pressed a finger to his lips.

'Later,' she smiled, 'we'll talk later.'

Brodie reached a hand up to her face, one finger tracing a line of moisture.

'I love you,' he said, pulling himself up on his elbows, his body readjusting to the simple acts of life.

'And I love you too,' Sysa said, half-crying, letting him pull her close so that their tears entwined, sticky and moist as her cheek pressed against him.

She felt his lips brush against the corner of her mouth, the salty tang of them biting against her like the call of the sea, beckoning her home.

'What a tender scene!' Rogart's voice cleaved the air, sending whatever wave had been caressing them retreating.

The Giant was striding across the beach now, arms pumping the air as he thumped towards them, the line of his jaw set under his coat of downy fur. Behind him, Sysa's family and William stood over the chasm, helpless and watching, faced only with the smooth lines of Rogart's back; rippling muscle and sinew. Sysa flashed a look towards

Brodie, licking the salt from her lips, willing the heat of the fire that crackled in her hands.

As if in response, Brodie sprang to his feet, looking down at his own hands. He watched them for a moment, curling them into fists, fingers spread wide as they unfurled. Sysa felt it then, a spark in the space between them, as if a tiny fire had whispered.

Brodie reached out his arms, a wave of bright light flowing like a ribbon from his hands.

Sysa watched, eyes wide as she flashed him a glance in question.

Brodie arched his eyebrows, an expression that suggested he was as bemused as she was by the revelation streaming from his hands.

Sysa just nodded, steadying herself as she felt the spring of light escape from her own fingers, crackling inside the tips before leaping out, like someone jumping from a cliff edge. The streams arced into the air, meeting with Brodie's, twisting and entwining like a rope, before combining to a single bright shock of crackling power that surged outwards and met with Rogart's chest.

Sysa and Brodie watched as Rogart careered backwards, flying through the air and landing with a thud against the rocks in front of them. Sysa flicked a look over her shoulder at Frode, who nodded back at her, arms folded across his chest, as he stood with the others who were waiting like a shield wall on the beach. Sysa turned again towards Rogart, no more than a second passing before his arms and legs began to twitch, then flail about on the shingle beneath him. His hooves dug into its carpet, frantically seeking purchase on the sand.

Sysa saw the gleam in Brodie's eyes as his Father began to stand up again, uncurling and straightening, like a wall of thunder lifting itself from the shingle. His eyes burned with anger as he began to run towards them, a huge roar leaving his mouth, almost knocking them backwards as they met with the force of it, a hard wind slamming suddenly against steel.

'Now!' Sysa called as Rogart made his final few bounds towards them.

She looked to each side, as her friends arced between she and Brodie, lifting their arms to push out every bit of light their combined union could invoke. The rays weaved into one another, tilting to a rope, a gleaming lifeline in the semi-darkness.

Rogart knew this was no lifeline for him though. As it hit him, Sysa saw the hard lines of his face change, dissolving into an expression that might have been confusion.

Or, she thought with a glance towards Brodie, it might have been closer to relief.

Rogart's almond eyes looked out into the world, hard features slackening as the realisation of what was happening swept over him. Sysa saw his gaze flicker towards Brodie before he was thrust backwards for the second time, his body arcing like a dark horseshoe on the beach. He lay there, still and quiet, a strange echo of the lifeless form Brodie had assumed just minutes earlier. For his part, Brodie's face had emptied of all expression, his thoughts betrayed only by the moisture that shone around his eyes. Sysa flicked her head in Rogart's direction, urging Brodie forwards, raising a palm at her rear to steady Frode and the selkies. Together, they inched ahead across the shingle, both seeking the other's hand as they looked down on Rogart, his huge dark form spilled out like blood across the sand.

'Finish it!' Rogart whispered, opening one eye to a slit that peered up at them, his voice rasping as his hooves grappled against the shingle.

'Finish it now. Do it, boy,' he croaked. He gave a bitter laugh, and Sysa felt Brodie flinch beside her, the movement sending a shiver down her spine.

'What's wrong, are you too weak to kill me?' Rogart continued when Brodie didn't answer, instead looking down at his Father, a sudden film of hurt and disappointment laid out across his features.

*He's waiting*, Sysa thought to herself. *After all this, he thinks Rogart might still change.* As if hearing her thoughts, Brodie stiffened, whatever hope he'd had disappearing as though it had never been, like mist under the gaze of an early morning. Sysa watched as he lifted his arms up, ready to satiate whatever need now burned in him.

'Brodie,' she whispered. 'You don't have to do this.'

'Look at me, Brodie. It doesn't have to be this way.'

Sysa ducked behind him, placing a palm on his back, feeling his muscles tighten in a sort of latent, determined fury. But as she dropped her head against his skin she felt a loosening, like a knot uncurling, escaping out into the world as he grunted an exhale. His shoulders slackened and his arms fell to his sides again, eyes drifting up to where Arno hovered in the half-dark sky above them. When Brodie looked at his Father again, Sysa saw it was with another kind of determination. He fixed Rogart with a blue stare, and when he finally spoke, his voice was strangely mild.

'No, it won't be this way,' he said, as if Rogart had only

just appeared on the beach, and none of his previous terrors had been known to them.

'There's another way, a better way – and a way that will end all this without anyone else dying here today.'

Sysa saw Rogart's eyes widen; small slits curving into round pools as he absorbed his son's words, realisation washing over the Giant's features like water trickling down a rocky crevice. Sysa watched, then, as Brodie exuded that light again, as it came pouring out of his fingers, whipping under and around his Father's body and lifting it from the shingle, Rogart hovering suspended, his eyes opening and closing in small, defeated blinks. Sysa felt the twitch in her own fingers then, scratching and bristling there as she spread her hands out like stars, joining the light that streamed from her with Brodie's in a web of blinding luminosity.

A web that wrapped Rogart in a ball of twisted rays, until they could no longer tell what remained behind its glow.

Brodie shot an enquiring look at Sysa, his blue eyes slanted in concentration. She nodded once in answer, and let her arms fall to her sides. She watched as Brodie pulled his hands back, releasing his tombed father like a stone fleeing from a catapult. For a moment, the sky itself seemed to pull away from them, catching its breath before sending Rogart hurtling through the grey and out onto the wind.

★

For a few seconds, everything was silent. The only sounds on the beach were the quiet breath of onlookers and the *whoosh* of Rogart's body flying through the air. Arno took up the space behind the light ball, Brodie nodding at the bead-like eye that sought out his instruction. As the bird's wings beat, Sysa saw a sudden flash of light, the white of it searing behind her eyes. The white dissolved into an image – a heathered mountain, Rogart imprisoned there and sleeping. A place where a giant could go unnoticed, shielded from the world under mounds of darkened earth. Sysa felt herself gasp, and as quickly as the image had come to her, everything went black, her view returning to the dark red curtain of her eyelids. When she opened them again, she found the bird and the ball of light disappearing into the distance, fading to tiny dots and then swallowed, as if stolen by the vastness of the sky.

'It's over,' she whispered as she turned to Brodie, who was staring out into the distance, his blue eyes misted with emotion.

'It's over,' she repeated, finding her voice again as her hand travelled upwards to his cheek.

He turned slowly, covering her fingers with his, trapping her hand against the skin there.

'We did it,' he said hoarsely. His face inched forwards until his forehead rested against the dampness of her own.

And then Sysa saw it: the golden light that hovered at the corners of her vision. This time not the bright light of the unicorn, but a yellow warmth that dappled across the shingle at their feet. Lifting her eyes she turned towards it: a wave of light that enveloped them, reclaiming every corner of the darkness. She watched as it spread across the sky, pouring liquid gold across the land below. As the light made its advance the sea shimmered and then blazed, puffed white clouds forming above the water, like plumes of steam escaping from the waves beneath them. Between the crevices of the cliff edge wild flowers of pink and yellow suddenly spurted, eager for release from a confinement that had lasted far too long. From the sky, Sysa heard the cries of birds that flapped around the ledges, the sound of their calls seeming to give voice to the rise of a new beginning.

'It's so beautiful,' Sysa whispered.

'But Grandfather…' Her voice trailed off as Brodie's arm arced round her waist, his hand encircling hers, squeezing gently.

'I know,' he whispered, his words disappearing into her hair as he pressed his lips against her head.

They watched as their friends stood agape, looking on at the scene, matching expressions of wonder veiling every feature. The world seemed to stop for a moment as Sysa watched their faces reflected in a pool of never-ending gold. The light unfurled like a blanket, carpeting the land above before dropping like a waterfall from the cliff edge. It fell towards them, pooling on the beach, binding the chasm between Sysa and her family before sealing along a line of something resembling molten gold. The two pieces of beach seemed to join magnetically, prompting a brief shuddering within the shingle, pieces of shell and sand spitting out into the air like tiny arrows loosing. Sysa watched as her parents wobbled briefly, before the land stood still again, the molten lava withdrawing like a finger curling back into the earth.

'Mother, Father!' she cried out, rushing towards them, meeting in the space where the chasm had been, no trace of its existence lingering. She slammed into them like a wall then, crushing herself into their arms, her Father's lips against her forehead, the weight of his palm pulling her roughly to his jaw.

'We thought we'd lost you,' he croaked out, as Elise showered soft kisses around her cheeks, her nose, her forehead.

'I know.' Sysa answered in a whisper.

'You didn't though.'

She lifted her eyes to Elva, who was standing at the periphery, gaze firmly rooted on her feet.

'Elva.' Sysa reached an arm towards her sister.

Elva looked at it for a moment, blinking against the sun which seemed to coat Sysa's outstretched limb in gold. Elva finally raised her eyes, meeting Sysa's with a look of pain that altered quickly to relief as Sysa urged her forwards. Elva's face creased into a smile, the soft, quick thump of contact pushing Sysa's breath out as the gap between them closed.

'Our daughters,' Bruan whispered, his voice heavy with emotion.

'We love you both so much,' said Elise, her eyes glistening in the warmth.

'I'm so sorry,' Elva whispered, her voice trembling, the air damp with tears and the heat of breath that mingled in the space between them.

'I got it all wrong, I never should have gone with Rogart. Will you forgive me?' Her voice choked as she spluttered tears that dribbled in hot tracks across her cheeks.

'Hush, now, it's over,' said Bruan, drawing himself out of the huddle and placing his arms on Elva's shoulders, holding her body away from him and crouching to meet her eyes.

'We love you Elva. We're a family and always will be, whether the world be full of light or full of dark. You're back with us now and nothing else matters.' Bruan looked around at his family, his eyes wet with moisture.

'You're everything to us. Both of you.' Beside him, Elise nodded, tears spilling down her face.

'Thankyou Father,' Elva said, falling into the embrace Bruan offered and burying her face into his body.

'I love you all so much,' she said, her bright eyes flickering across them from the refuge of Bruan's solid chest. Instinctively, Sysa glanced towards Brodie and then back at her sister, a crease settling in the space between her eyebrows. Elva, seeing the question in the movement, stepped forward, fingers curling like petals around her sister's hand.

'It's all right, Sysa, it's all right about you and Brodie.' Elva looked between them, a watery smile tugging her lips around the corners.

'I know how you feel about him, and he you, I can see that. I was wrong about it all. I was wrong about my own feelings, when I met William I could see that, the way that I felt for Brodie – it got smaller somehow.'

Elva tossed a look at Brodie, who was standing on the edges of the conversation, observing proceedings with a sort of detached wariness, the hard planes of his jaw mirroring the lines of caution around his face.

'Don't worry, I still love you,' Elva laughed. 'Just not in the way I thought I did. So you two together' – she waved her arms around in the space between them – 'it's all right, I don't want you to worry. I've found William now and everything is fine.'

267

William, who had been lingering behind Elva watching the unfolding scene, stepped forward at her urging, drawing a deep inhale that puffed his cheeks out awkwardly. Apparently thinking better of advancing, he immediately took a step back again, prompting a small smile from Bruan as he and Elise exchanged a silent, knowing look.

'Come here, William,' Elva encouraged, her voice clipped with a casual air of authority that gave no doubt as to the dynamics of the new relationship.

William obliged, taking his place next to Elva, slipping his hand into hers as she lifted her head with the faintest expression of triumph on her face. Sysa smiled, noticing the way William rubbed his thumb lightly over Elva's knuckles, the way he leaned into her and looked at her, his eyes pooled with tenderness and affection. She didn't have to worry about William, now, she knew that.

At least, she inwardly corrected herself, she didn't have to worry about William where her sister was concerned.

Instinctively, Sysa glanced towards the far side of the beach where Luna had been standing with the others. Sysa couldn't be sure what part – if any – the mermaid had played in Rogart's departure, but the prickle of trepidation that traced her spine suggested letting Luna join them had most likely been a mistake. The mermaid stood, eyes like stone, looking at Elva and William, her fists bunched in angry contemplation. Elva responded by raising her chin a little higher, while William looked between the two, his eyes darting about, a look of undisguised terror falling across his face. Luna's eyes narrowed, surveying the assembled group slowly, casually weighing up her options and evidently finding the odds uninviting. With a flick of her golden hair she turned, stepping towards the sea before throwing a final look over her shoulder as she strode into the waves. She walked out until the sea curled around her waist before casting one last look at Sysa, her expression entirely undefeated.

*She'll be back,* Sysa thought, feeling Brodie's hand on her arm as she took a step towards the water.

'Let her go,' he said quietly. 'Enough today.'

Sysa stopped, and watched as a flash of silvery tail disappeared quietly into the sea.

She stared out into the blue; all trace of Luna swallowed by the sparkling water. Somewhere behind her, she was aware of William shuddering and shaking, the vibration of his movements reverberating through the sand.

'She's gone,' she heard Elva say, as Elva patted William like a dog and offered other murmured reassurances.

'It's just us now.'

Sysa swivelled on her heel and conjured up the brightest tone she could.

'Well, it's nice to meet you, at least properly, William,' she said, offering her hand as William was lost in a sea of introductions.

'It's nice to meet you all too,' he stammered, glancing at Elva, who nodded back, encouraging him to carry on. With a gesture that encompassed Luna, Rogart, and everything that had passed between them on the beach, William continued.

'And thankyou.'

Sysa saw the look that passed between her sister and William and felt a wave of relief surge over her. She felt the weight of Brodie's gaze, and knew he was feeling the same way. The eyes that rested on her face were blue again, the dark rim of grey receded almost to nothing. They were a mirror of the blue sea behind him, as bright and as bold as the new sky that had risen like a mountain above his head.

# CHAPTER TWENTY-FIVE

'I think perhaps you and Brodie could do with a bit of time to talk privately, Sysa,' Bruan said, emerging from the group with a smile some time later.

'And after that, perhaps Elise and I could have a word with you too,' he said, cocking one eyebrow towards the younger man.

If Bruan and Elise felt any surprise at the revelations about Elva's feelings for Brodie – and indeed Sysa and Brodie's for each other – they hadn't shown it, thought Sysa, noticing the tips of Brodie's ears redden slightly. Then again, she reflected with a shudder, there had been rather a lot of revelations to contend with for one day. She opened her mouth to speak, but Elva's voice rang out in the gap, eyes fixed on Brodie and glinting with a trace of mischief.

'Yes, what was that?' she asked, with no one in any doubt about the nature of the 'that' she was referring to.

'Where have you been hiding those talents?'

Brodie's lips curved to a lopsided smile, staring at Sysa as if the answer were somehow to be found around her person.

He finally shrugged in that easy way of his, making Sysa shiver.

'I don't know Elva. I'm still trying to work that out myself.'

★

Sysa and Brodie walked silently toward the rocks at the far end of the beach, passing Frode and the others in a throng of back slaps and congratulatory murmurs. Sysa felt her hand cupped gently in Brodie's, aware of the light pressure of his fingers against her skin. She felt at once exhilarated by his presence and at the same time terribly exposed by it. There were so many questions hanging in the air between them but to form them would be to puncture this moment where all that mattered was his hand in hers. Instead, when they rounded the arc of the cliff away from the others she turned and pressed her lips on his, feeling the warmth of his mouth and the breath of the sea; salty, sweet and wonderful. Brodie responded, at first softly and then with a heightened urgency as they stumbled against the rock, his back pressed against the stone. His hands tugged through her hair, and up and down her back, before at last he pushed her face away from him, cupped his hands around her jaw, and drank in every one of her features.

'I love you so much,' he said breathlessly.

'I know. I love you too,' she replied, finally exhaling and dropping her forehead against his.

They stood like that for a while, letting the kiss release everything that had gone unspoken between them. Eventually, when they were both sufficiently recovered, Brodie took her hand and traced a finger along her palm. He looked down at it, savouring it for a moment, still mesmerised by the small act of touching her.

'I'm so sorry I said I didn't,' he said, lifting his gaze towards her, blue pools meeting the question in her eyes.

'Why did you?' Sysa said, knowing the answer but asking anyway. Brodie shook his head and Sysa saw the tightening of that familiar line along his jaw.

'I didn't think you'd want me when you knew I was his,' Brodie said, his features stained with an unbearable sadness.

'And I didn't know if I was going to end up like him – you know, evil,' he said with a hollow laugh, his gaze drifting to the water beyond the rocks.

'But then I could feel the darkness growing in me after I made the decision to stay away from you. It was getting worse and worse until what happened on the beach back there.'

He flicked his jaw, silently articulating what he had done to his own Father on the sand.

Sysa nodded, trying to convey encouragement and understanding, before swooping under his chin to give him a long, soft kiss that she hoped would tell him more about her feelings.

'I need you,' he whispered, when she finally pulled away from him. 'When I felt like I had lost you I could feel myself just sort of slipping away from the world. Nothing seems to make sense without you Sysa. Without you I'm not sure I could keep that darkness out.'

'So when did you find out? I mean, that he was your Father?' Sysa asked, looking into Brodie's eyes as she stroked gently at his forearms, enjoying the softness of his skin and the small tug of her nails across the hair there. Brodie gestured towards the rocks nearby and they sat alongside each other, staring out at the silvered surface of the sea.

Sysa took his hand and squeezed it, renewing the physical contact that seemed to be a channel for communication about anything other than their powerful feelings for each other. It occurred to Sysa as she sat there how little she actually knew Brodie, and he her, despite the deep-seated understanding they seemed to share that their souls were connected somehow. It was as though each had removed their own soul in a place where they had inextricably twisted and entangled. Trying to unravel them now would be futile – the only thing they could do was work backwards to fill the spaces they had left.

'It was after I went into the water that day at the cave with Luna,' Brodie said, sighing loudly.

His words seemed to drift off on the air and into the water as he watched a wave roll in, its white and blue fingers reflected in his eyes.

'The time I kissed you,' he said, turning to her, smiling that lopsided smile again.

'As if I could forget,' she laughed.

'Go on,' she encouraged, lifting their joined hands before dropping them back onto the solid mound of his thigh.

'It was after that first kiss that I felt these *powers*' – Brodie said the word as if he himself could scarcely believe it – 'these powers start, like a strength growing inside me. It sounds stupid Sysa,' he shook his head, looking down at their clasped fingers and curling his pinkie around her own.

He paused before speaking again, as if considering his

words carefully, only to let them tumble out of him like a waterfall.

'It was like you'd poured something inside me when we kissed back there.' He shook his head, peeking a half-shut eye at her.

'Ridiculous, I know.'

'But – the same thing Grandfather did when he told me stories,' Sysa pondered, her eyes reaching out to the horizon, searching for understanding.

'Yes, a bit like that, I suppose,' replied Brodie.

'Apart from the kissing bit, of course,' he added, jabbing Sysa with a playful nudge across the ribs.

'So anyway,' he continued, picking up the thread of his story. 'I hadn't had these powers before that. Before that I didn't really know what I was, but I knew now I was changed. Changed by you, I think. I hadn't even used any powers, I just knew they were there now, waiting. It was like my insides had been clad in steel or something. Very strange. Very difficult to explain.' He looked around, his eyes casting about as he sought out her hand again in reassurance. Sysa gave it to him, pressing the tips of her fingers hard into his palm.

'I can understand that,' Sysa said, thinking of her own arrival in Fyrish and how impossible her situation had seemed to her.

'And so what happened after you went into the water?' she asked, anticipating that whatever the answer, neither of them would fully understand what it all meant.

'That's when Frode and the others found me out on the sea,' Brodie replied, his dark hair streaked with gold in the sunlight.

'That's when they took me back to Selkie Island and told me who I really was.'

'They were your friends,' Sysa said, almost to herself, remembering their conversation at the ceilidh. She thought of the visions Grey had given her, the image of the selkies rescuing the baby, Brodie's dark hair, slick and wet and silky, and wondered how she had managed not to see it all before.

'Oh yes, I'd known them all through my childhood,' Brodie interrupted, apparently oblivious to her thoughts, and the sudden, irresistible urge she felt to run her fingers through the dark mop that crowned him.

'I used to go back and forth between them and your family. I always felt drawn to the selkies somehow, but they never explained why and I suppose I never tried to ask.'

'Why not?' Sysa asked, her wits suddenly returning. 'Didn't you wonder why you wanted to spend so much time with them?'

'Yes,' Brodie replied, rubbing his thumb slowly along the pink lines of her palm.

'And I thought it must have something to do with my parents. But I didn't really want to ask them. I didn't want to find out what I thought about my parents' – he hesitated for a moment – 'that they didn't want me – was true I suppose.'

He looked away to the sea again, a flicker of shame hardening the smooth planes of his face.

'But that's not true…' Sysa interjected, pressing her fingers to his jaw so that he had to turn and face her again. Brodie gestured vaguely, waving away the turn of conversation with a weak smile that didn't reach his eyes.

'It's all right,' he said. 'When Frode heard what had happened he knew it was time to tell me everything. My mother was a selkie – she was Frode's sister – and for some reason she fell in love with... *him*.' Brodie's face contorted in disgust.

'But she lived in the human world and only returned to Fyrish once every human year. One year, she didn't return, and not long after that I turned up in the water where Frode and the others found me. After that they discovered what had happened to me. That's when Frode got his scar, you know – he went back to the human world to find out what happened to my Mother, and that's when he was attacked.'

'Oh,' Sysa said, thinking of the scar Frode wore on his chest and mentally piecing together all the things that Brodie and Grey had told her.

'So you aren't a selkie then?' A quick flash of her question to Brodie at their first meeting echoed around her mind.

'No,' said Brodie, shaking his head and pushing away the strands of hair that fell around his forehead.

'As I was born in the human world and never showed any sign of being anything other than human, Frode assumed I would remain that way, and never told me who my Father was. But then you came along and whatever's been waiting inside me seemed to be awoken. Frode could see that, and he knew the time had come to tell the truth.'

'That must have been – shocking.' Sysa hesitated, devoid of any language to convey the magnitude of the revelations Brodie had been faced with.

'Sort of,' Brodie replied. 'In a way I knew there was something Frode was holding back.' He shrugged, as if sending his thoughts about the whole thing rolling off the angles of his shoulders.

'The worst part was thinking that there was no way you could ever love me when you found out who my Father was.'

'But I do love you!' Sysa burst out, a note of frustration coating her exclamation.

'Even with everything with Elva, I mean, I would have understood.'

'I know that now,' Brodie replied, kissing her once in reassurance. 'But at the time all I could think about was what an evil monster I might become. I couldn't consider putting you in a position where I might hurt you, Sysa. So I made the decision to stay away. And that's when the darkness started. Trying to make you believe I didn't love you was the hardest thing I've ever had to go through. Like ripping my soul away.'

His eyes clouded over, a dark echo reflecting the memory of his pain.

'So how did you end up coming to live with my parents?' Sysa asked, trying to divert the conversation to something more hopeful.

'Oh,' said Brodie, his eyes clearing. 'That was Frode's idea. He was afraid that Rogart would come for me again after he realised I was still alive. He thought placing me under the protection of the King and Queen would be safer for me. So he and the selkies left me on the beach outside the castle, watching to see if they accepted me. And as you know, your Mother did. The sealskin I was wrapped in that day was my own Mother's. Frode found it when he went back to the human world and realised she was dead.'

Sysa sat beside Brodie considering the story he had told her, turning it over and over like a coin between her fingers.

'But you still went back to the selkies as you grew up – and you were safe then?' she asked, trying to close the gap between the conversation and her thoughts.

'Yes, it seemed so,' Brodie replied. 'I had them all to take care of me. Rogart seemed happy to ignore my existence until he saw me with you that first time in the woods.'

'And my parents? They didn't know? That you were Rogart's son I mean?' Sysa thought back to Elise and Bruan.

'Not that I know of,' Brodie replied, his eyes darkening as he tugged a hand roughly through his hair.

He paused for a moment, tracing his way through a thousand childhood memories.

'Well, if they had any suspicions, they never mentioned them to me.'

Sysa considered this for a moment, wondering if privately her parents had understood more than Brodie realised.

'I'm so glad you had them,' she said eventually, lifting Brodie's hand to place a quick kiss on his skin.

'Me too,' Brodie replied, inhaling deeply. 'They've been so good to me.' He lifted his hand to her cheek, his thumb tracing a path towards her jawline.

'And it was being with them all these years that led me to being here with you.'

'When we were on the beach back there – before everything, I mean, I heard you tell Frode you were going to leave,' Sysa said in answer, a prickle flashing down her spine as every part of her alerted once again to the danger of losing him.

A vision of Brodie and Frode talking pinched at her, the memory of what she had heard searing inside her like a blade.

'Yes, I was going to leave,' Brodie answered, a blanket of sadness opening up across his face as he looked out again towards the horizon. Sysa followed with her eyes, imagining their words tumbling over the edge like a waterfall where the sky and water met.

'Being near you but not being able to be with you was just torture, Sysa,' Brodie continued, his face creased in lines of remembered agony.

'I can hardly breathe without you, let alone be able to properly function or exist. I'd made up my mind that I was going to go after the battle with Rogart, to find somewhere I wouldn't have to see you or think about you. But the moment I saw you in danger I didn't care about anything anymore, all that mattered was you, and that you were going to be all right.'

'I felt dead inside anyway, so what difference was Rogart killing me going to make?' He looked back out to sea as if the waves might pick up his unwelcome memories.

'I was giving up, then, when he was strangling me, I didn't care about my life in any way at all. And then, just at the end, I saw you whisper that you loved me, and it was like this sense of peacefulness came over me. And then everything went dark. And then I felt something dropping onto my face and I knew you were holding me in your arms and I remembered that you loved me. And I knew what your Grandfather had done and why you were crying, and how much you loved both of us.' Brodie's words came quickly now, tumbling out of him like water gushing from a stream.

'And then I felt that feeling again, the powers coming back, but this time not a force for darkness. I felt them all coming back to me then. They came back to me because you came back, Sysa. They came back to me with you.'

Sysa looked at Brodie's open face and thought how freely he gave away his emotions. She didn't know if this was the normal way of things – despite her limited experience she suspected it was not. But as he took her hand again she knew that this was to be the way it was between them, that no other way existed. He had said he couldn't breathe without her, the same was true of her own capacity to live. Her Grandfather had known that; she saw that now, that he had made his sacrifice gladly.

*'He believed your love could save us,'* Bruan had said back at the castle.

Sysa saw that it wasn't just the love within her Grey believed in; it was the love between her and Brodie, irrevocable as the sky above their heads.

'And Elva? What about Elva?' Sysa asked, the only remaining question she had to ask of him.

'Did you think about Elva after you kissed me, when I said I couldn't be with you because of her?'

'Not really,' said Brodie, offering a quick smile in apology.

'I've known Elva for so many years that I knew she didn't love me in the way you thought she did. And I knew when you kissed me what you felt about me – you don't kiss people like that unless you feel something for them.'

Brodie flashed Sysa a broad grin that stoked a burst of pink across her cheeks.

'I still had plenty of hope that we could work it out

somehow,' he continued, 'but then everything went wrong and I found out about my Father and that Elva had taken off with Rogart, and it all seemed so hopeless. It felt like there was nothing I could do.' He looked down, the darkness in his eyes returning with a flash before flickering away against the light of the watching sun.

'Elva seems happy with William.' Sysa spoke almost to herself as she stretched out her legs to meet the sunlight.

'She does, she seems very happy,' Brodie replied, taking a strand of Sysa's hair and rolling it between his finger and his thumb.

'So it's not hopeless anymore?' Sysa asked, turning her face to him and tilting her head up to meet the blue eyes that felt like a mirror to every part of her.

'Not hopeless at all,' Brodie said, tipping a finger under her chin and lowering his gaze unapologetically towards her mouth.

'In fact, quite the opposite,' he murmured as he moved his body towards her, swivelling slightly as he pressed himself against her.

As he found her lips, Sysa closed her eyes, feeling the shields she had built inside herself slip away, quietly taken by the fingers of a wave.

# CHAPTER TWENTY-SIX

'I hate him. Lavellan, I mean,' Sysa said some time later when Brodie finally pulled away from her.

'Ah, Lavellan. Yes, he's not my favourite person either,' Brodie said, a wry look on his face as he twisted, brushing another wayward strand of hair back off his brow.

'But hate? Sysa, I've been quite well acquainted with hate lately and I can tell you, it's not an emotion I want to keep close to me.' His eyes burrowed into her, blue rounds of tenderness pleading with her.

'And it's not something I want for you, either.' He touched her cheek lightly.

Instinctively, Sysa pulled away, shuffling her rear across the rock.

'Brodie. He killed my Grandfather,' she said, the hard edge of her voice mirroring her irritation.

'And he nearly killed you too, back on the cliffs, remember? Or have you conveniently forgotten about that?'

'Of course I haven't. I haven't forgotten anything,' Brodie said, his jaw twitching slightly at the memory. 'But I'm still here. And I think maybe your Grandfather wanted to be killed.'

'Wanted to be killed?' Sysa shook her head, wincing at

the thought of Grey's sacrifice. She knew Brodie was right of course, but that didn't mean she had to agree with him. She couldn't forgive Lavellan for what he'd taken from her, for all the evil things he'd done.

'If it weren't for Lavellan and Rogart, my Grandfather would never have been in a position where he *wanted to be killed,*' Sysa said, her face twisting as she parroted Brodie's statement.

'I'll never forgive him. And now he's out there somewhere' – she waved her hand around – 'goodness knows where, and no doubt plotting out his next move. And Luna, too, we let her get away,' Sysa continued, flashing a look at Brodie, her eyes lighting up with accusation.

As the mist of her anger faded, she saw the look of sadness on Brodie's face, and instantly felt guilty. She exhaled loudly, slumping on the rock as she felt the burst of anger leave her, floating away on her breath and drifting out to sea.

'I'm sorry,' she sighed, reaching her hand back across to Brodie, who took it, squeezing her fingers gently.

'I just feel so angry. And I don't understand why Lavellan did it – I mean, if he wanted you dead, then why did he kill Grey? He must have known that it would save you. I don't know what he's up to, and now he's off out there somewhere, probably in cahoots with Luna and planning how they can get back at us for Rogart, and for Elva taking William away.'

Sysa dropped her head, rubbing at the space between her eyebrows with her finger and her thumb.

'It's fine Sysa,' Brodie said, shifting so that he knelt in front of her, hands pressed against her forearms.

'You're exhausted.'

'I don't know why Lavellan did what he did either Sysa. And yes, you're right, he and Luna will probably be back. But we're together now, and from now on we face everything together, including them – or whatever else comes our way.'

He ducked his head beneath hers, dropping a quick kiss on the edge of her nose, which Sysa realised was moist with the track of an errant tear she hadn't noticed falling.

'With you I feel like I can face anything Sysa,' he continued, wiping the tear away and cupping his hands around her face, so that she looked up at him, her eyes wet and squinting.

'Promise me that from now on, it's you and me always,' he said, searching her face with a desperate, tender look.

'I promise,' Sysa whispered, her voice broken and cracking.

Brodie stood, offering an outstretched hand, his fingers streaked with strips of sunlight. Sysa let him pull the weight of her, the remains of her tears disappearing in the warmth as she rose and turned her face into the light.

*

*'I have another story for you, Sysa,' said Grey as Sysa wriggled onto his lap in front of the peat fire and watched a strand of smoke rise up towards the roof of the cottage.*

*'What's it about?' Sysa said, peering up at him, her eyes clouded as she inhaled the intoxicating scent.*

*'It's about love. Or rather, what happened when two people fell in love, I suppose,' Grey answered, looking back at the fire, the small reflected glow lighting up his features.*

'Who fell in love?' Sysa asked, suddenly forgetting her prior sleepiness. 'Was it you, Grandfather?'

'No, not me, not this time at least,' Grey laughed, his green eyes creasing in amusement as he patted at her knee.

'This was a girl a bit like you, who fell in love with a boy, much like any other boy in fact,' he continued.

'But together they were something special – they were able to defeat a Giant, and send him away somewhere he couldn't cause any more trouble in their kingdom for a while.'

'Oh!' said Sysa, fidgeting on Grey's lap in excitement at the prospect.

'How did they do it? Did they shoot him with an elf bolt?' She flicked an imaginary bolt with her thumb and finger the way Hugh had done at the market, picturing it flying into the fire and exploding with a bang.

'No,' said Grey, shaking his head. 'They didn't shoot him. But they did use their powers to send him somewhere he wouldn't be able to cause any mischief for a very long time. And while he couldn't cause any trouble, there were less Fae folk meddling in the human world. And so for a time, at least, the faeries and the kelpies and so on disappeared from the human world, and the humans started to believe that they no longer existed, perhaps that they had never even existed at all.'

Sysa's eyes widened at the thought.

'But they still existed back in their own lands, of course,' Grey continued, dismissing the notion of a world without faeries with a quick hand flick.

'And in the meantime, the two young people who had fallen in love watched over the kingdom, because they were both' – Grey hesitated for a moment – 'well the girl in particular I'd say – they were both very clever folk. They realised it was up to them to keep darkness out of their Fae lands.'

*'And they did it? They kept the darkness away?'* Sysa asked, riveted.

*'I don't know,'* Grey said, his eyes clouding in an unfamiliar manner. *'That's where my story finishes.'*

*'I hope so, though,'* he said, turning towards Sysa with an expression she didn't recognise.

*Then she understood completely: it was the same look he wore when he was seeking an answer in the sky.*

★

'Home.' Brodie's voice brought Sysa's thoughts back into focus as the spiked turrets of Steel Castle appeared in the distance, pricking at the pale blue sky above the treetops.

'Yes,' said Sysa, as they paused for a moment along the path, fingered leaves whispering in the breeze to greet them as they completed their journey back. Sysa glanced over her shoulder, to where her parents and the others followed, keeping a polite, if curious, distance.

'They're young and in love – they need a little space to get to know each other,' she'd heard her Mother chide Bruan when he'd made to set off beside them earlier in the day.

Bruan had hung back at his wife's request, dropping his head with a wry smile and flashing a hopeful look towards Elva and William. Elise had lifted her eyebrows in response, and before long, Bruan had positioned himself behind the two sets of lovers, a resigned, if contented, sort of expression on his face.

'It is home now,' Sysa said eventually, drinking in the

287

sight of the bluebell-strewn woods, and the pebbled shore to their right that hugged the path towards the castle.

She thought back to her other home then, the one in Caithness, where the skies had been as vast and open as the days of her childhood, and Grey had laughed as she'd run barefoot down the hill. She thought of the butterflies that kept pace as she'd twisted and turned through the long grass that leapt up to meet her fingers. She looked down, feeling the tiniest flutter of movement on the back of her hand, no more than a whisper tracking its way across the skin. A blue butterfly was roaming a path around her hand, tracing her thoughts in tiny, roving circles. Sysa raised her hand up, inviting it to leave her if it wished to. It hesitated for a moment before fluttering away, flitting from flower to flower, sprinkling her memories like raindrops on the leaves.

Tears pricked at her eyes as she knew they would so many times in the future.

'My home is where you are,' Brodie said, gathering her into his arms, his mouth pressed against the dark folds of her hair.

'And for me too,' she said, catching the hand he raised towards her face, lifting his palm towards her lips so that she could kiss the skin there. They stood like that for a moment, just looking at each other, until Sysa heard the crunch of feet against twigs, and turned to see her sister's face tilted towards them, curiosity escaping like trapped air from the curves of Elva's open mouth.

'So your wandering days are over, Brodie?' Elva interrupted, her eyes narrowing in an expression that bordered on amusement.

Behind her, William emerged, looking between Elva

and Brodie in his usual startled manner, as if he had only just stumbled into the Fae lands and was surprised to find a collection of faeries conversing quite naturally in the woods. Bruan, Elise and the others came to a halt behind Elva too, looking far less shocked, Sysa noted, by the turn of conversation than William. For a moment Sysa regretted the highly sensitive hearing abilities of faeries: with the exception of the human, she thought to herself, cheeks colouring, they had all heard everything, no doubt.

'Yes,' replied Brodie in answer, lifting his chin a fraction towards the assembled party. He glanced towards Frode, who was watching with interest, one hand linked through Krystan's, the other tracing a path through the pleats of Modan's shining mane.

'Wandering days over,' he said with a note of finality, before looking back at Sysa as if there were no one else in the world around them.

'I know now where I belong Elva. From now on I follow only her.'

There was a pause before Bruan coughed, breaking the tension that hung in the air like the last breath before a thunderstorm.

'Glad to hear that,' he said finally, looking at Elva, who nodded back at him, apparently satisfied with what Brodie had said.

'I hope you'll still come and visit us now and again, though,' said Frode, as he stepped forwards into the clearing, his arms opening to Brodie in invitation.

'Of course I will,' Brodie said, flashing a grin towards the seal-man and entering a rough embrace with him.

'But from now on, I'll take Sysa with me too.'

Sysa looked around at the family and friends she had found since her arrival in Fyrish; her parents, Elva and William, Frode, Krystan and the selkies, Modan and the kelpies, still in horse form, who had paused at the burn which meandered through the woods.

She thought of the others, the people who had run to them as they had advanced back towards the castle, the folk who had come clutching flowers and pressing their palms in gratitude and relief. And for now there was no more light and dark here, just the world there had always been, and the night and day that had always lived beneath the surface. Sysa looked at Brodie, thinking of the light and dark that would always be in him, and knew they were hers to watch over, to turn gently between her fingertips like a ball of precious glass.

'Well, don't leave it too long until your first visit together,' Frode said, interrupting Sysa's thoughts as she snapped her head back round to face him.

'Now that things are settled, we must go back to Selkie Island. It's time for us to leave you.' Frode slapped Brodie on the back, ruffling the dark mop of his hair with a large hand before he moved towards the shore.

Sysa caught Krystan's eye as she stepped away, taking the hand Frode held out to her.

'I'm going with them,' Krystan smiled, cupping Frode's hand as if it held a precious bird that could take flight at any moment. And then, almost as an afterthought, she lowered her knees into a curtsey, head bent low, the golden timepiece that had been returned to her twinkling from underneath the neckline of her dress.

'Of course, Sysa, if that's all right with you.'

'Of course it's all right with me,' Sysa said, shrugging off the gesture and wrapping her arms around Krystan as soon as the faerie rose up again.

'I hope you'll be very happy together.'

'We all do,' said Brodie, echoing the softly spoken words that murmured around the remainder of the group, who were arced in a half-circle, facing towards the shore. The horses looked up from the burn, surveying their companions, who were suddenly lost in a haze of farewells and backslaps.

As the sun fell in shafts through the trees, illuminating them with its golden, outstretched hands, Modan snuffled contentedly. Rays of light landed in pools on the forest floor beneath them, quietly accepting of the parts its fingers could not reach.

★

Sysa watched as the group disappeared into the distance. The silvered backs of the selkies shone against the sunlight, like curling mirrors that rose and fell in a sea studded with a blanket of tiny jewels. Krystan rode Modan, her face fixed on Selkie Island as they cut through waves painted with brushstrokes of sweeping silver. Sysa stayed on the shore until the outline of their figures resembled small dots on the horizon, until she could no longer tell who was faerie, who was selkie, who was horse.

Eventually she turned, ready for the final part of their journey back to the castle. Then a tug at her sleeve: it was Brodie, pointing a finger back out towards the sea.

'It's Arno,' he said, a smile of recognition spreading

across his face as he looked towards the eagle. Sysa watched as Arno closed the space between them, soaring over the island, their friends, and across the jewel-strewn sea. All at once she saw his huge wings in front of her and felt the rush of air as he arrived closer to his target.

'Arno?' Brodie called out in question, his hand raised to his forehead, his face shielded as the eagle beat a path closer, momentarily blocking out the sun.

Arno hovered for a moment, in silent commune with Brodie, the outline of his long-fingered wings silhouetted against the slivers of sun remaining. Brodie held the bird's gaze, unblinking, and then nodded, releasing Arno into an upward spiral and back into the sky.

'It's done,' he confirmed, seeking out the questioning faces of the others who huddled closer around him.

'Rogart is far away now, he's part of the mountain.'

'Sleeping,' he added after a pause, his expression unreadable. 'He won't be bothering us for a long time. He won't be bothering anyone in fact.'

There were nods and murmurs from the group, more the sounds of relief, Sysa thought, than the roars of outright victory. She looked at the faces around her, seeing loss in each expression – not just the loss of Grey, but the loss of a Giant, whom she could see in her Father's face had once been entirely something else. And then there was Lavellan, and Luna, and whatever would become of them. Sysa felt a trickle of ice run down her spine and shivered. She steadied herself, lifting her chin into the sun. This moment was about Grey, and everything he had done for them. As that thought entered her head she felt him around her then, as if the air had once more rushed towards her, without an eagle to send it flying. The air wrapped itself around her, and for a moment she was encased in its cocoon.

'Thankyou Father.' Sysa heard Bruan's voice, and she knew he felt it too, as she watched his face, so empty of its usual expression that it was almost unbearable to keep her gaze there.

Elise nudged closer to her husband, curling her hand over his forearm and murmuring soft reassurances as she inclined her head to make contact with his cheek. Sysa looked between her Father and Brodie, who each stared out into the same horizon, both now Fatherless, both consumed in their own internal workings. Finally, Bruan sighed, looking out into the distance as Arno rose higher like an arrow, taking their words and streaming them across the vast and open sky.

'Goodbye Grey. I love you,' Sysa whispered as she watched Arno disappear into the distance.

She felt the air that had encased them pull away, wrapping itself around the words and carrying them off. As tears rolled down her cheeks she felt the breath of a whisper graze them like a feather touch.

*'I love you too,'* it said before surrendering itself to the ocean, where it was lost in the sound of the waves that carried its gentle murmur off to sea.

# CHAPTER TWENTY-SEVEN

Brodie watched as the stone he had set flying puttered across the water, meeting briefly with the surface one, two, three times as it ventured further across the sea that stretched in front of them like a blanket. He followed its progress before flashing a sideways grin at Sysa.

'Not bad, eh?' he said brightly, eyeing her as she stretched out on a rock, her tanned legs shining in the sun.

'Pretty good,' she replied, arching her back and tilting her face up to meet the warmth that had enveloped them since that day on the beach with Rogart. She closed her eyes, smiling to herself. Through the curtain of her eyelids, she felt Brodie looming over her, the sudden nearness of him sending a shiver of anticipation down her spine.

'I can show you how to do it,' Brodie said, as she opened her eyes, to find his face over hers, one eyebrow arced in question.

'Oh thank you,' Sysa smirked, reaching out her hand to meet the one that was being offered above her head. Brodie pulled her up, simultaneously wrapping his other arm around her, pulling her close to him.

'Couldn't resist,' he smiled, his face millimetres away from her. A few seconds later, when he had released her mouth from his, he grinned broadly, grabbed her hand and pulled her towards the shore.

'Come on.'

Brodie adjusted himself behind her, raising his arm to the side in unison with the one he'd instructed her to lift upwards.

'Like this,' he murmured, pressing the stone into her palm and manipulating the angle of her hand. Sysa felt his breath on her neck and felt the skin tingle so that she raised her shoulder to meet it.

'Like this?' she enquired, eyes wide to his instructions.

'Yes, exactly that,' he replied. 'Now swing.'

Sysa drew her arm back and watched as the stone skimmed repeatedly against the surface of the sea.

'You knew how to do that.' Brodie nudged at her, a quick prod to her side as he watched the stone journey, his face squeezed against the sunlight.

'Of course I did,' she laughed, ducking out from under him and running the few remaining steps towards the shore.

'I'll get you for that,' he said, in mock anger, darting towards her like a pouncing animal.

As their feet met with the water, Sysa felt its familiar rush as they wriggled against each other. Breathless, they paused for a moment, laughing, tasting the salty bite of the wayward droplets that flailed around their heads. Brodie looked at Sysa, taking in every one of her features.

'There,' he said, leaning forward and pushing a strand of wet hair that clung to her cheek and placing it very slowly behind her ear.

'We better get back,' Sysa murmured, holding his gaze for a moment. She looked back towards the castle, where her parents and the other occupants would soon be waking up. She took in the familiar scene of the white turrets, partially cloaked behind the comfort of the trees, her eye tracing an arc from the rear of the castle, down through the walled garden and out through the gate to the shore which she and Brodie had retreated to on waking. Since returning to the castle they had become accustomed to snatched moments, kisses in long corridors, muffled giggles as footsteps rounded corners, well-timed coughs that heralded an advance. Sysa had become used to waking early and peering round her bedroom door, where Brodie would be waiting for her, his face a study in concentration as he sat on his haunches, hands on his knees, his fingertips resting against each other like a church steeple. He'd spring up at the sight of her, his face brightening in a sort of realisation, as if, each day, he had wondered if she would still emerge. Each morning he looked at her with that same open face, as if he couldn't quite believe it. Then he would grab her, kiss her, and then pull away, dragging her gently by the hand along the corridor, and they'd scramble through halls and down the long winding staircase before bursting through the heavy wooden doors of the castle and emerging out into the world.

'Five more minutes,' Brodie said, looking over his shoulder and following Sysa's gaze to the castle.

'They'll know where we are,' he continued, dipping down to snub her nose with his finger, pushing his bottom lip out slightly and giving her a big-eyed, pleading look.

'All right,' Sysa said, her lips curling at the sight of him. 'Just five minutes, okay?'

She wrapped her arms around his neck, fingers interlaced, and Brodie stepped clownishly from foot to foot, turning her in a circle so her face looked out to sea again.

'You are silly,' she laughed, as she pressed her face into his skin, his arms tightening around her as she peered over the hard line of his shoulder.

'You like silly,' he replied, pressing his face into her hair and tracing soft, tickling kisses down her neck that made her shiver in response to his warm breath on her skin.

'In fact, I believe you like silly very much,' he murmured, nibbling at her neck in a manner which usually made her dissolve into giggles against him. But this time, he felt Sysa stiffen, her whole body alert and rigid.

'What's wrong?' he said, returning to her eyes, crouching down slightly in front of her, searching her features in concern.

'Out there in the water, I thought I saw something,' she said, her eyes scanning the horizon, trying to pick out something in the vast azure expanse. Brodie wheeled round, flicking a glance over the water, and then turned back to her.

'I don't see anything. What was it?' he asked, his eyes returning to the water.

'I don't know, maybe nothing,' Sysa replied, her eyes still tracking across the sea.

'Oh never mind,' she shrugged at last, gesturing with her hand to wave away the moment.

'I probably imagined it.'

She smoothed her palm across her forearm, trying to wipe away the gooseflesh that stood up in hard bumps across her skin.

'Come on,' she said, already moving back towards the castle, her hand outstretched behind her.

'Okay,' Brodie replied, grabbing it. 'Time to get back after all I suppose. I need to have a word with Bruan if he's up.'

Sysa only heard part of what Brodie was saying, her mind was adrift, looping over and over what she'd just seen in the water. Out amongst the waves, a face she remembered from that day so very long ago with Grey. Slanted eyes that had watched them intently, slick fur scraped back from familiar, icy features. Lavellan had watched as they embraced on the shore, watched as the last of Brodie's kisses had fallen on Sysa's neck like summer rain. He had watched as her body tightened in recognition, his eyes meeting hers in a kind of cool realisation; some sort of question lingering in the space that existed between them. They had stayed like that for a moment before Brodie's voice had released them – as he had spoken, Lavellan's head had dipped beneath the water, a flash of tail following behind it before the sea stilled and there was no trace of him ever being there at all.

How had she been so stupid, Sysa thought, as to let him slip away from them at the cliff edge? Of course she'd known that he'd be back, and here he was, and no doubt Luna, too, could not be far away. She remembered the strange expression on Lavellan's face as he'd looked down at her from beside Rogart that day, the hard line of Luna's mouth as she'd looked from William to Elva, her eyes narrowed in bitter recognition.

*How could I have thought this might be over?* Sysa seethed to herself, inhaling air that now burned her throat and lodged there, her fingertips crackling with eager lightning. She turned, ready to fly back into the water, to breach the waves and cleave the sea around them.

And then she heard the hum of Brodie speaking, his words tugging at her like the pull of a distant wave.

She turned to look at him, and the face that stared into hers, so bright and clear and beautiful. She had him, and he had her, and right now she wanted to focus on this moment, and push whatever she had seen out there – and what it might mean for them – out and away into the world. Rogart was gone, and her home was here now. She had her Father, her Mother and Elva – William too, she supposed, as he trailed about after her sister like a puppy on a leash. She had all these things and the life that they had given her, the life that Grey too had given her, in a field dotted with wildflowers and on the edge of a cliff against inky skies that had rolled above them. This life was hers now – wild, magical and full of possibilities, and what might come before or after, for now could not be her concern. For Brodie was here beside her, two souls entwined, shielded from the world in their own protective cloak of ivy. Like a mirror to another world, she saw that she was his, and he was hers – it must always be this way, they must never be disentangled, pulled apart. She knew this truth as well as she knew the beating of her own heart inside her chest, she saw it all so clearly. The crackling fell away from her fingers like the dying embers of a hearthfire.

It would all wait for them.

She turned back to him, tuning back in to the remnants of his words.

'So what do you want to speak to my Father about?' she asked, once again alert to the feeling of her hand in his, his eyes upon her own eyes.

'Oh you know, he wants to talk to me about my

intentions towards his daughter,' Brodie laughed, casting her a sideways grin that reached out and clutched around her heart.

'And what might those be?' she asked, one eyebrow arched, every part of her being turned towards him.

He looked at her, unbelieving, as if she'd asked him a question he'd answered a hundred times before.

'That I want to marry you, of course,' he said, the world opening up with a promise that stretched out into the sea and enveloped the sky around them.

For a moment, it was just them, and those words that existed in the world as he took her hand and pulled her in towards him. And the world held on to that promise as it answered for her, the future hanging in the air, restless and eager against the breeze.

# LAVELLAN

walked away from the cliff, the pain in my hand searing up into my arm and along the heavy blades of my shoulders. It cut at me, striking its way through bone and sinew, beating a path of hard lightning that flew like an arrow, targeting everything that abided as it passed. I clamped my other hand over it, my fingers meeting with blood that trickled from my fingertips and met with the burgeoning heathers. Was it my blood, or his? I couldn't tell in the half-light. Behind me, the rays of his inner sun were pouring over the cliff wall, its edges spilling in front of me, lighting the track I followed like the reflection from a knife.

My powers were draining, draining like the blood that had spilled from him, over the milk white fur of his chest and onto the beach beneath him. My strength would return, I knew, with rest and quiet – albeit changed perhaps, altered somehow by what I had wielded on the cliff. His power would not return, nor would his life – that much was unequivocal. It was hers now, and she would wield and bestow it as she must.

Something hard pricked at me then as I thought of the look she had given the one who lay dying on the beach before her. I thought of the look she had given me, then, the same one she had given me back on another cliff, and at the place where she had danced in silken, wafting robes. Contempt. Hatred. I felt bile rising into my throat as the tang of the blood wafted towards me like a feather. It pinched at my nostrils, clouding my vision in a mist of unending, molten red.

I walked on, feeling once again that strange sense of pulling against my ribcage. It was as if something clung to the bone there, tethering me to the cliff while I tried to slip away. I braced myself against it, clenching my teeth together as if I could break it, bite it. It would not yield or give way though. It just drew tighter, reeling me in, leaving a part of me back there with her on the beach.

I thought of the mermaid, and wondered if she could be of any use to me. I doubted it – it was much more likely that I could be of use to her. No doubt she would come to me soon, seek out a new alliance. We were, after all, part of the same family. I shrugged off the idea, lowering my fangs from their recesses, trying to scorch the invisible line that stretched behind me. Again it resisted, a needle that seared at my insides, branding me. My flesh curled around it, moulding itself into a new and willing form.

I saw, or perhaps felt, the flash of bright light behind me. It would be over soon – or at least it would be over for today. I heard her cry out, then only silence. I paused for a moment, the tug of the incessant line caressing me. I bit down hard, tasted blood, then stepped forward, seeing only light behind my veil of misted red.

A few steps later, and I heard the crackle of lightning from her fingers. I heard the crackle from his too, as they joined in unison on the beach. A sense of realisation fell on me, thudding deep into the pit of my stomach – something both known, and unexpected. I heard a low growl rumble in my throat, passing my lips and straining. It was stained by the blood there, as it passed through and escaped into the air.

I felt a rushing, as if the wind was chasing itself behind me. I would not turn to see it, but felt the heat of Rogart's wrath withdrawing through the sky. Then the beat of the sky seer's wings, *sent to follow him on his journey. Then my own heart beating, feeling the pulse of what had grown between them. It thumped like an echo, grinding and twisting in my chest to bait me.*

*I did not answer. Hauling myself over the land that awoke beneath me, I carried on.*

# TO BE CONTINUED IN
## *PIECES OF SKY AND STONE*

# ABOUT THE AUTHOR

Gail Brown is a writer and blogger from Caithness who writes the blog *Wellies on the School Run*. Her work has featured in anthologies, websites and magazines.

Gail is passionate about life in the far north and enjoys living quietly with her husband, their two children and their Hungarian Vizsla.

*Castles of Steel and Thunder* is Gail's first book.